ON THE UP

ALICE O'KEEFFE

ON THE UP

A Novel

CORONET

First published in Great Britain in 2019 by Coronet
An Imprint of Hodder & Stoughton
An Hachette UK company

This paperback edition published in 2020

2

A CIP catalogue record for this title is available from the British Library

Paperback ISBN 9781529303360
eBook ISBN 9781529303377

Typeset in Charter by Palimpsest Book Production Ltd, Falkirk, Stirlingshire

Printed and bound in Great Britain by Clays Ltd, Elcograf S.p.A.

Hodder & Stoughton policy is to use papers that are natural, renewable
and recyclable products and made from wood grown in sustainable forests.
The logging and manufacturing processes are expected to conform to the
environmental regulations of the country of origin.

Hodder & Stoughton Ltd
Carmelite House
50 Victoria Embankment
London EC4Y 0DZ

www.hodder.co.uk

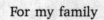
For my family

'THE FANTASTIC FUTURE COMETH'
Graffiti, Brighton

1.

Measuring Out My Life
With Coffee Spoons

'SEASON'S Greetings from the Hackney Council Anti-Social Behaviour Unit! You have reached Bill Baker. I am away from my desk until 3rd January. If the problem is urgent please phone the police on 999. Do have a very happy – and peaceful – new year!'

I paused for a moment after the beep, wondering whether to leave a message. Clearly, I had known when I called that Bill was not going to be at his desk. He would be all tucked up and dreaming in his little semi in Enfield, or some other nice, quiet suburb. I had just wanted to do something, to take action. I needed reassurance, and nobody reassured me like Bill.

'Hi, Bill!' I said to the answerphone. 'Sorry for calling so late. It's just that it's only three hours before I'll have to get up, and . . . it's been a bad night.' I paused. I made sure to breathe. 'I've been writing it all down in the logbook, like we discussed.'

The baby stirred in my arms, the tiny shell of his ear

moving up and down as he suckled. I hugged his warm body a little closer, readjusted his blanket with my free hand.

'Anyway. You're not there. If you do by any chance get this message, do call me back. Any time.' Then I remembered, and added, 'Happy new year!' before ending the call.

I picked up the logbook from its position on the living-room window sill and re-read the entry I had just written.

Incident No. 253. 1st January, 3 a.m.

Wow, I am feeling inspired. I am feeling – appropriately, as I meet this box-fresh year – brand new. Why? Because I'm listening to the uplifting lyrics of 'New York' by Alicia Keys featuring Jay-Z. For the 10th time tonight.

So yes, I feel inspired . . . to break something. Possibly my own head.

Total hours' sleep: 3 (broken). The Toddler will be bouncing on my poor tired body in another three.

New Year's resolution: get Dawn some new music.

After a moment's thought, I added: *Something soothing. Mozart?*

Sleep felt a long way off, so I flicked back through the pages. Dawn moved in downstairs just before The

Toddler, aka our older son Larkin, was born. He was now nearly three. The logbook was started as evidence for the Anti-Social Behaviour Unit, but it had become a record of my entire journey through motherhood so far. The first entry transported me back to when Larkin was just five days old, a red-faced, scrawny newborn, and Dawn's anti-social behaviour was also in its infancy.

3rd March, 1 a.m., it read. *Burning smell. Man's voice shouting 'Put it out, you plum.' Went downstairs. D answered door in stilettos and dressing gown, holding mop. Floor under several centimetres of water.*

Ah, I thought nostalgically. Those were the days when I still bothered to go down there to ask her to shut up. The days of hope. I flicked forward a few pages.

16th July, 4 a.m. Thumping. Cause unknown, perhaps D has forgotten to take medication again. Broom against ceiling? Head against Wall? V loud. Hopefully not head.

The more recent entries were terser, in a scratchy ballpoint. On the page facing my current entry was the one from Christmas Eve.

*24th December, 3 a.m. 6 straight hours of Rihanna.
Happy Christmas, one and all!*

In small letters underneath I had written *Help. Me.*

Should probably Tipp-Ex that out before submitting it to the council.

I put the book back on the ledge, and sank my head against the chair. The living room was dark and, outside, moonlight glittered on the reservoir. I sometimes enjoyed these witching-hour feeds, alone with my baby while the rest of the estate was asleep. Eliot, or That Baby, as his older brother lovingly called him, was four months old, and needed feeding every night at about two or three. I had put the armchair by the window, so I could look out over the water and watch for the family of foxes that lived on the bank.

The view from this window was my favourite thing about living in Priory Court. From the outside, the estate looked like your average low-rise 1950s council block: six floors on three sides of a square, striped with walkways looking out over a tarmacked forecourt and, beyond that, the traffic rushing along the High Street.

Only we, the residents, and possibly a few estate agents, knew that the reservoir was even there. You couldn't see it from the road. But from our living rooms we could watch the water as it changed colour with the light, from silver to deepest midnight blue, reflecting the sky, giving us a sense of stillness and space. This view was our little secret; Obe and I called it the Hackney Riviera.

On Dawn's balcony downstairs, a man with a cracked, throaty voice was shouting loudly into a phone.

'Nah, it's one of those old blocks off the High Street, the boys are all coming here, let me get the address, hold up . . .'

The balcony door creaked, letting the bass loose into the night. The vocals whined through a wall of Auto-Tune. Dawn only ever played two songs, at unpredictable times of the day and night, and always at top volume: 'New York', and 'Diamonds' by Rihanna. After three years on constant rotation, I knew them so well that they played over and over in my head, even when it was quiet.

Obe and I had decided not to go out for New Year's Eve, as staying up late didn't appeal much any more. At this rate, I thought bitterly, I could have been better rested if I had gone to an all-night rave.

With a quiet click, Eliot let go of my nipple. His eyes were closed, but his lips still moving – dreaming a lovely breast-filled dream. I stroked his soft caramel cheek with my finger. Dawn's noise didn't bother him. Priory Court didn't bother him. Nothing bothered him except food, sleep and cuddles. How ridiculous, I thought, that adults were supposed to teach babies to walk, and talk, and think, and be like us. 'Don't ever let me teach you anything,' I told Eliot silently. I often talked to him like this, communicating directly, mind-to-mind. 'What adults really need to do is learn to be a bit more like you.'

Wrapping him carefully in his blanket, I lifted him onto my shoulder and carried him ten steps down the skinny, windowless hall to the bedroom. The noise from downstairs was more muffled in there, just an insistent thump of bass and the odd shout. Somewhere under the bunched-up duvet lay Obe.

'Hey,' I whispered. 'She's at it again.'

From beneath the duvet came a muffled grunt.

'Isn't it keeping you awake?'

There was an angry flap, and a tousled afro emerged. 'The only thing keeping me awake,' he said, 'is you.'

Chastened, I put Eliot carefully down in his cot and climbed into bed, tugging the slightly-too-small duvet firmly over to my side. I closed my eyes and tried to become one with the beat. My whole body ached, torn between the opposing poles of sleep and rage, but with some effort I directed my mind towards my well-worn happy place.

I am walking through a large, white, spacious living room. In front of me are French windows, which I open, and step out onto a paved patio, furnished with a wrought-iron table and chairs. It is a sunny day, but the patio is shaded by a pergola, from which deep purple blooms of wisteria hang like luxuriant grapes. I cross the patio and sink my feet into a soft lawn. As I walk towards a potting shed at the end of the garden, my garden, I can hear birds trilling, and the bees buzzing in the blooming lavender.

Peace. Finally, after a long and confusing series of misunderstandings, the world makes sense again. This is my place. It is quiet, it is tranquil, and it is mine. My house. My garden. My life.

Clinging to this alternate reality as if my very existence depended on it, I tumbled gratefully towards sleep.

'Mummy!' came the yell, followed by an agonising blast of light hitting the back of my retina. Larkin's face loomed towards me, chubby and cheerful. 'It's my birthday!!!'

I grabbed back the duvet and cowered.

'Obe!' I croaked. 'Obe, please!'

Obe made an irritable I'm-not-awake-yet noise.

'You've got to get up, babe. I can't do it, not yet.'

Larkin started bouncing on the bed, casually jabbing at my kidneys with his foot. 'It's my birthday!' he cried. 'I'm getting my presents!'

'Obe, please!'

'All right, all right.' There was a rustle and an arpeggio of grunts as my not-quite-husband heaved himself into a seated position.

For a few blissful moments, the bouncing ceased, and I retreated into warmth and darkness. But just as I was about to drift off, another cold blast of light as Larkin lifted the duvet and got in beside me, wriggling and kicking. His body, warm in its Batman onesie, radiated energy. From the moment he woke until the moment he dropped like a stone into sleep every night, The Toddler never stopped bouncing.

He grabbed my cheeks between two hands. 'Can I have my presents now?'

Obe gently lifted the duvet, picked Larkin up, and kissed him. I gazed up wearily at them, two of the three men in my life, their matching 'fros framed by the grubby white light seeping through our too-thin curtains. 'Larkin,' Obe said, 'it's not your birthday. Not until the twenty-third of February. Nearly two months.'

'Oh.' Larkin's face momentarily fell, but he was used to this daily disappointment: he'd thought it was his birthday every morning since Boxing Day. 'Can I have my presents anyway?'

'No,' said Obe firmly, carrying him out of the room. The drawer banged and the cupboard creaked as I heard him get the cereal and bowls out. I closed my eyes and tried to drift off again, but in the cot beside the bed, That Baby was stirring. Any minute now, he would greet the new year with a hungry cry.

New Year's Day was warmer than it should have been, but that almost went without saying. The summer had been a scorcher, the hottest since records began. On the news, Australians were standing in the burned-out remains of their homes, or picking their way down the cracked, parched beds of dry rivers. In north-east London, the impact was less dramatic. Just a slow drip, drip of things being slightly off-kilter: the crocuses blooming at Christmas; so much rain that the park's new trees had rotted before they even put out leaves.

Eliot and I were back in our customary position, he suckling, me watching sheets of rain sweep across the reservoir. Meanwhile, in the kitchen next door, Obe brewed our first strong coffee of the morning. An iron band of tiredness was tightening around my temples, and The Toddler was bouncing up and down the hall: THUMP THUMP THUMP. THUMP THUMP THUMP. The one good thing about having a neighbour as noisy as Dawn was that I never had to tell him to be quiet.

'Let us go, then, you and I,' said Obe, to nobody in particular, as he unfolded the table and sat down. He suited his full name, Oberon – a legacy of his father, a postman and frustrated actor who had named both Obe and his sister Titania. Shakespeare's Oberon is King of the Fairies, but the name also means 'bear-like'. My Obe had both of those qualities: otherworldly, but also solid and huggable. While other people got caught up in everyday concerns, he kept his eyes firmly fixed on the horizon.

Right now, for example, he was thinking about poetry. During our nearly four years together, I had learned that in any given gap in the conversation, Obe would be thinking about poetry.

He stirred his coffee carefully; the cup was so full that every stir risked overflow. I worried about the amount of coffee we were consuming, that it was getting out of hand. Over the last few months I had started to worry about a lot of things, both large and small. Somehow the largest things seemed to bleed into the smallest, and vice versa. Like the weird weather, for example, and the fact that if Obe died suddenly of a coffee-related heart attack I'd be left on my own with two kids, and I doubted I could cope with that, especially if some kind of environmental apocalypse was on the cards.

'Do you think we should give up coffee for new year?' I said.

'When the evening is spread against the sky,' murmured

Obe, gazing into his cup. 'Like a patient etherised on a table. Let us go!'

'I mean, starting tomorrow, obviously,' I went on, finishing my coffee in three heavenly gulps. I passed That Baby to Obe and took a deep breath, making a mental list of all the things I would have to do before we could get out of the door. In another lifetime, I had skipped gaily out into the world carrying nothing but a handbag. Now, I was an explorer preparing to leave base camp. The terrain was hostile; I couldn't rule out crocodiles. Every move involved planning, and equipment, and supplies. Motherhood, after all, was about survival.

Meanwhile, Obe was now in fully caffeinated fun-dad mode.

'Morning, fella.' He pulled a face at Eliot.

'Bah. Dah,' said Eliot, and reached for Obe's nose, which he loved to grab.

'Not the nose, man.' Obe dodged the claw-like grip, burying his face in squishy baby tummy while Eliot cackled with joy. 'You'll never take the nose.'

'Dah,' said Eliot, and blew a raspberry, his latest trick. As Obe laughed, Eliot, quick as a flash, hooked his claws into his father's nostrils.

'Noooo!' cried Obe, grasping his face in mock horror. 'The teeny-tiny razor-sharp nails!'

More cackles as he put Eliot across his knees and

tickled. Sensing he was missing the action, Larkin came bouncing over. 'Tickle me, Daddy! Tickle me!'

To a soundtrack of their shrieks and giggles, my preparations began. I cleared up Larkin's cereal bowl, wiped the table, wiped the floor and the wall. I looked for the waterproofs in the normal place – they weren't there. After five minutes of fruitless searching I found them in the cupboard with the plastic bags. I changed Eliot into his rainsuit, and then cleared up the breakfast things, including the fancy coffee-maker that Obe, every single morning, left unwashed in a drift of coffee grounds next to the sink.

By the time we were all ready to leave, the caffeine high had worn off, my body felt like lead, and all I wanted to do was go back to bed. Obe took a final swig from his stone-cold cup, stood up and clapped his hands.

'Let us go, through certain half-deserted streets!' he cried, giving me a frazzled grin. I sometimes wondered if he even knew who did all the clearing up, who washed all the clothes, who opened the bills and paid them and filed them, who made sure the kids had snacks and drinks and changes of clothes. Perhaps he thought it was the fairies.

'There will be time, there will be time . . .'

* * *

There was indeed a time, a carefree time, not so very long ago, when Obe had landed in my life like a lunar spacecraft. It was the morning after a big night at a festival; my sister Lou had persuaded me to sign up for eight hours of litter-picking in exchange for a free ticket. Looking out over the carnage – thousands of squashed plastic cups, fuzzy outcrops of mud-matted clown wigs, a couple of capsized shopping trolleys, an orange rash of road cones, and something that looked like the insides of a giant accordion – it was impossible to remember why this had seemed like a good idea.

'Here,' said a voice from somewhere above my head. 'Take one of these.'

A bear-paw was extended out in front of me, with a small white packet of pills in the palm. I looked up and met a pair of shockingly kind golden eyes. The face around them was chestnut brown, high-cheekboned, topped off with a chaotic fuzz of curls. It radiated a kind of serene joy.

'What are they?'

'No idea,' replied this vision. He, like me, was clutching a bin bag, but the carnage didn't seem to be fazing him. 'I just found them on the floor.'

I popped a pill out of the packet, and looked at it closely. Ritalin, it said, in tiny print.

'What does Ritalin do?' I asked, and his face crinkled into a smile, which intensified the dazzling effect so much that I blinked.

'Not sure, but I just took three of them and I'm feeling *fine*.'

I still don't know what Ritalin does, but when we kissed later that afternoon, it was with a particular concentrated focus. We were telling each other something with that kiss, something so deep that six months later I was phoning Obe in shock after two lines appeared on the little white stick.

With the benefit of hindsight, perhaps we could have done things differently; waited to have a family, got ourselves financially stable first, got the house and the car. But that was a line of thought that didn't really get me anywhere.

We left for the park, Obe pushing the double buggy. But when the lift doors opened on the ground floor, the front wheels met an obstacle. I peered over the top; it was Dawn, lying curled in a foetal position on the tarmac, snoring lightly. I had to credit Dawn with some brave fashion choices. Despite being overweight and in her fifties, she was wearing a tight silver mini-skirt and high heels, and had bright blue eyeshadow smeared liberally over the top half of her face. Her bird's-nest hair was strung with tiny beads of drizzle.

'Don't worry now,' came a voice from above. 'She just sleeping. She all right.'

Winston was peering down at us over the parapet wall. I'd never been quite sure whether Winston had appointed himself Priory Court's concierge, or whether he had some more sinister reason for always hanging around outside his flat on the first floor, watching people come and go. It was probably best not to know. That morning he was braving the weather in a fetching zebra-print dressing gown. At his slippered feet was a half-empty bottle of Wray and Nephew's.

'She's not that all right, is she?' I said tetchily. My temples were throbbing; the caffeine hangover was kicking in, and the iron band was tightening around my head. 'It's raining. And we can't get the buggy out with her lying there.'

'Just wake her up then,' said Winston, lighting a cigarette and leaning out to get a better look. Obe squeezed around the edge of the buggy, crouched down, and shook Dawn carefully by the shoulder.

'Dawn! Dawn, it's me, Obe, from upstairs. Time to wake up now.'

Dawn's eyes snapped open. 'Am I in Disneyland?' she said.

'No, Dawn. You're in Priory Court, and you've fallen asleep outside. Let's get you up and into bed, shall we?'

Dawn sat up slowly. The lift doors were opening and closing repeatedly on the front wheels of the buggy, and beneath the rain cover I could see Larkin's face, peering at me questioningly. I gave him what I hoped was a cheery smile, and went to help Obe. We hooked one arm each beneath Dawn's shoulders and heaved, managing to get her upright, then staggered to the lift, wedging her into the small space where the buggy wasn't.

'Easy as you go,' called Winston, helpfully.

The first floor clanked past. When the doors opened on two, I got out with the buggy and Obe half-carried Dawn out to the front door of her flat. He leaned her against the door frame and fumbled in her pocket for keys. Dawn opened her eyes and, with a yellow, wrinkled, toothless, but radiant smile, bent over unsteadily to inspect That Baby. I winced as she reached out a long-nailed finger and chucked him on the cheek.

'I remember when my son was a baby, he cried and cried, he never stopped.' She inclined her head dreamily. 'So I pinched him,' she said, and her eyes darted up at me with a wicked little glimmer. Obe pushed the door open, and Dawn staggered unevenly inside – one of her high heels was still lying on the floor of the lift. 'Thank you, kind ladies,' she called, slamming the door behind her. There was a crumple and a thud as she hit the floor on the other side.

'Boy,' said Obe, wiping sweat from his brow as we headed once again for the ground floor, 'I have genuinely never needed a coffee more.'

Café Aroma was filled with the people from the leafy streets, with their Bugaboos and scooters. The park café used to be owned by the council and run by people from the community college, but it had been sold off to a private catering company and renovated: lattes and croissants instead of Coke and chips. I followed Obe as he pushed the buggy into the high-ceilinged room. It really was a nice space: white walls, a poured-concrete floor, and little round tables with green chairs.

'You've got to admit, it is nicer now,' I said, making my way over to a table by the window. 'Even if it is a little bit pricey.'

'Two-fifty for a cup of tea!' responded Obe. 'It's a scandal.'

I sat down, arranged Larkin in a high chair with a breadstick, and settled down to feed Eliot. Obe went up to the counter, and in his soft Brummie accent I could hear him ordering a coffee for himself, a peppermint tea for me, three croissants, and the obligatory babyccino.

Obe always refused, on principle, to say the word 'babyc-cino'.

'I'd like a warm milk, you know, for the boy. With a bit of froth on top and some chocolate.'

The waitress looked at him patiently. 'A babyccino?'

'What? Er, yeah, one of those.'

He returned to the table. 'You all right, Syl? Did you get some sleep?'

I looked down at my hands. There was something wrong with them recently; the skin wasn't stretchy any more, it was cracked and parched as one of those Australian riverbeds. They hurt every time I moved my fingers or touched anything, which was all the time. Obe took one, turned it palm-up, examined the deep, raw-red fissures running across the joint of each finger.

'Ouch.'

I flinched and pulled it back. 'It's just dry skin. I'll get some cream.'

The waitress came over and placed our order carefully down in front of us, with the bill folded in half on a little saucer. The coffee had a heart swirled into the foam, and the croissants were served on slate tiles instead of plates. I peeked at the bill and then wished that I hadn't.

Before having children, I had never believed people who told me that they were expensive. I was used to thinking about costs in terms of transactions: specific moments when you hand over your money to someone else. I hadn't appreciated that the true cost of children is abstract. It's the time you don't spend working, the money you never earn because you are looking after them. It's the mental capacity that you might once have used to progress up the career ladder. Financial crisis was now a constant feature of our lives.

Obe was still examining the witchy hand. 'You're worrying again, hey?'

Sometimes Obe's kindness made things worse; I could collapse into it, like an old sofa. My head sagged beneath the full weight of my tiredness. 'I can't handle Priory Court any more,' I said. 'Obe, we need to move out.'

He sighed; we had been here so many times before. Obe saw no need for us to leave the estate. It was real life, he always said. I used to feel that way too, when I first moved in. I loved the bustle, the mystery of other lives unfolding in the flats around me. I followed each storyline like a soap opera: the Kosovan woman who was always hoovering, and her daughter, who never took off her roller skates; the Hasidic family, who rarely met my eye; the Turkish lot who had delicious-smelling barbecues in the communal garden all through the summer.

But deep down I'd always assumed that Priory Court

would be temporary, that someday I would move out, into a nice quiet terraced house on the leafy streets. I grew up on the leafy streets, and some part of me still felt that was where I belonged. Obe, who had been brought up on an estate much like this, had no such delusions of grandeur.

'Okay, let's think about it,' he said carefully. 'Where would we move to?'

'Beckstow.'

'Where?'

'East. North-east. Not that far. You know, up by the North Circular.'

Obe looked nonplussed. He didn't want to leave zone two.

'It's on the up! Didn't you see that link I sent you last week?'

I had tagged him in a post from the Hackney Parents page. 'Why move to Beckstow?' read the headline, and underneath:

Property pundits have been plugging Beckstow for years, to no avail. It remains one of the best value and nicest places within easy reach of central London . . . good news for those trying to get a foot up on the property ladder.

'They're calling it "Little Hackney",' I told Obe.

He threw his head back and laughed. 'Just like they're calling Hackney "Little Islington". And Islington "Little Chelsea". Everybody wants to be somewhere else.'

Except you, I thought to myself. You never want to be anywhere other than right where you are.

The Toddler had finished his croissant. He grinned at us crummily and kicked his wellies a few times against the table leg. I was still distinctly hungry as we trundled home, despite having spent a quarter of our weekly food budget. Above the steady swish of traffic, I could hear Obe reciting quietly to himself: 'For I have known them all already, known them all – / Have known the evenings, mornings, afternoons, / I have measured out my life with coffee spoons . . .'

2.

Extinction

Incident No. 254. 8th January, 6.07 a.m.

Nightmare scenario: has D taken up the trumpet? A new noise started about half an hour ago. I can't think of anything else that would sound like this: piercingly loud, brassy, parping. Definitely too high to be a French horn. Could it be a saxophone? Or a crumhorn (NB what IS a crumhorn)? When I wished for soothing classical music, I did not mean this.

For the last hour I have been lying in bed staring at the crack in the ceiling directly above our bed. It definitely looks bigger than it did before. Note: if it reaches the light fitting, call the landlord.

Hours' sleep: 3, night feed, and then a light doze before the Dawn chorus.

'You can't go on like this,' said Frankie. 'You have to move.'

I nodded miserably. A warmer-than-average raindrop

snaked down the back of my neck. The Christmas holidays were but a memory, Obe was back at work, and my best mate Frankie and her son Caleb had come to meet us in the park. Despite the appalling weather conditions, Frankie managed to look stylish, in a yellow mac and ankle-length wellies, which matched her red Bugaboo. I was wearing my leaky black boots, and the ancient Puffa jacket I had owned since university. My tank-like double buggy was festooned with plastic carrier bags. Larkin and Caleb were in full waterproofs, feeding the ducks.

'Obviously we have to move,' I said, idly nibbling at some birdseed. 'But try telling Obe. He won't consider it.'

'You suggested Beckstow?'

'Vetoed,' I told her. 'He really struggles outside zone two.'

'Just ignore him,' said Frankie, in that confident way of hers. 'Beckstow would be a great investment. It is really on the up.'

'He thinks Priory Court has poetry.'

'That man could find poetry anywhere. In a bin, or a dead pigeon. He'll find poetry in Beckstow, all right.'

Thoughtfully, I threw a few crumbs to a friendly-looking lady mallard. But before she could get her beak anywhere near them, a Canada goose barged her out of the way and wolfed down the lot. Cheeky beggar! I threw another handful, deliberately closer to the mallard. But the same thing happened again.

'Hey, Franks! Since when did these geese move in?'

Frankie was too busy fiddling with her phone, unbothered, but I leaned in closer to work out the duck dynamics. There was no doubt about it – there was a new pond hierarchy in place. The mallards used to have a comfortable spot under the weeping willow. There were a few moorhens and pigeons, sure, but they seemed happy to scoop up whatever crumbs the mallards left behind.

But now the whole front section by the fence, prime breadcrumb territory, was occupied by scores of thick-necked Canada geese, with beady black eyes and determined expressions. The mallards were lurking hungrily in the water, way out of breadcrumb range. They looked miserable, ousted; their once-sleek feathers ruffled and drab.

A deep empathy kicked in as I looked at those mallards. I knew exactly what they were going through. I felt the same way myself, walking around this area, the place I had lived all my life, seeing the chino-clad bankers and stockbrokers strutting around the leafy streets like they owned the place. I set my jaw in resolve. I was going to get my birdseed to those mallards, by hook or by crook.

Perhaps if I climbed up onto the fence and got just the right angle . . .

'Jesus, Syl, what are you doing?'

'Just hold my hand,' I said, wobbling. I hurled my seeds, high and wide. Immediately the Canada geese started to advance in a menacing flock. But the lady mallard had their number. She was quicker off the mark. She was smaller, and more agile and, dammit, she wanted those seeds more than the geese did. Before they got anywhere near, she had snapped them all up and glided away.

Frankie helped me down off the fence. 'Well, that was worth risking life and limb for.'

I didn't bother explaining. There were some things Frankie would never understand.

Frankie and I had been friends since school. It had been clear to me, even aged eleven, that things were simpler for her. We both lived in Islington but went to a grammar school in the suburbs, so we had a long train ride together every morning. Frankie always made some small but well-judged alteration to her school uniform – a pair of sparkly Converse instead of dull Clarks T-bars, or a bias-cut skirt instead of scratchy nylon pleats. Often during the forty-five-minute train ride she would give me a 'style makeover'. She'd pull my hair back into a topknot, apply a tiny bit of eyeliner right in the corner of my eye, or roll my skirt-waist up and shorten my tie. I would emerge at Silver Street looking, and feeling, like someone not-quite-myself. As soon as we got to school, I'd rush into the toilets, roll my skirt down, and wash off the makeup. But somehow, the next time Frankie offered to make me over, I'd always say yes.

Soon after we met, Frankie invited me to her house. Mum dropped me off; Frankie's parents lived just around the corner from us, on one of the grandest streets in the borough. As we approached the Greek-pillared front door, Mum coughed, and made an odd face. *My goodness, it's a whole house,* she whispered, *on Highbury Place. What did you say her parents do?* I told her what Frankie had told me: her dad was deputy head of the Bank of England. It didn't mean much to me, but Mum seemed to find this significant. *I wish you'd told me, Sylvia.*

When Frankie's mum, Judith, answered the door, all smiles, Mum fluffed her perm nervously and said she couldn't come in for tea. *Another time that would be lovely, but I must get going.* Frankie had waved from the bottom of the stairs as I stepped into the cool, marble-tiled hall, scattered with her coats, bags and roller skates. Frankie's house felt solid, like a fortress.

Or maybe it was only later that it felt that way. After my dad died, very suddenly, of a heart attack, and Mum had to take on more shifts at the hospital. My little sister Lou was sent to after-school club, so our house was always empty when I got home.

I started going back to Frankie's after school, as often as I could. Judith would make us tea and toast, and Frankie would try and fail to teach me dance routines. I would relax for a while in that safe and solid place, and then after tea I would leave and trudge back around the corner to our smaller, sadder house, where something heavy would settle around my shoulders, like a cloak.

'So where's Mark at the moment, then?' I asked, as we made our way slowly towards the tennis courts. Mark was Frankie's husband. He was a barrister, and they lived in a large red-brick house on Jubilee Walk, one of the leafiest of the leafy streets. From the living room with its designer sofa to the bathroom with walk-in shower, from the period fireplace to the wisteria curling around the door, it was the Platonic ideal of a family home.

'Afghanistan,' said Frankie. 'He's writing their constitution.'

That sounded impressive, even for Mark. 'How does he know how to do that?'

'I guess he's just picking it up as he goes along.'

'Is that possible,' I asked carefully, 'with something like a constitution?'

Frankie shrugged. 'I guess so,' she said. 'At least, it is for Mark.'

Most of the time, I managed not to mind how differently things were working out for Frankie and me. It was just the natural product of a refined evolutionary process. Frankie would never have married someone poor and impractical like Obe. It would never have crossed her mind; just as it never would have crossed my mind to marry someone rich and respectable like Mark. The most aggravating thing about our financial situation was my suspicion – no, my knowledge – that I had somehow chosen it.

Not that Frankie's set-up was perfect, of course. Mark's work on international human rights cases was very important and highly paid, but it also demanded constant foreign travel, which was why Frankie had given up her job in telly – her award-winning job in film – to stay at home with Caleb. But if she minded giving up her career, Frankie never said so. She took it, as she took most things, easily in her stride.

On the fence around the courts there was a laminated A4 sign: 'Meet Here for the Workshop: Making a Hotel for Minibeasts'. It was one of a series put on by the council; others had included building a loggery and weaving a tunnel out of living willow. According to the leaflet, such activities helped children to 'participate in risk-taking tasks and build a sense of connection to the natural world.'

Whatever that meant, I was all for it. I'd booked places weeks ago for Larkin and Caleb. This morning Frankie had suggested that, as it was tipping it down, we could just go to the soft play centre instead, but I pointed out that their generation was probably going to need some survival skills. 'That's a cheery thought,' said Frankie, who seemed to find this amusing.

'Just being realistic,' I replied. 'A guy on the radio was saying it's much worse than we all think. A three-degree temperature rise is probably the bare minimum, which means a permanent melt of the entire Arctic ice sheet. By the time these guys are out of short trousers we could well be underwater.'

But Frankie had tuned out, rummaging in her bag for something: an umbrella, tissues, nutritious snacks. I counted on her to remember all these essentials.

'Yoo-hoo!' came a call from the other side of the courts. A woman in khaki waterproofs was striding towards us, smoking a roll-up. She chucked the butt into the bushes and clapped her burly hands. 'You here for the workshop?'

'Yes!' said Frankie enthusiastically. We extracted the boys from their buggies and they stood, swathed in waterproof suits, blinking drizzle from their eyes, staring silently at the instructor. She took off a large rucksack and put it down on the sodden grass. Then she disappeared behind the tree and re-emerged dragging a pallet painted bright blue. 'This,' she said triumphantly, 'is our wonderful minibeast hotel! Just imagine how cosy our minibeasts are going to be in there!'

The bright blue paint looked toxic to me, but it seemed churlish to quibble. It occurred to me that we should have explained to the boys beforehand what minibeasts were, and why they would need a hotel. But I also felt a little hazy on the details.

'Come on, Larkin!' I said gaily. 'Shall we make a bedroom for the bees?'

'Bees don't need bedrooms,' he replied. 'They're insects.'

The instructor nodded approvingly. 'You know a lot about bees!' she said. 'That's excellent. The human race is going to need people like you. Now, I've got some goodies here to make our hotel extra cosy!'

The instructor opened her rucksack and produced several jute bags filled with bunches of lavender, broken plant pots, sheep's wool, straw and dried seed heads. We encouraged the children to pick them up and put them into the pallet. That took about two minutes, and nobody seemed quite sure what to do next. The rain was intensifying from a light drizzle to a steady downpour.

The Toddler's eyes brightened momentarily when the instructor produced a power drill from the tool box, and set about fixing another pallet on top of the first.

'He's like Bob the Builder,' he said, admiringly.

'She,' I corrected him in a whisper. 'It's a lady.'

'No, it isn't,' he replied firmly.

Caleb was standing over by the fence, where a row of gardens backed onto the park. He had his eye pressed to a crack between the panels. Larkin trotted over to join him. What were they doing? I followed and peeped through the gap. On the other side was somebody's back garden, and on the lawn sat . . . a bright red, shiny, toddler-sized plastic car.

'Broom, broom,' said Larkin.

'Beep beep,' replied Caleb.

I smiled apologetically at the instructor. Clearly this was not quite the risk-taking, natural-world-connecting play we were supposed to be encouraging.

'Come on, boys!' she said, valiantly. 'Let's put another layer of lavender on top to attract the bees!'

But alas, it was too late – we had lost them. 'Don't want to build a hotel, Mummy. I want to play on the broom-broom car.' The instructor smiled kindly at me and shrugged. She knew her number was up.

'And that,' I observed to Frankie, as we loaded them both back into their buggies, 'is why the world is going to hell in a handcart.'

Later, back at Frankie's house, we got to looking at properties online. This was one of Frankie's favourite activities – as the owner of a whole house in zone 2, property chat was fun for her. Before Caleb was born, Frankie and Mark had their place redesigned by an architect. They'd removed several of the original walls; it was all spare, light-filled spaces and skylights. We were sitting downstairs in her large, airy kitchen, which opened out into a living-room-cum-play-area. On a rational level, I knew a room like this couldn't actually be the answer to all life's difficulties.

'Ooooh, look at this one,' she purred, tapping on a picture of a magnificent double-fronted Edwardian home just around the corner. 'Look at the period features! Isn't it gorgeous?'

I took the tablet and flicked guiltily through the pictures. I had promised Obe that I would kick my GoodMove habit. It had been at least three weeks since I last looked – but now, surely, with all this talk of a property crash, it was worth having just a quick browse. Frankie was right – the house was beautiful. It had ornate fireplaces and a kitchen with a huge table. There was no wisteria, that I could see, but I could always plant one. It was, in short, my dream home I didn't bother checking the price.

'Well, of course it's gorgeous,' I snapped. 'But what's your point, frankly.'

The boys were getting all the toys out of Caleb's bespoke wooden cabinet; Frankie didn't buy furniture from IKEA.

'I've got a new digger,' I overheard Caleb telling Larkin. 'It's the biggest digger in the whole world.' The new digger was indeed enormous, shiny and yellow. Larkin's eyes widened.

'Make sure you share it, Caleb,' Frankie called over. I put the tablet to one side and looked down at That Baby, who was supposed to be feeding. He must be nearly ready for weaning, as he kept breaking off to stare at the lunch Frankie had set out: pots of houmous, baba ganoush, French bread, cherry tomatoes, pre-chopped carrots and celery. Frankie did all her shopping at Waitrose online, she never went to Lidl or Aldi and probably never considered crossing the threshold of Poundland. That was the other reason I liked going to her house.

I sat Eliot up and experimentally gave him a celery stick to hold. He stuck it in his eye first, thought about it for a bit, and then located his drooling, gummy mouth. 'That's it, little 'un,' I whispered to him, softly. 'Keep going like that, and soon you won't need me any more.' Which would be just as well, as my return to full-time work was looming – three months, four days.

Frankie sat down and grabbed a carrot stick. 'So. Anything interesting?'

'No. I mean, I didn't really look.' My voice was flat; this was not a good topic. 'I'm just not sure now is a great time to buy,' I went on, scooping too much baba ganoush onto a piece of bread. 'I mean, what with the state of the nation.' Frankie's sympathetic expression conveyed that she felt the state of the nation was a side issue. Politically, her instincts were unfailingly generous, but somehow distant and fuzzy, like the world was a game that had nothing to do with her. I guessed it was easier to feel that way once you were a property owner.

'Are you stockpiling yet?' I asked provocatively. I was, as far as budget would allow: one extra tin of tomatoes every time I went to the shop. As long as I had tomatoes, I told myself, things couldn't get that bad.

'That's hilarious,' said Frankie. 'Of course not! It'll all work out in the end. It has to.'

Eliot, who obviously shared Frankie's hilarity, cackled

loudly. He had dropped his celery stick on the floor, and I had picked it up for him. He grabbed it, and very deliberately dropped it again.

'Anyway, stop it, Syl,' said Frankie, sternly. 'You're going down The Hole.' The Hole was her term for a dark place I sometimes went to. Not so much a physical place, as a mental one. It hadn't occurred to me that I was anywhere near The Hole, but this is the joy and pain of having very old friends; they know you better than you know yourself. 'Look. Give me that.'

She snatched the tablet, scrolling and tapping with quiet efficiency. Meanwhile, there was a yelp from the living room: Larkin had snatched Caleb's digger, and was ramming it repeatedly against the bespoke cabinet while Caleb cried helplessly. I jumped up and separated them. 'Sharing is caring,' I told him, 'remember'. But after I returned the digger to Caleb, Larkin stuck his tongue out. I let it pass.

'Unbelievable,' said Frankie. 'Look at this.'

She handed me the tablet again, and this time the picture was much less prepossessing. It was a grainy photograph of a small, pebbledash 1930s two-up-two-down in Beckstow. There were only two images of the house, both of the exterior: nothing from inside. 'In need of modernisation', read the blurb.

Frankie scanned the pages with an expert eye. She

scrolled around, enlarging the pictures and peering at them. 'You could almost afford this, couldn't you?'

Through my brain-fug I attempted some mental arithmetic. We had inherited some money when Obe's mum died, just after Larkin was born. It was a lot of money, or rather in any sane world it would have been a lot of money, the proceeds of selling her flat in Birmingham. But in reality it was just barely enough for a deposit. During my two maternity leaves, the balance had been gradually dwindling.

Inside my mind, the arithmetic exploded, firing out a heap of random numbers. 'Possibly.'

'I think you should look at it. Wrecks like this never come onto the open market. It's unheard of. They always go to developers.' My pulse rate was rising. 'Crash or no crash,' said Frankie, 'think of all the desperate families just like yours who have been waiting years to find something at this price.' But I didn't want to think about all the desperate families just like ours; I only wanted to think about ours. She snapped the tablet case shut, put it down on the table, and reached for her phone. 'Right,' she said. 'I'm calling them now. We've got to move fast.'

Frankie drove us all out to Beckstow that afternoon in her nippy new hybrid car, buggies folded in the back.

Down the High Street, past the artisan coffee places and the arty cinema, we reached Clapton roundabout, and then turned onto the unfamiliar territory of Lea Bridge Road. The subtle taupe shopfronts gradually gave way to primary colours: Betfair, Western Union and Chicken 4U blinked garishly through the drizzle. The people on the pavement were hunched into cheap overcoats, pushing buggies and shopping carts, battling through the rain and the traffic.

'How far out is this place, then?' asked Frankie.

'Just keep going,' I said, examining the blue arrow on my phone. 'If you hit the North Circular, you've gone too far.'

The house was in the furthest-flung part of north-east London, the 'burbs proper. This area was hanging onto the capital by its fingertips. The streets were quiet, almost eerily so; here and there, a determined tree fought its way up through the tarmac. Eventually we came to the turning; Jewel Road was a small cul-de-sac lined with vans. The houses were small and square, with two windows at the bottom and two at the top, like a child's drawing with all the colour removed.

Parked on the curve of the cul-de-sac was a big black car with tinted windows. As we approached, the driver's door swung open, and a very shiny man emerged, jangling a set of keys.

'Rob Crockett,' said the estate agent, holding out his free hand. I waited in vain for him to tell me his name was a joke, but he simply said, with polished sincerity: 'Believe me, ladies – this place is a diamond in the rough.'

His hand was damp, his face was nearly as glossy as his suit, and his large black shoes were mirror-bright patent leather. They tapped smartly on the crazy-paved path as he made his way up the drive. The house had a patch of front garden with a straggly rose bush and a tangle of overgrown grass. It was small and grey, or maybe that's just the way it made me feel.

'As I'm sure you know, this area is on the up,' Rob Crockett continued, as we followed him towards the front door. 'Don't believe what they say about a housing crash. I've got people lining up at every open day, buyers with cash deposits from mum and dad. Fastest rising house prices in London last year, so there's no doubt that this would be a fantastic investment.'

The door stuck halfway, and Rob Crockett rammed it hard with his shoulder. Frankie and Caleb went in first, while he gallantly helped me over the step with the buggy. Somehow, he managed to keep talking.

'You see, I'm not like other estate agents. I've been in this area all my life, seen its little ups and downs, so, believe me, I know: this is one place where values will hold. We opened two more branches last year, that's how confident we are.'

Inside, the hall was dark. There was a swirly orange-and-brown carpet and a strange smell that brought the word 'putrid' unbidden to my mind.

'Dis-GUS-ting,' said Larkin, seizing the chance to put one of his favourite words to good use. He clutched his nose with a chubby hand.

'Ah, the smell. There's a story there,' said Rob Crockett, ushering us into the living room. It was poky and square, and the carpet was still swirly, but blue this time. Double doors led through to a back room, with the same carpet, worn away where a dining table had once been, and a warped old back door. 'The previous resident was an old lady who went doolally, bless her. She was going down Tesco's every day, buying meat and fish, and keeping it all in her kitchen for months. The smell got so bad the neighbours called up her son – who is now the vendor. They thought she'd died!'

As I looked at him, I remembered the naked mole-rat at London Zoo. We had taken Larkin there to see the lions, but they were all asleep, and we ended up trans-fixed instead by this trembling, eyeless creature scurrying round and round its plastic tube like a fragment of nightmare brought to life.

'And had she?' I asked.

'What?'

'Had she died?'

'Oh no!' Rob Crockett laughed like a drain. 'He put her in a home. That's why he's selling it.'

Perhaps sensing that he was losing me, he swiftly changed tack. 'You'll have to use your imagination,' he said, gesturing around at the splintered bay window, the rusting gas fire. 'Just blank out what it actually looks like now, and think about . . . the potential. And if you need any high-quality furniture, you need look no further. I've got five antique shops out in Epping, so just say the word and I can kit you out.'

'You're quite the entrepreneur,' I said, flattering him. 'Watch out Alan Sugar.'

'I once thought about going on *The Apprentice*,' said Rob Crockett, in a wistful tone, 'but when you think about it, it's really not worth it. The prize is only half a million quid.'

From the hall came the sound of Caleb and Larkin shooting each other. They'd been doing this a lot recently, despite Frankie and I both having blanket bans on plastic guns and violence of any sort. 'Pow pow. You're dead.'

'You're deader.'

I stood in the middle of the sitting room and closed my eyes. If I held my breath as well, I could imagine I was in a nice Victorian terrace, French windows, distressed pine flooring. I could almost forget that I was in a two-up two-down just off the North Circular. Almost, but not quite: the hum of traffic was audible.

'You might want to take this out, to make a through lounge,' said Rob Crockett, banging on the double doors, which wobbled like the set of a cheap soap opera. 'And you'll need a new kitchen, obviously.'

The kitchen was almost as small as the one in Priory Court. A wall cabinet was hanging loose at a 45-degree angle, and the door on one of the cupboards had come off. The smell was particularly intense by the fridge. After all the excitement of racing to Beckstow for the viewing, my heart was sinking fast. We couldn't live in this house. It was uninhabitable.

I shrugged apologetically at Rob Crockett. 'I'm sorry,' I said. 'We may be wasting your time. It needs an awful lot of work. More than we could take on.'

'Hey, Syl,' called Frankie, who by now had made her way methodically through the house and was now in the dining room, by the back door, 'just come in here a sec.' Rob Crockett followed me over, but she fixed him with one of her smiles. 'If you wouldn't mind,' she said, 'I'd just like to talk to my friend in private.'

She took me by the arm. 'I know it doesn't look like much now,' she said, 'but actually, he is right. You have to think about the potential.'

'Frankie,' I said. 'It's a dump. It's disgusting. It stinks.'

'It stinks *now*,' she said. 'But just think about this. You could knock through into the kitchen, remove the back wall, and create a lovely light back extension. You could even hang lots of lovely pots on this side, create a kind of green wall.' She gestured at a large expanse of pock-marked wallpaper. I followed her gaze doubtfully. 'Seriously, it would look amazing,' she said. 'I saw something like that in Elle decoration.'

Before they moved to their current place, Frankie and Mark did up and sold three flats; she knew everything there was to know about home renovation. Frankie got a buzz from plans and quotes, plumbers and plasterers, doorknobs and light switches, for me, one glance at the IKEA catalogue induced a combination of intense stress and overwhelming boredom.

'So you'd knock down the entire back wall?'

'Yup. Take it out. Extend out into the back garden. Skylights, French windows. Breakfast bar. Utility area.'

Eliot started to whimper; he was hungry again. I settled down to feed him cross-legged on the swirly carpet with my back to the grubby flock wallpaper. I was tired, so tired. Everything Frankie said was making me tireder.

'And, er, how much,' I ventured, in a small voice, 'do you think all that might cost?'

Frankie ticked the main points off on her fingers as

she did the calculations. 'The bathroom, the kitchen, the extension, garden landscaping, replastering, new electrics and plumbing – you may as well, while you're at it – tiling, complete redecoration . . .'

She then named a figure that almost made my eyes bleed.

'But the main thing,' said Frankie, her face pressed up against the glass of the back window, 'is out here. Check this out.'

She summoned Rob Crockett, who produced another set of keys from his shiny jacket pocket. It took several shoves before the back door opened. Larkin dashed outside first, and once Eliot had finished we followed him onto a cracked concrete step. Before us was a sea of brambles. But the sea seemed to go on for ever. The back fence was far away in the distance, beyond a huddle of gnarled old apple trees; an orchard, I thought, grandly.

I had no idea that gardens like this existed in London. It was big enough to get lost in; big enough for two small boys to have endless adventures; big enough for my veggie patch, for a shed – for two sheds, one for Obe, one for me. He could write free verse and fulfil his long-held ambition to learn spoon-whittling; once I'd slept for a month, I could start work on my blueprint for a better world.

'It's got a park!' Larkin was half way to the fence,

beating back the brambles with a stick, Caleb bringing up the rear. They looked like miniature colonial explorers laying claim to a new country.

'Quite something, isn't it?' said Rob Crockett, with a narrow smile.

'Quite something,' I repeated to Frankie, feeling a little dazed.

She nodded. 'It really is.'

Larkin came rushing back with a question. 'When we live here, will That Baby come and visit?'

I sighed and tousled his frizzy hair. 'Your brother will be coming with us, love.'

'Let me give you a little bit of advice,' said Rob Crockett as he showed us out. 'Think about it, but don't take too long. You see, my dears,' he leaned towards us conspiratorially, 'I know things are tough for young families these days, and I like to do my best for you. My colleagues think I'm a mug. "Why do you bother, Rob?" they ask me, "just sell it to a developer." But that's not the way I like to do business.'

I nodded sagely, taking in the true magnitude of Rob Crockett's contribution to society.

'Believe me, my dear,' he said as he closed the door. 'If you manage to buy this place, I'll be on your Christmas card list for years to come.'

3.

Reaching out

Incident No. 255. 9th January, 2 a.m.

I might even miss Dawn's R'n'B medley once we move out. Perhaps, if I ask her nicely, she would make me a mix tape.

I've noticed a strange smell coming from down there: rubbery but sweet. Like marshmallows, but more . . . chemical.

The crack is definitely wider. I must ask Obe to check it when he wakes up. How does he sleep through this music?

Do men hear a different frequency, like dogs?

Hours' sleep: a pleasant nap between 9–11.

THERE was something going on outside, some kind of unusual bustle in the communal garden. 'Who Let the Dogs Out' was playing on a tinny stereo. I went out onto the balcony to take a look: there was a flimsy blue gazebo set up on the lawn, flapping away in the wind and the drizzle. Beneath it I could just make out the figure of

Brenda: wide, sturdy, her steel-grey bob slightly mussed up by the elements. Immediately I tried to duck down behind the plant pots, but it was too late – she'd already spotted me.

'Hey there, Sylvia!' she boomed up, in her broad Glaswegian accent. I guessed Brenda was in her sixties; she lived on the ground floor with her husband, Ian, who was as narrow as she was wide, as meek as she was formidable. I waved awkwardly, hoping she hadn't noticed me trying to hide, then fiddled around with the watering can in a futile effort to look like I had things to do. 'Come on down, I need to talk to you!'

I knew what she wanted, and it was going to take all the cunning I had to get out of it. Brenda was the head of the Priory Court Tenants and Residents Association, and exactly the kind of community-spirited person I wanted to be, one day – just not quite yet. She wanted me – she wanted everyone – to Get Involved. And I wholeheartedly endorsed that, in theory. What Priory Court could do with, more than anything, was a bit of community spirit. But right now, I couldn't get roped into endless TRA meetings, bulb-planting mornings, bus trips to Southend . . . I could barely get my own shoes on in the morning.

'I'll be down in a bit, Brenda.' That was good – non-specific, non-committal. 'Just a bit busy with the baby.'

'Bring the baby!' yelled Brenda, in what was clearly an order.

Soon enough, I found myself down there, coated up against the weather, Eliot on my hip. Larkin ran off to play on the swings, with the roller skate girl. I had never seen her in ordinary shoes. She spent even the greyest afternoons swooping in wide loops around the forecourt, with a look of pure liberation on her face; even watching her felt like flying.

I gave her a little wave. I liked roller skates; she was a free spirit. Unlike her poor mother, a meek and mousy woman who spoke almost no English. She was a compulsive cleaner; her hoover whined constantly from their flat on the fourth floor. I wondered what she was saying through that hoover.

'Soooooo,' said Brenda, drawing out her extravagant Scottish vowels. She smoothed her grey bob, which always made me think of a tin hat; as Priory Court's organiser-in-chief, she needed one. 'Lovely to see you. Welcome to our little awareness-raising event.'

When Brenda said 'our' it was purely figurative; she was dearly the only person raising awareness. She picked up a leaflet from the picnic table under the gazebo and offered it to me.

'Before we get into all this, though, tell me: have you had any luck with the council, about, you know – '

she nodded her head up towards the second floor, where Dawn's balcony door was flapping open – 'our friend?'

'Not yet,' I said breezily. 'We're just making records, you know, documenting it all – I know Bill is on the case.'

'They take forever,' said Brenda. 'How long has it been now?'

'Nearly three years.'

'We're lucky with our neighbours, mind. The worst we get with old Ethel is *The Archers* on too loud. But who knows how long we'll be lucky for – you had Cora before, didn't you?'

Cora was a quiet old lady who had lived downstairs when I first moved into Priory Court. She'd been there ever since the estate was built, one of the older generation of long-term council tenants that were now dying off. They had been replaced by large families on temporary tenancies, people like Dawn, who should have been in an institution, or at least cared for in the community, or buy-to-let landlords who rented out the flats at commercial rates to 'young professionals' like Obe and me.

Cora told me once that in the '60s all the mothers on the estate would meet every day in the communal washrooms, they all knew each other and brought up their children together. 'It was a lovely place, then. People looked after it,' she said. 'Now, nobody cares.' Nobody stuck around these days. Tenants came and went mysteriously, leaving only the pile of mouldering mattresses by the communal bins as evidence of their stay. Brenda's was a lone communal voice in the wilderness.

'If you want to bring up the anti-social behaviour stuff, you should do it at the next Tenants and Residents Association meeting – just let me know if you'd like me to put it on the agenda.'

'Thanks, Brenda, but I won't make it, unfortunately,' I said, cutting her off quickly before this could go any further. 'It's hard for me to get out in the evening.' After all, Obe and I had been considering embarking on *Game of Thrones*. 'Maybe when the kids are bigger . . .'

Slowly but surely, a scattering of Priory Court residents was gathering around the gazebo. There was Zeynab, one of the Turkish mums, in a floral headscarf, with her son Hassan; the father from one of the Hasidic Jewish families in full flowing robes, clutching, for some reason, a small fishing net. Brenda handed out a few more leaflets.

'Welcome, welcome, everyone. Just a little bit of information here about some big developments on the estate,' she said. 'This is going to be really significant for everyone who lives here – so it's important we all get informed. Pull together, you know. Reach out to our friends and neighbours.'

I looked at the leaflet, which announced in big red letters that it had been produced by Hackney Council in Association with High-Class Homes. *Riverside Apartments* said the green writing, with a blue river looping around it. *Housing for the 21st century. Waterside living within 20 minutes of central London.* There was a picture of a ladybird, and a gleaming fox with bright white whiskers. *An eco-development,* it said. *Creating habitats, fostering bio-diversity.*

On the back there was a picture of our road, but it didn't look like our road. There was no traffic, or rubbish, and there were no drunk people sitting on the benches. In the picture, it was gloriously sunny. The pavements were wide and clear, and lined with trees. Computer-generated couples were strolling, arm-in-arm and laughing, around the bright blue reservoir. Children from a careful range of ethnic groups were playing on the banks. In the background loomed two gigantic, gleaming, glass tower blocks.

'This looks lovely,' I said, to nobody in particular. 'It just doesn't—'

'Look like Priory Court?' interrupted Brenda. 'Well, quite. We have a lot of questions about these plans.'

When she said 'we', I guessed that was figurative, too.

The Hasidic man was frowning at the leaflet. 'Madam, I am Abraham,' he said in an Eastern European accent, holding out his hand formally. 'Please: where is our block in this picture?'

'Your guess,' replied Brenda, 'is as good as mine.'

Zeynab elbowed her way to the front. 'What you mean?' she asked – Zeynab's headscarf framed a neat, unsmiling face. She was small but hard-as-nails, like one of those cute but snappy pug dogs with black, glittery eyes. She sounded a little aggressive, but perhaps it was just her accent. 'They gonna knock our block down?'

'We don't know,' said Brenda. 'They are calling it regeneration. But they're going to tell us more in a couple of months, at an Extraordinary General Meeting of the Tenants and Residents Association – here are the details.' She held up one of her familiar information notices, scrawled in black magic marker on a piece of fluorescent green paper. Brenda's garish posters were forever cropping up in the lift and on the communal noticeboards; everyone ignored them, as far as I knew. 'LEARN MORE ABOUT THE COUNCIL'S PLANS!!!!' this one said. 'COME ALONG AND MEET THE BIG-WIGS, HOLD HIGH-CLASS HOMES TO ACCOUNT. 15th MARCH, IN THE COMMUNITY ROOM.'

Zeynab tapped the details into her phone. I was beginning to feel like I might have to go to the meeting after all – Hassan was the same age as The Toddler, so my child-based excuses looked ever more flimsy. And *Game of Thrones* was probably too much of a commitment, anyway.

When Zeynab caught my eye I gave her a cautious smile. At one point I'd tried to make friends. I wanted to get to know my neighbours, and the leafy streeters were stressing me out, with their house-price chat and Danish-design baby clothing. I thought I might have more in common with the other Priory Court mums. But it hadn't proved easy, what with the cultural differences. I had bumped into Zeynab one morning just after That Baby was born, as I pushed him along the street in his pram. The conversation went wrong almost straight away. She peeped in to see him bundled up asleep, and made a little clicking noise.

'How old he is now?'

'He's six weeks.'

'Six weeks! He tiny! Are you breastfeeding or something?'

Never tell a breastfeeding mother that her baby looks small, it's like laughing and wiggling your little finger at a naked man. And she didn't stop there.

'Did you mean to have another? I mean, two very

hard. When you're paying landlord, you have to go back to work. Very hard.'

'No, I – I've always wanted two,' I stuttered.

'Ali would never let me work,' she said. 'He's out there day and night driving his minicab.'

This was not the comforting vibe I had been hoping for. I wasn't prepared for the little thrill of envy I felt at the thought of a council subsidised rent, and a husband who took full financial responsibility. I did not like that thrill, or what it said about me as a person.

'Your big one – what his name? Funny name, no?'

'Larkin,' I said. 'It's Larkin.'

'Larkin!' she laughed. 'So funny! Well, bring Larkin over to play with Hassan. Any time.'

I looked at Hassan but he didn't smile. He just stared back, rolling his lolly stick from one side of his mouth to the other. 'That sounds lovely.' I said politely.

I never did call on her, though. The Priory Court mums didn't seem to be the answer, after all.

Brenda's stereo was now playing 'Gangnam Style', and Larkin, Hassan and roller-skates girl all knew the moves. She broke into a rapid floss, which Larkin and Hassan tried to copy. Flossing on wheels; she was definitely the coolest girl on the estate. On the second floor, Dawn materialised on her balcony, gazing down groggily at our gathering below.

'She not good person,' Zeynab said in a low voice, lowering her head meaningfully in the direction of Dawn's balcony. 'She drink person, drug person.'

Dawn waved enthusiastically at us, and grinned, revealing three cracked teeth. Today's outfit was not her most glamorous: baggy black tracksuit bottoms, a tattered Puffa jacket, and an outsized black beanie. Her face was creased and yellow. When I saw Dawn, rather than just heard her, my anger mutated into something different, something heavier. She watched the kids for a moment, and with slow, jerky movements she started to floss.

'Look, Mummy!' cried The Toddler, pointing. 'She can do it!'

'I know! Well, so can I.'

'No, you can't!'

'I can!' I'd been practising in front of the mirror. 'Look.' I started slowly, moving my arms one way, my hips the other. Zeynab took one look at me and joined in, her hips and arms swinging rapidly. She was good – she must have been practising, too.

'Over the rainbow!' shouted Hassan, swinging his arms wildly above his head, his pudgy belly sticking out from beneath his Spiderman T-shirt. The Toddler flailed his arms so hard he ended up in a heap on the grass.

I tried to imagine what we would all look like to an alien visitor, this motley crew of people standing out in the drizzle, united in the floss. I glanced at Abraham, longing for him to join us, setting those robes swinging. But he kept his powder dry; with a small, shy smile he scurried off towards the reservoir, fishing net in hand. I wondered what he was catching, presumably he wasn't planning to eat it.

Obe got back late from work, because – big step, huge – he had been to see the Beckstow house. He clattered in once the kids were already in bed, and I was lying in the bath reading *Style* magazine. Peering around the bathroom door, he squinted at the cover and shook his head disparagingly.

'Reading that rag again? I thought you hated it.'

'I do hate it,' I told him. 'That's why I'm reading it.'

There was little point in explaining the intricacies of my relationship with *Style* magazine to Obe. He thought I read it to lust after all the pretty dresses. In fact, I was training myself not to want things. It was going quite well. I had already decided that I did not want a pair of Yves Saint Laurent mules, a chandelier made from plastic antlers, or a diamond-encrusted necklace in the shape of a pineapple. I was still working on not wanting a fitted farmhouse kitchen in warm wood.

'So,' I said warily. 'What did you think?'

'Hmmm.' He sat down heavily on the lid of the toilet, his knees thudding up against the bath. He had an even dreamier look in his eyes than usual. 'Actually, I liked it.' This was big. I put down the magazine. 'It has a lot of potential.' Obe paused, scratched his head, sending his curls springing. 'The place has something about it,' he said. 'An intangible essence. A soul. I even liked the carpets, they're kind of retro.'

That snapped me out of it; here, I had to draw a firm line. 'Only if vomit is retro,' I said. 'The carpets have to go.'

But he was off and away. 'We'd need to get the chimney checked out,' he said, 'but a wood-burning stove would be cosy for cold winter nights. And the garden! Those trees! I sat out there listening to birdsong as the sun was setting.'

I smiled internally, imagining Rob Crockett's impatient jangling as Obe rhapsodised over sunset birdsong.

'And what about the area? Can you imagine living out in Beckstow?'

He pulled himself up straight, closed his eyes. 'My true home has no walls / no man can buy it, sell it / or knock it down.'

'Is that a yes?'

'That haiku just came to me on the way home.' He reached down and dipped his fingers into the water, tickling my ankle. 'You know, Syl, it doesn't really matter where we are.'

'So do you think we should make an offer?'

Obe's jaw clenched. 'Well, if we're going to do that, we need to talk tactics.' He had been planning our approach: we were going to play hardball. If the estate agent thought he could have one over on us, just because his suits were shiny and his patter was cockney, he'd got another thing coming. Because we had one clear advantage here – we were not desperate for this house. If the price wasn't right, we would simply walk away.

Let's face it, Obe went on, warming to his theme, the place was a dump. It had no functioning kitchen or bathroom, it smelled strongly of rotting meat, and it was situated less than a minute's walk from a major ring road. No one in their right mind would want it. Rob Crockett was lucky we were around to save his bacon.

'We make our offer, and we don't go a penny over,' he said, almost snarling. 'And if he doesn't like it, well he can stick it.'

'Okay,' I snarled back, impressed. I'd never seen Obe's hardball side before.

Before getting out of the bath I slid my head underwater and stayed there for a moment, temporarily removed from the real world. I had baths every night that winter, long ones, boiling hot, after both kids were in bed and the day was finally nearing its end. It was the only place where I didn't feel cold to my bones. Submerged in water, my whole body loosened. I remembered heat and how it felt to let go. I remembered the summer day when everything changed. When I told Obe the news I was pregnant he couldn't stop laughing.

'Oh, that's brilliant,' he said, as if I'd just cracked a great joke. I was sitting on the patch of grass outside my office with the phone pressed against my head. I watched a boat chug past, along the River Thames, and wished I was on it; anything not to go back into the office with red eyes and sore breasts and the overwhelming feeling that I had bitten off more than I could chew.

'Do you think so?' I said anxiously.

'Don't you?'

There was a pause. Obe's breath crackled down the line. In the background I could hear the familiar shouts and bangs of the playscheme where he worked, in Haringey, on the other side of the river. I imagined jumping in and swimming across, turning up at the gates dripping wet, so Jase and all the other autistic kids could bear me in on their shoulders like a vanquished princess and deliver me to Obe on the deck of the wooden pirate-ship climbing frame.

'It's amazing,' I said. 'It's just . . .' I lay back on the grass and put my hand on my belly. Was that the baby fluttering inside, or was it fear? Clouds were moving steadily past the office block above, and for a moment I imagined that it was falling. We'd have to move in together, now. We'd have to stop pretending, and become proper grown-ups. 'Are we going to be okay?'

'The future can be promised to no one,' said Obe.

'That's not the answer I was looking for,' I said.

'Okay, then,' he said. 'We'll definitely be one-hundred-per-cent brilliant.'

When the bump was just starting to show, Obe moved into Priory Court. All he had to show for thirty-two years on this earth was a suitcase, two cardboard boxes of books and a plastic bag filled with what looked like old receipts. It wasn't even enough to fill a van; he just brought it over in the back of a taxi and deposited it on the bed in the spare room.

'Is that all you have?' I asked him as he unpacked and carefully stowed a Beastie Boys 1990 tour T-shirt, apparently bought at the original gig and now laced with holes.

'Who needs stuff?' said Obe. 'It just weighs you down.'

Back then, I was only just starting to identify problems that had never occurred to me before. Like the fact that Obe was on minimum wage at the playscheme; like the fact that thinking-about-poetry was not a career. I had come of age in one of the wealthiest cities in the world, at the peak of capitalist excess; my generation was weaned on ecstasy, alcopops and cheap credit. It had taken me a while to work out that money didn't just magically appear when you needed it.

'We'll be happy, you'll see,' Obe used to say, whenever I woke up in the night, pulse racing, mouth dry, feeling the small, unfamiliar flickering of the thing that would one day become The Toddler. And he was right: we had been happy, most of the time. It was only after That Baby was born that the fog started to gather around the edges of my brain, shutting out the light, obscuring all the good things in my life. Some mornings, that winter, I couldn't see through it at all.

But now Obe liked the house and, who knew, perhaps that would solve the problem. I lay there and let the water creep into my ears, then my eyes, blurring out sound, blurring out vision, blurring out everything.

4.

Nudge

Incident No. 256. 10th January, 3 a.m.

Party downstairs. Even the foxes can hear it. Cub 1 and Cub 2 are out there rolling about in the nettles, biting each other's necks. Mummy Fox watches them protectively from underneath a tree. Sometimes Daddy Fox is there too, but not now. He is probably skulking around the bins on the estate, looking for choice morsels to bring back to his family. He's a good father, providing for them.

Another of Priory Court's little mysteries: there is somebody sitting down by the reservoir, dressed in black. What on earth is he doing?

Hours' sleep: 5, so far. Feeling pretty fresh.

BILL took ten days to respond to my desperate New Year's plea for help, but as soon as I heard his voice on the line I forgave him. Bill spoke in the scrupulous monotone of a man who had truly heard it all.

'Sorry for the delay, Sylvia,' he said. 'I was away over

New Year. And we've had redundancies here at the Anti-Social Behaviour Unit, so we're focusing on urgent cases.'

It occurred to me to wonder why, after three years of R'n'B hell, mine wasn't an urgent case. But somehow I couldn't hold it against Bill. He had called, and that made me happy, and besides I was sure he must have a very good reason.

'I quite understand, Bill,' I assured him. Over the three years that Bill had been my Anti-Social Behaviour case-worker, he had assumed a key role in my life. He had never been able to do much about Dawn's anti-social behaviour, but in other senses our relationship had blossomed. Bill had become a valuable source of support on matters ranging far beyond his council-approved remit. In fact, sometimes I felt that he was the only person who really had my back in the whole wide world.

I painted a brief portrait for him of Dawn's activities downstairs since New Year: the music, the parties, her tendency to pass out in or near the lift. Bill sucked his teeth. 'Dear, dear,' he said. 'No improvement there, then.'

'None at all, Bill. Is there anything you can do about it?'

'We are still at the evidence-gathering stage,' said Bill. 'Then we will move on to formulating the action plan. Are you writing it all down in the logbook?'

'Oh, yes,' I said, glancing over at the logbook on the window sill and admiring its stern, administrative appearance. 'I'm keeping extensive records. You know you can rely on me.'

'I do, Sylvia.'

There was a mutually satisfied pause, before I said, 'Anyway. Seeing as you can't actually do anything about Dawn right now, could I ask your advice about another issue that's been on my mind?'

'Fire away,' said Bill.

I took a deep breath. 'We're hoping to move out of Priory Court – to buy a house.'

'That is wonderful news!' said Bill, with an enthusiasm that I trusted had nothing to do with the prospect of being able to close our case.

'But there is something worrying me,' I went on. 'Do you think it's wise to take on a large mortgage at this point? Obe – my not-quite-husband, you know – doesn't earn much. It will rule out any possibility of me going part-time. So both kids will go into childcare – and I haven't even worked out the cost of that, yet.'

'That's a tough one,' said Bill, sympathetically. 'The mother-baby attachment at this age is so critical. And as much as I'm sure you'd consider yourself a feminist, there is a lot of pressure on women who are primary bread-winners when their children are small.'

'Exactly,' I said, feeling that warm glow I always got from my little chats with Bill. There was a brief pause, and some deep, sonorous breathing. I pictured Bill staring wisely into space, perhaps stroking his beard – I was sure he had a beard.

'What does Obe like to do? Does he have any dreams, plans, passions?'

'He loves poetry.'

'Writing it?'

'Occasionally. But mostly just – thinking about it.'

'Hmmm,' said Bill. He had an answer for most things, but I was really challenging him here. 'How about teaching?'

'I've always wanted him to train as a teacher!' I cried. How did Bill know that I nursed a fantasy about Obe doing teacher training? I could picture it so clearly: it was the summer holidays, 2025. We'd packed the kids off to some kind of boot camp, and we were on a walking holiday in Tuscany. The sun was shining, the wild flowers blooming. We were staying in one of those places where twinkly-eyed Italian farmers grow delicious food and their wives feed it to you. We were, in other words, fully-fledged members of the professional middle classes at leisure.

When I let myself dream this dream, I could almost feel the sun on my neck, the chilled Chianti as it slipped down my throat . . . God, it felt good. It felt like finally, after all the fretting and squabbling and messing about, order had been restored to the universe.

Deep inside, I knew that the reality of teaching was sure to be stressful and underpaid, but that didn't matter. This was not about reality. It was about me clinging desperately to the idea that there was a vaguely realistic solution to the financial crisis; a way for us to achieve the standard of living that we deserved.

'OK. Well, if that's what you want, play the long game. Don't nag, don't plead, but rather employ some basic nudge tactics. Have you come across nudge? It is a school of sociological thought, which argues that people are more susceptible to subtle, well-placed hints than to straightforward information-based arguments.'

This was the beauty of Bill: he made me feel more in control of things. As long as I didn't expect him to sort out the Dawn situation, he was always happy to help me out, in matters large and small. I felt lighter, happier, less tense, as I bid him farewell.

'Where are you moving to, by the way?'

'Beckstow,' I replied. 'It's really—'

'On the up,' said Bill. 'An excellent investment. They're calling it "the new Hackney".'

* * *

As soon as That Baby had gone down for his nap, I got out a pen, paper and a calculator. Before phoning Rob Crockett to play hardball, I was determined to do the maths, and work out what we could actually afford. Soon my calculations covered an entire page in numbers, squiggles, brackets, asterisks and crossings-out. It looked a little like the Rosetta Stone, and made about as much sense.

If we offered the asking price, used up Obe's mum's money, and borrowed the rest, I noted down the following options:

1. We both work full-time, put the kids into childcare.
2. Obe goes part-time and I persuade my mum to do the rest.
3. Work at home and look after Eliot at the same time, using a combination of Calpol and CBeebies.

But no matter what I put on one side of the equation, the number on the other remained the same: 100. We would have a maximum of £100 left over each month, after paying our mortgage, childcare, bills and food. That would need to cover clothes, petrol, travel to and from work, lunch, activities, car and house maintenance, birthdays . . .

I took one more look at the piece of paper, and then

slowly, in a mature, considered fashion, screwed it up and hid it right at the bottom of the bin.

As my finger hovered over the call button, a shadow of doubt flickered across my mind. The offer we had decided on was significantly less than the asking price – did we really have a hope in hell? As Bill said, we didn't want to get laughed out of town.

I gave Obe a quick call at work. When I got through, there was laughter down the line, and then a distant shout: 'Jase, give my phone back, or I will come over there and . . .'

'Hello, Domino's Pizza.'

'Er, can I speak to Obe?'

'Would you like extra cheese with that?'

'Hi, Jase.'

'Who is Jase?' said Jase. Obe had been looking after Jason at the playscheme since he was small enough to escape through the fence and raid the sweetshop down the road. Jase was a big eater. His other favourite trick as a child had been eating fridge magnets, of which his mother had a prized collection. Now he was seventeen, and so huge that Obe could no longer playfight him. The sad day was looming when Jase would be too old to come to the playscheme. Special needs childhood could be pretty good, said Obe. It was adulthood you had to worry about.

'I'll have ham and pineapple, please,' I told Jase. 'With extra cheese.'

'Thank you for your order, that'll be one million pounds,' said Jase. There was a brief scuffle.

'Hello?' said Obe, panting.

'I've been thinking,' I said. 'About the house. Perhaps it would be more realistic to go in a little higher. We don't want them to think we're not serious.'

'Okay,' said Obe after a millisecond's thought. 'Yeah, you're right, whack another ten grand on there. But if he doesn't accept that, we just walk away.'

'Absolutely. Just like that. We're walking.'

Rob Crockett greeted me with feigned surprise. I told him this was our highest offer. The line went briefly silent.

'I'm gonna be honest with you, now,' he said, in the manner of somebody who was never honest with anybody, ever. 'I want you guys to get this house, you know I do. But at that price it's not gonna happen. Just last week I had people queueing up to view the house across the road, better condition I grant you, but it was on for a hundred grand more.'

A hundred grand more! For a tiny two-up two-down in the outermost reaches of east London! I got a sinking sensation in my tummy. We hadn't got a chance. I pulled myself together – hardball. I was walking away, and I wasn't looking back.

'Well, I'm sorry to hear that. Let me know if you reconsider.' I hung up. For about a second I was proud of how I'd played hardball. Then a feeling of crushing despondency washed over me. So farewell, then, to my lovely garden with a picnic table, and space for the boys to play football. Goodbye to the book-lined study, the cosy wood-burning stove. Goodbye to a kitchen with space for a kitchen table. Goodbye to all that, hello to an entire lifetime spent in Priory Court, listening to Dawn's evening entertainments and eating dinner on a folding table.

I called Obe again, and he answered this time. 'He said no.' My voice cracked slightly. 'I think we should offer the asking price.'

'Okay,' said Obe immediately. 'Just do it.'

I waited what I considered to be a decent amount of time – exactly two minutes – and called back to offer the asking price. To his credit, Rob Crockett did not laugh.

Now all I could do was wait. I sat in the feeding chair, That Baby at my breast, phone at the ready on the windowsill. Around the reservoir, all was still. A blue plastic bag was floating on the water, like a small, doomed ship.

On the windowsill, my phone buzzed. I swiped and barked 'what did he say?' without even checking who it was.

'Pardon?' replied my mother, in her perfect Queen's English.

'Oh sorry, Mum, I thought you were someone else.' I took a breath, and my heart-rate slowed. 'How was the meditation retreat?'

Mum had become a Buddhist a few years ago, and it had transformed her. Her pale blue eyes had become as pure and sparkling as a mountain stream. She was retired now, so the long years she had spent working 12-hour shifts in the hospital ward were but a distant memory. Now, she meditated every morning, and once a week went to sweep the floor of the Buddhist centre. I sometimes wondered how much meditation and sweeping it would take for me to become as calm as her, but the very thought of it made me tired.

'It was very powerful,' she said. 'We were practising spiritual death and rebirth.'

'Ooh, what's death like?' It was a genuine question, but she just laughed.

'I don't think anyone knows that, darling.'

Disappointing; I hoped that Buddha might have come up with something more definitive. As far as I could make out, death was a door slamming. You could be here one moment, all warm and real, smoking Rothmans, drinking Foster's, and saying *ey-up, chuck* in a fake Northern accent, and then the very next moment be laid out behind a weird mechanised curtain in the morgue, cold and pale and gone. But although everybody knew this, somehow other people seemed able to put it out of their minds. Since having children, I had thought about it every single day.

Mum had taken Lou and me to see Dad's body. We went into a small dark room, where a man in glasses and a lab coat pressed a button and the red curtain inched back, like something off *The Paul Daniels Magic Show*, to reveal . . . Dead Dad! I didn't touch him, just stared. He had a sheet tucked up to his chin, and his face looked different because it wasn't moving. You don't realise that you can see someone breathing, until they aren't. For years afterwards, I had no mental image at all of Alive Dad, whenever I tried to summon up the image of him in my mind, all I got was that.

I readjusted Eliot in my arms. On the bank, one of the fox cubs had stuck its nose out of the hole to sniff the air. As Mum nattered mildly away about her roster of activities – her life these days was an endless whirl of chamber music concerts, watercolour classes, circle-dancing and book groups – I said *hmmm* and *oh really?* in all the right places, but my mind was elsewhere. I'd found that lately, if I really tried, I could summon up Alive Dad.

I always had to start with his smell, a 1980s-man blend of old sweat, fag-smoke and Pears soap. Once I had that, I could feel his arms around me, the scratchy wool of his patterned tank top, the nobbly bone of his shoulder. Sometimes, I could even take myself back there, to bedtime in my childhood house, its dull, comforting tones of brown and moss-green. I could be wearing my Winnie-the-Pooh nightie, and peeping around the door of the front room, where he was sitting bent over the typewriter, in the glow of the Anglepoise, cigarette in hand, smoke pluming upwards.

He would look up when he heard me and say, 'is it that time already?' and I would nod, and run over and climb onto his lap for our nightly ritual. 'What are you writing?' I would ask, trying to make out the last word he had typed through the little peep-hole where the keys hit the page. He would tell me he was writing a story. 'Who is it for?' I always asked, but I already knew: it was for me. It was always for me. 'And what's it about?'

The beginning was always the same. 'Once upon a time, there was a small girl with eyes the colour of seaweed, and her name was Sylvia . . .' Sylvia had all kinds of adventures. Sometimes they were exotic – she was hunted by killer iguanas in the Galapagos – and sometimes less so – a drunken gang of squirrels kidnapped her baby sister in Finsbury Park. She faced many trials, the most terrifying being an alien super-race with heads like cabbages. But although she was often scared and terribly outnumbered, she always won through in the end. 'Because although she was only small, Sylvia had a secret weapon,' Dad said every time. 'She had brains. She knew there was a better way.'

On the end of the line, Mum was coming to the end of an in-depth account of the latest meeting of her book group. A woman called Alison always dominated with her views, which tested Mum's new-found calm to its limit. 'So anyway, darling, what's your news?'

I took a deep breath and forced myself back in the room. 'Well, actually,' I said, 'Obe and I are trying to buy a house in Beckstow!'

'Goodness – really? Um . . . where is Beckstow?'

I sighed. 'Quite near the North Circular. It's very up-and-coming.'

'I'm not sure anywhere is up-and-coming, right now,' said Mum.

I thought about explaining that our plan was to get a big mortgage, buy the place as an investment, and do it up over the next few years, when, er . . . but I couldn't say the key phrase, 'when you sell your four-bedroom house and give us some money'. It would never do to say that, I didn't want her to feel under any pressure to sell her home and share the proceeds with us, of course not. That had most definitely not ever crossed my mind, not for a second. Obe and I needed to sort ourselves out and stand on our own two feet. Of course we did.

'I've got this vision of family life in my head,' I told her instead: 'I want them to grow up playing in the garden! I want them to have their own rooms! I want . . .'

'You want them to have a childhood like yours,' said Mum. 'And that's understandable. Your father and I were very lucky. We bought our house for ten thousand pounds, you know, and after having you and your sister I never had to work, until—'

She stopped, where she always stopped. Even after twenty-five years, his death was a wound so raw that neither of us could touch it.

'But it's like you say – things are different now. And sometimes –' I could almost feel the intense Zen vibrations coming at me down the line – 'it is better to try and accept life as it is rather than break your back struggling to change it.'

Something had seized up inside my throat. This

acceptance stuff was all very well if you lived a peaceful and lovely life on a leafy street. I was pretty sure that even the Buddha himself would have trouble trying to accept Jay-Z at four in the morning.

'Thanks, Mum,' I said, after taking and releasing a deep breath. 'I will bear that in mind.'

Rob Crockett finally called back later that afternoon. Satan's Horseman, read the name on the screen; I'd been having a bad day when I entered his number.

'I have consulted with the vendor,' he said, in a studiously neutral tone. I sat very still, frozen in position. I felt like I was in the boardroom, waiting for Sugar to tell me whether I'd been fired. 'Obviously I made the case that this has always been a family home, and that you would be planning to raise another generation in the property – some vendors do like to think about other factors, too, you know.'

'That's very kind of you, Mr Crockett,' I said, employing the tone of a grateful Dickensian urchin.

'I made the point that you are a charming young mother, with those two delightful boys, and very much in need of the garden, et cetera.'

I waited. I breathed. I managed to contain the part of myself that was screaming out: *Whatdidhefuckingsay?*

'And he is very pleased to accept your offer.'

I sat, still frozen. This was not the answer I had been expecting.

'He said yes. The house is yours,' said Rob Crockett slowly and loudly, as if addressing somebody hard of hearing. 'If you want it.'

'Yes! Yes, we do! Oh Mr Crockett, thank you, thank you! I'm putting you on my Christmas card list. I'm doing it now!'

After hanging up, I hugged That Baby tightly to my chest. He stopped feeding and looked up at me, his black eyes startled. 'We're on the up, baby!' I said joyfully, picking him up and bouncing him in the air. Eliot did not look amused. He just wanted to carry on with his snack. 'I know you don't understand just yet,' I told him silently, as I put him back on my breast and sank back into the too-soft cushions of our saggy old sofa.

Eliot paused before latching on again and looked straight at me. 'Bah,' he said, chattily. 'Dah.'

'It's funny,' I went on. 'When you grow up, you won't even remember this place. You'll think that you were always meant to live in a sweet little house with stripped floorboards and a great big garden. It will be as if Priory Court never even happened.'

* * *

That night, the nudge campaign began. The boys were in bed, and Obe and I happened to be watching a heart-warming reality TV documentary featuring inspirational teachers. On the screen, a girl called Tracey with silly eyebrows had just thrown a chair at the good-natured Mr Omar.

'Have you ever thought about – you know – teacher training?' I asked Obe.

'Nope,' said Obe.

On the screen, Mr Omar was dabbing at his head with a tissue while Tracey slammed out of the classroom.

'Just think of the holidays!' I said to Obe. 'And the salary! And the fact that you would be making such a huge contribution to the wellbeing of the younger generation!'

'But . . . I'd have to be a *teacher*,' Obe pointed out. Obe had been one of only two brown boys in his school, and his teachers couldn't make sense of the fact that he loved Wordsworth and could recite Shakespeare soliloquies. That all came from home; Obe's dad Earl was obsessed with the Bard. But then he split up with Obe's mum and went back to Jamaica. Now and again, when the fancy took him, Earl would send Obe a postcard written in his elegant cursive. 'Blue and dewy mornings here,' the last one had said. 'Haze over the mountains. Eat fish once a week, and greens daily.'

School hadn't served Obe, and he had no desire to ever set foot in one again. When he told the careers adviser he wanted to be a poet, she laughed and suggested he train as a mechanic. They'd settled on care work, which Obe had found that he loved, and that he was good at. His plan had been to perform at spoken-word events in the evenings, try to find his way into the arts world that way. But little by little, the day job had taken over. Obe loved the way the kids were just themselves, not projects for improvement.

As the credits rolled, I reached over and typed 'teacher training' into Google, and scanned the list of job requirements.

'You see? You could do it. You're perfectly qualified. You've got a degree, haven't you?'

'Yes,' said Obe, looking glum.

'And experience working with young people?'

'Fifteen years of it.'

'There you go. And obviously the GCSEs in English, maths and science aren't going to be a problem . . .'

'Actually,' Obe brightened. 'They are going to be a problem.'

'Why?'

'I've got English, but I haven't got maths or science.'

'Let me just get this straight,' I said, swallowing hard. 'You haven't got GCSE maths?'

'Nope!' Obe beamed, triumphantly. 'Unless you count a grade U.'

'I DO NOT COUNT A GRADE U!' I cried, my head sinking into my hands. Gaudy tatters of the dream billowed around in my mind. Ruined. No sun, no Tuscan holiday; chilly, cramped summers holidaying in the Thames Estuary stretched ahead of me like a punishment for I-knew-not-what.

Then I grabbed the laptop again and typed in 'GCSE distance learning courses'. The dream might have been dying, but it wasn't dead yet. It wasn't. Dead. Yet.

5.

Keeping in touch

Incident No. 257. 15th February, 5 a.m.

Perfectly quiet down there. No sign of life outside, neither man nor fox. Am I the only creature in the whole of Priory Court who is awake right now?

In just a few hours I am going to be back in the office, in Executive Wear, for my Keeping in Touch meeting. The plan is – no guarantees, now – that I will have brushed my hair and teeth. I will have caught up on the news, and thought of some intelligent, topical things to say to Hari.

It would just be so much easier to do all that if only I could sleep. I almost wish that crack in the ceiling would open up and swallow me.

Hours' sleep – none – I can't blame Dawn, or the children. Just my own stupid brain.

UK Housing Market Experiences New Year Chill, read the top headline on the BBC website. I hovered the cursor over it, but couldn't bring myself to click. I also decided against stories about another stabbing in east London, and record temperatures in the Arctic. Dancing Penguins Cause Sensation at London Zoo, ran the line above the novelty feature at the bottom of the page – now that sounded like something I could deal with.

'Hey, this came through the door,' said Obe, who had been about to leave. In a rehearsal for our forthcoming back-to-work routine, he was supposed to be dropping The Toddler at nursery. But in his hand was a large, brown envelope that looked too important to wait. 'I think it must be the survey.'

We looked at each other with matching expressions of silent fear. 'Go on, then,' I said. 'You open it.'

He sat down at the table, carefully avoiding the splodges of mushed-up cereal and banana, pulled out the chunky booklet and leafed through it slowly. Unable to cope with the suspense, I got up and peered over his shoulder. The surveyor had employed a 'traffic light' system; each section of the survey had a spot next to it in the page margin to indicate the gravity of the problem. A green spot meant all was fine, orange indicated that the issue was not urgent. The pages of our survey looked like they were covered with livid red measles.

'When he says the roof is "sagging",' I asked. 'Is that as bad as it sounds?'

'I don't think it's "sagging" in the way you or I would

understand it,' said Obe. 'When a surveyor says "sagging", it's a technical term.'

He turned the page, revealing another rash of red. We had known about all the obvious damage – the mouldy cork tiles in the kitchen, the festering avocado bathroom suite, the persistent smell of rotting meat and fish – but we had been clinging to the hope that a deep clean and a quick lick of paint would sort it. But it seemed there was another level of structural wrongness, the financial implications of which we could only guess at.

'Replacing the ceiling joists,' I said. 'Sounds pricey.'

'"Eventually",' Obe pointed out. 'He says "eventually".' He flicked to the final page, where there was one isolated green dot. 'And look here, this is good news. He says there are "no visible signs of an infestation of wood-boring insect".'

I read on a little further. 'Although he does say we should get a second opinion from a pest expert.'

Obe slammed the booklet shut, and stood up. 'Come on, fella!' he called to The Toddler, who had just taken his shoes off again. 'The thing about surveyors,' he said, as he grabbed them and shoved them back onto Larkin's small, wriggling feet, 'is that they'll always give you the worst-case scenario. They have to cover their backs.'

I slugged down my coffee and turned back to the laptop, clicking on the penguin story. There was some footage of the penguin pair performing their adorable, waddly dance routine. Obe, The Toddler and I watched it together, sharing a moment of love and laughter.

'Now that,' he said, kissing the back of my neck before he dashed for the door, 'is a great way to start the day.'

I stood in front of the mirror turning this way and that, assessing the situation. I might not have achieved actual executive smartness, but I was definitely presentable. That Baby was strapped into his vibrating chair in front of an extra-long Peppa Pig YouTube compilation while I put on my grey Jigsaw skirt – bought in the heady days when I could shop somewhere other than TKMaxx – and a nice flowered blouse. I had blow-dried my hair smooth. I had applied a thick layer of foundation all over my face, with extra concealer on the under-eye area.

I peered a little closer. I had new creases in the corner of my eyes; if not crow's feet, yet, then at least one crow's toe. But I hadn't put on weight after having kids, not with The Toddler or That Baby. If anything, I looked slimmer than I had before. The skirt draped in a pleasing way from my hips, and the blouse still fitted, with room to spare. I put on my boots with the little heel, and stood up a bit straighter. In the mirror my eyes met the eyes of a ghost of selves past. That self had been a promising Young Professional. People had told her she would Go Far. She had felt Important and Purposeful. There had been a sense that the Future Was Hers.

She had dashed around in taxis, scheduled high-level meetings, lunched with ministers and journalists. She had wanted to be important and influential.

Could I be that person again?

The other day I'd read an article in *Style* magazine by an important woman about how we should all try harder to be more important. For a brief moment I thought she was right. Then I threw the magazine into the bin and squidged a dirty nappy in there, too, right on top of her smug self-righteous face.

Right now, I literally couldn't think of anything worse than being important and influential. The very idea of having even one molecule more responsibility sent a shiver down my spine. All I wanted was to be relaxed and maybe even happy; it was a different kind of ambition, and one I had no idea how to realise.

Aesthetically speaking I was ready. I put the sling over my blouse and strapped That Baby into it, putting my smart coat on top. Checked the mirror again: she was still there. And there was still time to think about current affairs on the tube.

On the way to the station, I stopped at the newsagent's to buy a paper. Queuing up to pay, my eyes alit upon a big red sign on the counter. 'What would you do?' it read, and underneath: 'National Lottery. Life Changing™'. After I had finished wondering how it could be possible to trademark the phrase 'life changing' (could they sue you if you applied it to something other than the national lottery? Childbirth, for example, or death?), it struck me as a good question.

'What would I do?' I said silently to That Baby, but he was too busy craning his neck to look at the sweets.

Okay, obviously in at number one: buy a house. And just as obviously, not the one we were currently buying. I would buy one that did not smell of rotting meat, had a functioning kitchen and bathroom, and did not need, as Rob Crockett put it, 'a bit of work'.

Come on, happy thoughts: what else? I'd renew the car insurance. Take Obe on a romantic weekend mini-break. Buy lots of totally unnecessary shoes. Buy Lou lots of totally unnecessary shoes. Get that ice-cream maker I'd been lusting after. But this was all small fry. I needed to think bigger. Would I move back to Islington?

Send my kids to private school? I really didn't think so. I genuinely wouldn't need millions to possess everything I wanted in life. Around half a million would probably do it.

That wasn't much, was it? Not in the grand scheme of things. Even a lucky break on the *Antiques Roadshow* might do it. Could that odd trippy painting we inherited from Obe's mum be a little-known Picasso?

My eyes strayed back to the sign. 'Life Changing™'. My fingers started to itch. I was feeling lucky. Perhaps I'd buy a ticket. I'd never played the national lottery before. Dad had always scorned people who bought lottery tickets. Whenever the advert with the big blue hand came on the telly – It Could Be You! – he would snort, and say: 'They're peddling dreams.' He told us that bookies gave better odds on bumping into Elvis in the frozen-goods aisle of Kwiksave than winning the jackpot. 'But here we all are, sitting around waiting for some big blue hand in the sky.'

Now I mostly just wanted that big ol' finger to point at me – me! Over here! Hello! Hello! Hello?

'Should I get a ticket?' I asked That Baby, silently. 'Are you feeling lucky?' He stuck his fist into his mouth. He was drooling more than usual; perhaps he had a tooth coming through.

The man in front of me moved aside. The grumpy

newsagent scowled and took my card. Now could be the moment, should I say the words 'and also . . .'? Was I still feeling lucky? But just as I was about to say 'a winning Euromillions ticket please', I felt it: a wave of disapproval so tangible that the words shrivelled in my throat. And I heard, or perhaps just felt, a voice that was both loud and quiet: *Come on, Sylvia. You've got brains. You know there's a better way.*

It was the oddest thing. I fumbled to unzip my purse. The newsagent was scowling even harder, unaware that his shop was hosting a voice from beyond the grave. And as I stood there I caught a trace of that smell, the Pears soap, and the feeling of that scratchy jumper against my cheek. He's here! Can you feel it? I asked That Baby silently. His deep black eyes met mine, and I knew he could.

'Come on, love, I've got a queue here, you're away with the fairies.'

Away with Dead Dad, I thought, paying for my paper and stepping out into the street.

The sky had brightened a little by the time we emerged from Westminster station. The gold trimmings on Big Ben and the Houses of Parliament were blinging away in the weak late-winter light. All the way here, I had tried to focus on the paper and formulate smart things to say, but the thoughts floated to the surface like bubbles, and then burst, leaving no trace.

'Behold,' I told That Baby, turning sideways so he could look. 'The towers of power.'

I carried him carefully along Embankment, up the slate-tiled pedestrian area, past the little raised beds planted with aggressively-pruned trees. Office workers rushed past us looking self-important, and I remembered when I had been just like them. Over the railing, the Thames was sluggish and murky. I hugged Eliot's pudgy body to my chest.

When I got my job at the Equality and Human Rights Department, fondly known to its employees as TEHRD, it had seemed like an excellent prospect. I'd made it as far as the lower rungs of journalism, but decided that celebrity tittle-tattle wasn't my thing; I wanted to make a difference. TEHRD had been established under New Labour, with a budget of tens of millions. Its aim, according to its zingy, Cool Britannia-style website, was to 'bring the campaigns for race equality, women's and disabled people's rights together into the heart of government'. I had no idea what that meant, but it sounded like A Good Thing.

Since then I had sat through endless meetings about the organisation's mission and purpose – what *was* equality, anyway? – but nobody ever quite pinned it down. One thing was clear: TEHRD could take action to tackle racism, sexism, ageism . . . anything but financial inequality. When I brought it up, Hari snapped: 'That's socio-economic, darling. We don't do that.'

With his confident patter and impressive range of Ozwald Boateng suits, Hari had been a New Labour darling. Somebody at a very high level – possibly the *highest* level – had appointed him to the Director, Communications role at TEHRD. On my first day, he took me out to lunch to tell me about the job. 'We need to do something spectacular, move the debate along,' he told me, over spaghetti with clams in Carluccio's. 'Like . . . project our logo onto the White Cliffs of Dover. You know?'

I nodded. Whatever it was I had expected to be doing, it wasn't that.

'With your experience in the popular press,' he said, 'you are just what this organisation needs. There are so many worthies around here – they're all stuck in the era of protest, the Birkenstocks and banners brigade. But those days are over. We're part of the establishment now. You know what I think?' He took a swig of his outsize glass of Merlot. 'If you play your cards right, you'll make Head of Comms one day.'

But the Head of Comms thing wasn't mentioned again, and once I got pregnant with Larkin, I didn't believe it ever would be. Once I got pregnant with Larkin, my position at TEHRD, like my residency at Priory Court, started to feel more permanent than I'd ever really expected.

When I was little I'd loved one of the necklaces in Mum's jewellery box. It was made from honey-coloured beads, each one slightly different, flecked with brown, or gold. In the middle of the largest bead you could see the fragile body of a fly, frozen as if it had been paused mid-flight. Mum told me that, a long time ago, the fly had flown unsuspecting into a sticky liquid. The liquid had hardened around it, and now it would be in there, for ever. That fly fascinated me. I wanted to break open the stone and set it free, so it could buzz about again. Despite everything, it looked ready to take off.

The glass lift hummed up to the seventh floor. Sanghita was sitting at the reception desk filing her long, pink nails; I was pretty sure she'd been doing exactly the same thing when I left the building, six months ago. But now the sleek reception desk was surrounded on three sides by towering stacks of cardboard boxes.

'What's all this?' I asked her, pointing at the boxes, when she had finished clucking at Eliot and telling me how handsome he was.

'Oh darling, don't say they didn't tell you?'

Fear sprouted in my stomach. 'Tell me what?'

'We're moving, innit?'

'Moving where?' There had been rumours about this ever since New Labour crumbled and first the coalition took over, then the Tories, but somehow, TEHRD had always hung on to its prime position in One London, a glitzy riverside tower block that housed legal firms and investment banks.

Sanghita lowered her voice to a whisper. 'To Tower Hamlets,' she said. 'An old library. It's practically derelict.' With a roll of her eyes, she nodded her head in the general direction of the senior management. 'They're killing us off, basically. Oh Sylvia, I tell you, you're best off out of it.'

Inside the cavernous open-plan office, there were floor-to-ceiling windows with a spectacular view over the Thames and Tower Bridge, and rows and rows of desks and computers with nobody sitting at them. Boxes were piled up everywhere.

'Hey,' I said, sneaking up behind Duane, the only person in sight. He was my fellow press officer and a true one-off: devoutly Christian, gay, the owner of five parrots that he refused to cage for animal rights reasons, which flew and shat around his living room all day while he was at work. When we got bored in the afternoon Duane would watch the parrots on a webcam on his phone. Duane loved his parrots almost as much as he hated his job.

I gestured around at all the empty desks. 'It's like a ghost town.'

'Cuts,' Duane said. 'All the casual staff have gone, and half of the permanents. We're fucked.'

'I can't believe nobody told me!' I said. 'I'm supposed to be talking to Hari now about coming back to work.'

'Oh yeah,' Duane replied. 'And Hari is leaving.'

'Leaving?'

'He's got some blinging new job at Deutsche Bank. Diversity adviser.'

'Oh wow.' My mouth had gone dry. 'Is that even a job?'

'A very handsomely rewarded one, apparently,' said Duane, sucking in his cheeks. 'We're all very pleased for him.'

I swallowed hard. 'Well. Forewarned is forearmed, as they say.'

'Yeah,' said Duane. 'But they also say ignorance is bliss.'

'Sylvia! Do come on in,' drawled Hari, when I poked my head around the door. Hari used to flirt with me, but since I'd had kids, this had morphed into an awkward kind of gallantry. He swooped over, gave me a peck on the cheek, and pulled out a chair. 'So,' he said, after a cursory glance at Eliot. 'You've probably noticed a few changes around here.'

Eliot wriggled in the sling. I undid the catch and lifted him out, stretching and yawning like a sleepy cat. His tiny body was so neat, so unassuming, so perfectly aligned. He seemed like the only real thing in that whole building. I draped a scarf around my shoulders and laid him in the crook of my arm, hitching up my shirt and unfastening my bra. Hari's eyes flickered down, and then immediately back to my face again, hard and smiling. He rapped his BlackBerry against the desk.

'You may have heard,' he said. 'I am moving on.'

'Yes, Duane told me. Congratulations!' I said, my voice failing to lift in quite the right way.

'Why, thank you!' he said, beaming. Then he glanced through the plate-glass partition, and added more quietly: 'A bit of advice for you: this place is screwed. Like the whole of the public sector. There's going to be another round of restructuring this year, and a word to the wise: your role will be cut.' He said this so plainly, so factually, that all I could do was stare. 'If I were you, I would take this time to explore your options.'

'Right,' I said. 'I understand.'

I was speaking just about normally, but I could feel the heat rising in my face. Hari saw it, too. 'Try not to worry too much,' he said quickly. 'You know what they say: a redundancy is only a disaster for the dead wood. For those who are worth their salt, it will open up new opportunities.'

I couldn't think of a reply to that, so I just sat there, turning over the idea of people who are dead wood and people who are worth their salt. I wondered which I was, and how I would find out. Eliot had finished his feed, so I put him over my shoulder and patted a gentle semaphore of comfort onto his back. My collarbone neatly cupped his head, as though it had been custom designed.

'I'm sorry the news isn't better,' Hari pushed his glasses up his nose. I knew he was trying to be kind. 'There might even be something for you at Deutsche Bank. Let's meet up for a coffee once I've got my feet under the desk. How does that sound?'

I gulped back my coffee, and told him that it sounded fine.

'How did the meeting go?' said Obe, when he got back from work. I'd put my tracksuit bottoms back on and given in to The Toddler watching just one more round of *Bob the Builder*, while I sat in the feeding chair with That Baby and looked out over the reservoir. The cubs were out again; they were playing happily in the nettles with an old tin can.

'Syl?'

'Um.' I focused on the foxes. The game was getting a little bit rough, it looked like the bigger one might push the smaller one into the water. But just in the nick of time, Mummy Fox appeared, and skilfully separated them, picking up the cheekiest cub by the scruff of the neck. As she gently groomed him, I felt a tear roll down my nose and hang, wobbling, from the tip.

'Syl?' said Obe again, bending to kneel beside me. 'Are you crying?'

'No,' I said, and sniffed. 'Yes.'

The tear dripped off my nose and plopped down into That Baby's ear, then another, and another. He twitched, and I covered my face with a sour-milk-smelling muslin.

'Hari tipped me off: they're going to make me redundant,' I said through folds of cloth. 'Later this year.'

Obe's face lit up. 'Now the heart sings with all its thousand voices!' he cried. 'You've been wanting to leave that place for ever.'

I lowered the muslin slowly. 'But Obe, without that job we'll never be able to move. They won't give us a mortgage without my salary. We'll be stuck here forever.'

I put down the muslin and buried myself in Obe's neck so he could soak up the tears instead.

'We're not *stuck* here,' he said, gently, stroking my hair. 'We are *living* here. Choose your words.'

I breathed in the smell of him, fresh like hay. I'd always loved Obe's smell. When we first got together, in the days when we could spend an entire day in bed without getting up, I used to bury my nose in his armpit and inhale it like a fine wine. 'Top notes of blackberry, and an undertone of old books,' I would whisper. We talked a lot of nonsense to each other back then.

Now that smell didn't give me butterflies any more, but it did feel like home – more home than any flat or house. I knew he was right. If I couldn't change our housing situation, I'd have to change how I *felt* about our housing situation. And that was something no estate agent, bank or boss could help me with. It was a project that I had no idea how to begin.

That night, something odd happened downstairs. It wasn't music, or swearing – I almost wished it was. Because the sound coming through the floorboards now was a moaning, keening sound, like an animal in distress. If sadness itself was a noise, this was what it would sound like. As I opened my eyes there was another howl, chilling and mournful.

'Obe,' I said, elbowing the sleeping form beside me. 'Can you *hear* that? What is she doing down there?'

He grunted, then turned over. 'You know she does weird stuff, when she forgets to take her medication,' said his muffled voice into the pillow. He lifted his head to listen. 'Anyway, that's not Dawn. That is the foxes.'

It was true that during mating season, the foxes did sometimes make strange cries, but not at this time of year. I reached for the curtains and peeped out. There was no sign of the fox family; the water glistened inscrutably in the moonlight. The moaning trailed off into a kind of yapping, sobbing noise.

'It's not the foxes,' I said. 'It's definitely Dawn.'

There was a long silence. 'There you go,' muttered Obe. 'It's stopped.'

I got up and went into the sitting room. I wrote *Howling. Foxes?* in the logbook. Then, looking out into the darkness, I saw a movement: he was there again, under the tree by the bank – the man in black. He seemed to be wearing a large hat, and he was crouching at the edge of the water, very still, just looking in. Was I dreaming? Who was he?

I went back to bed and lay there for a long time, tensely waiting for the noise to start again. Thoughts churned around my mind like clothes in a washing machine. Should we just forget the whole moving house plan? Without my job, we'd never be able to keep up the repayments. But, on the other hand, what if we *didn't* move house? Once I was out of work we'd never get a mortgage, and Priory Court would be our home for ever.

Round and round went those grubby old clothes, building up to the spin cycle. I tried to summon up the dancing penguins, but they disappeared in a waddly, black-and-white whirl. Instead, thoughts about the Arctic ice sheet crowded in, and the hideous geopolitical situation, the rise of populism, something terrible I read the other day about the situation in Yemen, and then of course there was Syria, children breathing chlorine gas, children bombed and dying . . .

I wrenched my eyes open, and cursed myself for wasting precious night hours worrying about things that were beyond my control. Perhaps it really was time to take up meditation, as Mum was always telling me. I took a few deep breaths, but it was no good, sleep was further away than ever. Eventually I just stared up at the crack in the ceiling, which was a little bigger every time I looked. I imagined it splitting open so floors four, five and six would fall on my head and then I wouldn't have to think about anything any more.

6.

Waterside living

Incident No. 258. 23rd February, 3 a.m.

Just a few hours until the birthday boy wakes up, and I am working up to the party spirit. If only it wasn't for this headache, this knot of tension between my shoulders . . .

By the sounds of things, Dawn is way ahead of me, party-wise. 'New York' is pumping, and the marsh-mallow smell is making me quite light-headed. I must ask Obe what he thinks it could be. Laughing gas? Anthrax?

Note to self: buy hand cream. My right hand is now so dry that it is frozen in an agonising claw-like grip.

Hours' sleep: 4

Hours until birthday lift-off: 3

A dream — sitting in the back of the car, I realise Eliot is driving. He can't reach the brakes.

I HAD worried that after months of feverish anticipation, The Toddler's birthday might come as a let-down. But far from it: he came thundering down the hall at 6 a.m., exploding through the bedroom door and flying headfirst onto the bed. He grabbed both of Obe's cheeks and shouted, 'IS IT NOW?'

'At last, big man.' Obe bundled him into a hug, and murmured into his soft curls: 'Because the birthday of my life is come / my love is come to me.'

For breakfast, Obe made toast and honey and stuck a candle in it. He showed Larkin his birthday postcard from Earl, featuring a dog with a Rasta hat on, and the slogan, 'Jamaica Me Happy'. He read out the looping writing on the back: *Happy Birthday, youngster. Remember, life is a test, and death the only outcome. Our remedies oft in ourselves do lie, which we ascribe to heaven. Peace and love, Grandpops.*

The Toddler took the postcard in his sticky fingers and looked for a long time at the dog in the hat. 'What does it *mean*?' he asked, and we all thought about it for a while.

A brown-paper-wrapped box almost as big as The Toddler himself had arrived from Titania in Berlin. As I put it down on the folding table, I tried to work out what on earth it might be; it made an odd chiming noise when you shook it. You couldn't really rule anything out, with Titania. She had moved to Germany to live in an artists' colony just before The Toddler was born. The last time we saw her had been at the opening of a group exhibition called 'Black to the Future' in a warehouse in Hackney Wick. Titania had contributed a series of photographs of herself standing in a field of sheep, naked and painted gold, wearing a feathered headdress.

As soon as I put the box down on the table, The Toddler ripped off the brown paper with fearsome attack. Obe opened the top flaps and peered inside.

'Oh Christ.'

'What is it?'

'Um.'

He got a pair of scissors, cut along the edges of the box, and folded down the sides. Removing the bubble wrap, we found ourselves in the presence of a tribal-style mask, made from welded-together tin cans. It was mounted on a long, slender neck of coiled copper wire, and framed by a soaring afro made from jingling, clinking bottle-tops. The whole assemblage was at least three feet high, and there was a label tied to the top of the head. 'For The Future, my bestest neph,' Titania had written.

'Does she have any sodding idea how small our flat is?' I asked Obe in a low voice.

Even That Baby was staring at the birthday sculpture

in awed silence. You had to hand it to Titania: the thing had an aura.

'Is it a goodie or a baddie?' asked The Toddler.

'It would fit on the table, as a kind of centrepiece,' suggested Obe.

'But where will we eat?'

Obe was scanning the room. 'It'll have to be over there, then. On the window sill.'

So now I would be eyeball-to-eyeball with the birthday sculpture every time I sat in my peaceful breast-feeding, reservoir-viewing area. Obe carried it over ceremonially and placed it right next to the logbook. It almost entirely blocked the view. He stepped back. 'Look! I actually think it does something interesting to the feng shui.'

The Toddler, That Baby and I regarded the sculpture suspiciously. It did indeed change the whole character of the room; I just wasn't sure it did so in a way that I would have chosen. The Toddler approached it and ran his fingers over the bottle tops, setting off a jingling arpeggio.

'I think it's a goodie *and* a baddie,' he said.

'Is That Baby coming to my party?' asked The Toddler before we left for mum's house. He was pointing at Eliot.

'Of course he is, love. He's your brother. Look! He's really excited about celebrating with you!'

Eliot was asleep in the buggy, but I took his fists and made *Saturday Night Fever* dance shapes to indicate his off-the-chart levels of excitement.

The Toddler sighed, unconvinced. 'I thought perhaps – just today – he could stay at home.'

I got the usual nostalgic thrill as we wheeled the boys through Highbury Barn. It always felt odd coming back to the area where I grew up. The old dry cleaner's had become an artisan bakery, the chippy where Dad had taken us on Fridays after school was now an organic butcher's and the Spar was a greengrocer's, painted dove grey with a few polished-looking vegetables displayed outside in rustic-style baskets. The only thing that had remained the same was the newsagent's: I waved at the old Asian guy behind the counter through the glass door as I walked past and, when he saw me, he raised his hand. I'd been going into that newsagent's since I was a child; I wished that we'd learned each other's names.

'It's hard to believe, I know,' I mused idly to Obe. 'But when I was a kid, Islington was not that posh. People like us lived here: social workers, teachers, nurses like Mum. Ordinary people, you know.'

'It's not that posh now,' he said, 'it just looks that way. Half the kids from the playscheme live in Islington, and believe me their families are not shopping here.' He gestured at a shop across the road, which had five pieces of cheese proudly displayed on pedestals in the window.

We crossed the road by the clock tower, and followed the footpath through Highbury Fields. The ancient plane trees towered over us, stretching their bare fingers into the white sky. I remembered these same plane trees towering over my buggy as Dad wheeled me along. Turning down Mum's road was like meeting a childhood friend who'd had a facelift: the houses were whiter, newly painted, with sleek cars parked outside. 'Imagine: I lived here when I was your age,' I told the boys, who weren't listening. 'With Aunty Lou, and Granny, and Grandad. Until—' I stopped, where we always stopped.

Mum answered the door wearing an elegant, possibly cashmere dress and a chunky wooden necklace. Her hair was gleaming white, her pale-blue eyes serene. When we hugged I inhaled the familiar smell of lavender and face cream.

'Happy birthday, darling!' she said to The Toddler, unbuckling him from his buggy. He bounced straight into her arms, burying his head in the folds of soft wool. The Toddler loved his granny; they had the same oval-shaped face, the same slightly hesitant smile. He showed her his prized birthday present: a *Bob the Builder* toolbelt, complete with plastic screwdriver.

'I've been looking for a handyman!' she exclaimed.

They nattered gently as Mum led Larkin into the sitting room. Obe followed her with That Baby, while I stood in the hall of her house, my childhood home, and took a deep breath. Everything was the same: the gold-framed mirror gleaming on the wall, the black and white tiled floor. Down the hallway, I could see a white pot of hyacinths on the kitchen table. There were no Lego pieces on the floor, no dirty nappies stuffed into dustbins, no splodges of cornflakes or mashed banana on the walls. But what I noticed most of all was the hushed quiet. There was no traffic, no shouting, no insistent thump of music. I could actually hear the trilling of a bird in the tree outside.

My sister Lou poked her head out of the sitting room.

'All right, sis?' I hugged her and ruffled her bright pink hair, which matched her pink leopard-print leggings and outsized fluffy jumper. 'It's been a while, hey.'

'Yeah, sorry about that.' I had promised Lou several times that I'd go out and visit her place, a squat on the outskirts of west London. I kept making excuses about the trains being difficult with a buggy, but the truth was I just didn't fancy it. Lou's squatty crew made me nervous. With their chippy air of moral superiority, they made me feel I had to justify my conventional life choices. How had I ended up being the one with the flat and the job and the family and the head crammed full of worries and responsibilities, rather than the one who spent her life going to festivals and parties with seemingly not a care in the world.

'You know what it's like,' I said. 'Kids, work . . .'

'Well, no.' Lou didn't have kids yet, and she didn't really work, either, unless you counted the laughter yoga sessions she ran at festivals. She spent a lot of time doing what she called 'community projects' with her boyfriend, who had changed his name from Shaun to Shanti and didn't wear shoes. These generally involved protesting against the injustices of the neoliberal capitalist system, such as the expansion of Heathrow airport, the use of inorganic, bee-massacring pesticides, and the deportation of asylum-seekers. In some ways, I admired her for reaching the grand old age of 32 without compromising to the prevailing neoliberal capitalist ideology. But in most ways it got right on my wick.

'Let's just say,' I explained, 'I've had quite a lot on.'

She gave me an understanding smile, with a reprimand buried in it. Over the course of three decades, my relationship with my sister had turned a complete one-eighty. When we were small, she traipsed around after me and did whatever I said, even when my demands were outrageous. If I asked for one of her toys, she would give it to me, mutely and submissively. I must have been about seven or eight when I found a yellow toadstool in the garden, and made her eat it. 'I want to find out if it's poisonous,' I explained to five-year-old Lou, with the air of a scientist conducting an important experiment. She just looked at me trustingly with her big blue eyes, and popped it obediently into her mouth. (Luckily for us both, it wasn't.)

Later, during Mum's absent years, I clucked around my little sister like an anxious hen. I used to have dreams, terrible nightmares, in which Lou died in an array of grisly and terrifying ways: falling off a ferry into a churning grey sea, or being taken by mysterious men with guns. My mission in life became to prevent what I saw as my sister's inevitable early demise. I was vigilant. I didn't like her climbing trees, and I hid her roller skates. In bed at night, I'd check she was still breathing.

So I took it badly when Lou hit her teenage years and developed a will of her own. Aged fourteen, she fell in with a cool, rebellious crowd at school. She would tell Mum she was going for a sleepover, when I knew she was going raving at Whirligig; I'd wait up until the early hours for her, planning the *Crimewatch* reconstruction in my head. She took to wearing a Rage Against the Machine T-shirt with the slogan: *fuck you, I won't do what you tell me*. It seemed to be the principle that had guided most of her life-choices since then.

'Aunty Lou!' Larkin was tugging at her hand, wanting her to come and play. Lou always had endless energy for games, and seemed to actively enjoy pretending to be Sue, Bob the Builder's right-hand woman. She was, I had to concede, more fun than me.

'No more excuses, come soon – and bring the kids,' she told me firmly, before she was dragged away. 'There's so much room to play! They would love it.'

Mum had prepared a birthday tea: cheese sandwiches with the crusts cut off, fairy cakes, a pot of tea, juice and crisps for Larkin, who busied himself banging loudly on one of the kitchen cabinets with his plastic hammer.

'Well,' said Mum. 'You are going to be helpful when you all move in to this new house. I hear it needs a . . . bit of work.'

I'd given Mum only a vague report on the survey results, skirting over the structural issues, and failing to mention the sagging roof. I hadn't told her about the redundancy. I knew she would tell me not to go ahead with the move, and that was advice I did not want to hear.

'Mum told me about you guys buying a place,' Lou

said. She didn't approve of home owning, or private property in general. 'It sounds like a total liability!' Her voice was slightly too loud and her cheeks were slightly too rosy from the Aldi prosecco, which she had been drinking rather more quickly than anyone else. 'You should tell that estate agent where to stick it.'

'Easy for you to say, Lou,' I snapped. 'We can't all live in squats and bloody yurts, you know.'

She either didn't hear this comment, or rose above it. 'How about a narrow boat? They're cheap as chips. Shanti has some friends with kids who live in one.' While I always appreciated Lou's blue skies thinking, I wasn't convinced she fully understood the accommodation needs of a young family. But she was on a roll. 'So. Here's what you do,' she said, waving her glass in the air. 'Sod the house. Buy a cheap boat, do it up, and go on a grand tour of the nation's waterways before the kids start school.'

Perhaps it was just the glow of the wine, but I had to admit that some aspects of this plan were appealing. Sure, a boat would be even smaller than our flat, but then the boys could play outside on the bank. We could pick daisies, make friends with some ducks. I'd have to get a couple of lifejackets, obviously. It could be idyllic – in the summer, at least. And no mortgage, or rent! We would be free!

'What do you think, Obe?' I asked.

'Mum took us on a narrow-boat holiday once,' he said, chewing on a cheese sandwich. 'Never been so seasick in my life.'

This elicited a peal of laughter from mum. She always laughed at Obe's jokes, even if they weren't jokes. Sometimes I felt that Mum and Obe had more in common with each other than I did with either of them; they could spend happy hours discussing the haiku, or Tchaikovsky, or the Buddhist principle of no-self. They both existed on a higher plane, while I grubbed around below, thinking about car insurance.

'Back in the days of the water gypsies,' Lou was saying, 'families of fourteen used to live in those boats. They'd keep the toddlers from falling in by sitting them on the roof of the boat and chaining them to the chimney.'

'Hmmm,' I said. 'Not sure you'd get away with that these days.'

As we got progressively lower down the bottle, more problems with the narrow-boat plan presented themselves. Where would we park it? It would be all very well if you got a nice spot near Hackney marshes, but it had been looking very crowded down there lately. Knowing our luck, we'd end up round the back of an industrial estate in Barking.

Extensive analysis revealed several key flaws in the

narrow-boat plan. 'It's a lovely idea in theory,' I concluded, as Mum got up to stick the candles in the cake. 'I just don't think a boat is practical at this stage.'

'You may be right,' Lou conceded, getting up and yogically stretching out one leopard-print leg. Then she straightened, her face lit up. 'How about a teepee?'

Before dimming the lights, Mum smiled her all-embracing smile. 'Well, I think the new house sounds like a great adventure,' she said gamely. 'There's no hurry, is there? Over the next few years, you can get the builders in, do the place up, can't you, fix it up just the way you like it.'

Larkin's ears pricked up. 'I'll fix it!' he shouted, springing out of his chair and grasping his hammer. As he battered on the floor, the table and the kitchen cabinet, we all joined in with a chorus of Larkin's favourite song: 'Bob the Builder, can he fix it? Bob the Builder, yes he can!'

Only if you can pay him, though, I thought grimly to myself, and took another large swig of prosecco.

It didn't take us long to tackle Obe's rum-and-raisin cake, boozily age-inappropriate, but compulsory on every birthday as it was a treasured family recipe. His mum, Roberta, had made it for us the last time we went to see her in Birmingham. We kept a photo from that visit on our living-room wall: Roberta, chemo-chic in a turban, holding baby Larkin on her lap, paintings covering every inch of the wall behind her. Roberta was a nurse, like my mum, but in the evenings she painted, Birmingham street-scenes rendered in rich, vivid colours.

'Welcome to our palace,' Obe said grandly, when I first stepped over the threshold of that small, cramped flat. And it was a palace, because Roberta had made it so.

She hadn't actually eaten any of the cake that day, as her tastebuds were shot by the treatment. But she had still baked, and we wolfed it down at the table in her tiny living room, while she had her first and final cuddle with her grandson.

When there was nothing left of The Toddler's birthday cake but a pile of crumbs, Obe disappeared off for his customary perusal of the bookshelves in the living room. Mum cleared her throat and said, in a low whisper, 'Girls: I've got some news.'

She had an air of having seized her chance. There was a barely discernible glimmer of excitement in the blue eyes, and she seemed a little breathless, like The Toddler when he talked about his Christmas presents (I was expecting the build-up to Christmas to start tomorrow). Was she even blushing, just a little bit? Lou and I glanced at each other. Could it be . . . ? Surely not.

But it was.

'On my New Year meditation retreat – in addition to some very fulfilling spiritual practice of course, I—'

'Mum!' cried Lou, boisterously. 'Did you get it on?'

'I don't know what that even means, Louisa,' Mum said, frowning and drawing herself up straight.

'You met a man?'

'Who is he?'

'Ring-a-ding dong!'

Lou and I were scrambling over each other in our excitement. This was huge: since Mum's spiritual conversion, we had assumed that she was sticking with a life of celibacy. Not that she'd ever seemed that interested in moving on after Dad died; she had gone for a couple of disappointing lonely-hearts dates in the '90s, before the Internet really kicked in, but had steadfastly, despite concerted nagging from both of us, drawn the line at online dating. 'It's like shopping in a supermarket,' she'd said, pulling a disapproving face, when we tried to set her up with a profile in the early 2000s. We got as far as 'soulful NHS worker seeks mature man for country walks', when she put her foot down.

'I just don't want to, girls. Please delete it.'

'But why? What are you frightened of?'

Mum didn't answer. She cleared her throat and patted her hair, like she always did when she was nervous.

'Are you worried nobody will pick you?' I asked. But really I knew: the only thing that worried Mum more than nobody picking her, was somebody picking her. Because then maybe she would like that person, and then maybe she would be happy, and then, one day, the happiness would end one day. There was no way she was risking that happening again.

'Just delete it,' she said, and that was that.

But now – now she was glowing. 'There is a connection,' she sighed. 'A deep, spiritual connection. He's the kind of man you really can talk to about anything. He has a wonderfully deep understanding of the Dharma—'

'All right, Mum,' said Lou. 'But is he hot?'

'Oh, for goodness' sake!' Mum's cheeks flushed from delicate rose to bright red. 'He is a seventy-year-old man!'

'A silver fox!'

'You know, Richard Gere is nearly seventy, and I'd still . . .'

'Girls!' Mum clapped her hands together, commandingly. 'Please. This is still very new. But yes, we've seen each other several times over the last couple of months. In fact, tomorrow night –' she paused, for dramatic effect – 'he's taking me to see a wonderful string quartet at the Wigmore Hall.'

'Dirty bastard,' muttered Lou under her breath. Fortunately Mum didn't seem to hear.

'That's wonderful news, Mum. He's a lucky man,' I said loudly. 'What's his name?'

'His name,' she said, shyly, 'is William.'

We left as the evening was drawing in. I winced as I hugged Mum goodbye, having snagged the cashmere of her dress with my scaly hand. Mum glanced down at it and frowned, taking in the scabs on my knuckles, which were oozing yellow fluid.

'What's the matter with your hands, darling?'

'Oh, I don't know. I keep meaning to get some cream.'

'Why don't you do that first thing tomorrow?' Mum stroked it, which was painful. 'Remember: you can't look after other people, if you don't look after yourself.'

'Thanks, I'll remember that,' I said, smiling through gritted teeth. 'And hey –' I leaned over to whisper, in case she didn't want Obe to know about her date – 'have a great time tomorrow!'

Obviously, I told him anyway as soon as we were out of earshot. It was past bedtime; both of the boys were fast asleep in the buggy, so we had decided to walk all the way back instead of getting the bus. The plane trees flickered sulphurous orange in the street lights, and our footsteps rang out in the damp, iron-tasting air.

'Maybe – just maybe – she'll move in with him, sell

her house, and give us some money!' I was saying, the wine running away with me a little.

Obe frowned. 'Really? That's the first thing that occurred to you?'

'Oh, come on,' I said. 'It's just a thought. It's not like she really needs that big house now. Surely anyone would think that.'

There was a pause; he was still frowning, and there was a hint of something – sadness? Disappointment? – in his expression. 'It hadn't occurred to me,' he said.

On the football pitch, some hooded kids were doing wheelies on a pizza-delivery scooter. Obe seemed to recognise them; and he gave a little nod as we passed.

'You know,' I said. 'I've been thinking. About this move. Since the redundancy thing, it is starting to feel a bit crazy. We can't even afford the car insurance right now. What if I don't get any more work? How will we pay the mortgage?'

'If you don't get any more work, we'll be screwed anyway,' said Obe. 'Look. We need to go ahead with this, not because there is anything wrong with Priory Court, but because you are so unhappy. You need to get out.'

This was obviously true, but also patronising. I felt obliged to show I wasn't bothered either way. 'Well, you never know,' I said. 'Maybe we won't even get the mortgage.'

We had sent off our mortgage application weeks ago, and we had not mentioned the redundancy. The whole application was basically fiction; we procured technically-true documents about my maternity leave, concealed Obe's dodgy credit history details, and provided some very optimistic estimates of our childcare costs. Perhaps the bank would see right through it.

We were on the High Street now. Here things started to rough up a bit, with the Polish grocer's display of too-pink salami, several pound shops and a grimy row of 'budget' rental estate agents, with dog-eared cards in the window advertising No DSS. There was a large crowd of Algerian men outside the shisha café.

'Let's think about other things,' said Obe. 'You know what? Follow me.' He grabbed the handles of the buggy and sped up, rushing past the Happy Man pub and the LightHouse: Pay As You Go Home Store, and taking the turning towards Priory Court.

'Obe, where are you . . .?' I called after him, trotting to keep up.

'Shhh!' Obe turned and put his finger fiercely to his lips. 'No arguments. Just follow.'

It wasn't raining tonight: the night was cool but clear. The visible stars were clustered together in the middle of the sky, holding out against the orange London glow. Halfway down our road Obe stopped, and fumbled with the fence between the pavement and the reservoir. A wooden panel came loose, and he lifted it up, creating a door-sized opening. I lowered my head and peered dubiously through. Across a wild patch of grass and weeds, the water winked in the moonlight. Nettles and brambles crowded around the other side of the fence, but there was a beaten-down path running through them.

Was this where the mysterious man in black got in?

'I don't think we're supposed to—'

'Didn't you hear me, Syl? Just follow.'

Obe pulled the buggy awkwardly through the gap, parking it in the undergrowth, and replacing the panel carefully behind him. I ducked under, and then picked my way through the nettles towards the glistening water. I'd never been down here before, and it was surreal to find myself within the landscape I had spent so many nights gazing at from my lookout in the living room. Years ago, starting off in journalism, I got a freelance gig as a pundit on *Sky News*, and I found myself sitting at the same newsreader's desk I watched every night on the TV screen. It felt like dreaming.

But this was real; this was beautiful. By the bank of the reservoir was the tree where the fox cubs played their games and, beneath it, a soft patch of grass. The water lapped quietly at the bank. Obe put down his rucksack, pulled out the muslin cloths from beneath the buggy, and spread them on the ground.

'The Hackney Riviera,' he said, spreading his arms out theatrically before sitting down. I lay next to him with my head on his lap. Here, the stars were bolder and more numerous than they had seemed from the road. On one side the reservoir was a flat darkness, with tower blocks silhouetted on the far bank; on the other Priory Court loomed above us. Lights were on in most of the windows. Ours was dark, but I could just make out the silhouette of the birthday sculpture in the living-room window.

There was no light from Dawn's flat below, but the balcony door was flapping open.

'Do you think she's in there?' I asked Obe.

'Who cares?' he said. 'I don't care what she does.'

I sighed, letting my weight rest on his legs, letting the tension go from my body. The air was cold, but despite its many holes my trusty old Puffa jacket was still warm. It was good to be outside. 'I can't wait until I don't have to think about her any more.'

'I can't wait until I don't have to think about you, thinking about her.'

'I just can't believe she doesn't bother you,' I said. 'Why doesn't she bother you?'

I felt him shrug. 'Other things bother me. Like why we are here on this planet, and whether there is a universal consciousness that unites us all, and whether we can access that through artistic endeavour.'

I let that sink in for a moment. 'It's a shame there doesn't seem to be any space for that kind of thing in my head.'

'Perhaps you need to free some up.' He tapped a curly temple. 'There's infinite space in here.'

I sat up and turned to him. His face, the one I saw every day, the one I knew every millimetre of, looked different here in the moonlight. I remembered when just one look at that face could make me smile. I remembered when Obe seemed like the answer, to some question I'd been asking for my whole life. Where had that feeling gone? He smiled at me, then reached into his coat pocket and pulled out a small, red box.

'Actually, Syl,' he said, fiddling with the lid. 'I have something for you.'

I looked dumbly at the box. We had discussed marriage years ago, in the brief window before I got pregnant with Larkin, but I had made it clear that I was not the kind of woman who cared about conventional things like that. Which was just as well, as there was absolutely no way we could afford to do it now. And even if money hadn't been an issue, I wasn't at all sure we were in quite the right place . . . But still I felt a weird flutter of something – nerves? – as Obe handed it to me. I slowly took off the lid. There inside, nestled in white tissue paper, was a heart-shaped potato. I took it out and held it in my palm.

'I found it in the veggie box this morning, and thought of you,' he said.

Silence stretched out between us. The dark water lapped gently against the grassy bank. 'That's lovely,' I whispered. 'Thank you, Obe.'

He smiled, just gently, his eyes on the glimmering water. 'My pleasure, Syl,' he said.

My teeth were chattering as we heaved the double buggy back through the hole in the fence and made our way down the road towards the entrance of the estate. It was still too cold, really, to be lying around outside. But our brief holiday on the Hackney Riviera had done something: I felt zingy, alive, ready for anything.

'You know what I think?' I whispered to Obe as we approached the car park. 'We should have sex every day for a week.'

Obe mulled this over. 'We could have sex *once*,' he said.

'It's been a while.'

'How long?'

'Long.'

There was a time when Obe and I had sex every day.

Sometimes more than once; our record in 24 hours, and this was a matter of some pride to both of us, was six (I'd just come back from a work trip; he'd spent three days alone, reading Anaïs Nin). My favourite feature was his shoulders, from which T-shirts hung in a good way. All our problems now were sex's fault, really. We'd never had to plan; we had just let our bodies do their thing. Obe always said that bodies were wiser than minds.

But that was all long ago, in a more youthful and less tired era. If we didn't get back on the wagon, Mum could soon be having more sex than me – I simply couldn't let that happen. Winston waved cheerily at us from the first-floor balcony. He was wearing the zebra-print dressing gown again, accessorised this evening with a pink pom-pom hat.

'Have you seen Dawn recently?' I called up.

'Who?'

'Dawn. You know, your neighbour. The one who . . .'

'Oh, crazy lady. Yeah, sure.'

'Did she seem okay?'

'Why don't you ask her?'

He turned towards the door of his flat. 'Someone asking for you,' he said.

Dawn's grizzled yellow face, topped with a tangle of reddish-brown hair, appeared over the parapet wall. She gazed at me unsteadily. Despite the fact that I had lived upstairs from Dawn for three years, I still wasn't sure she knew who I was.

'Oh, hi, Dawn,' I called, surprised. 'I just wanted to check that you're okay. I heard some strange noises coming from your flat the other night.'

She frowned, crinkling her face up so much that her features almost disappeared. 'Fuck awf,' she said. 'I was singing.'

Winston chuckled and put his arm around her, and for the first time a disturbing thought occurred to me: were Winston and Dawn a *couple*? I wasn't sure whether the prospect was heart-warming. What did they talk about? Did they have sex? That was all I needed now: to hear Winston and Dawn having noisy sex through the floorboards. What with Mum, and Dawn, soon everyone would be at it, except us.

'Hey now, darling,' Winston said to Dawn. 'Don't say that to the lady and gentleman. They just checking up on you.'

Dawn smiled at him soppily, and then lifted her hand and gave Obe and me a dignified, almost queenly little wave. 'Sorry, lovely lady,' she said. 'I'm fine thankewvery-much.'

7.

Sleepless

Incident No. 259. 28th February, 2 a.m.

Something hellish is going on with Eliot; his sleeping has gone haywire. For the last few nights he's been waking up every half an hour, all night long.

Perhaps it's because of the weaning. Perhaps he has picked up on the stress surrounding the redundancy, and the house move. Or perhaps there's some other, deep-seated psychological explanation that is no doubt attributable in some way to me.

Note to self: sleep training!! Consistency is key!!

Note to self 2: HAND CREAM!! Also, antibiotics?

Hours' sleep: 4 (broken). Poor. Very poor.

OBE and I still hadn't had sex. We hadn't had sex because I hadn't slept for more than half an hour consecutively in what felt like for ever, but might actually have been five nights. Reality became slippery, conversations went nowhere.

'Have you heard of the Fibonacci sequence?' he said,

as we lay, watching the dawn light creep around the edge of the curtains. That Baby had been howling for forty minutes, and I was grinding my teeth, trying with every ounce of physical and mental strength I possessed not to pick him up and feed him back to sleep. I had decided to wean him off night feeds, and I couldn't let him break me. Consistency, I repeated to myself like a mantra, my jaw clenched. Consistency was key.

'The Fibowhat?'

'The Fibonacci sequence. According to which everything in nature has a ratio of 1.61.'

Nothing made sense. I couldn't imagine why Obe had chosen this moment to try and explain a Concept Out of Science. Science was never my strong suit, and particularly not when explained to me at a senseless hour of the morning by Obe, whose grasp of the subject was even shakier.

'Isn't a ratio supposed to have two numbers in it, like "one to four"?'

'Fibonacci explains everything, from ears, to snails, to artichokes.'

'My God, now you're trying to explain artichokes?'

I tried to concentrate on breathing, long and low. Although I was lying down, my whole body was taut with effort, my muscles contracted. There was a spot on my back, between my shoulders, which was clenched as hard and tight as a fist. Could it possibly be right to leave That Baby crying, when it caused me actual physical pain?

Ah! Sweet relief! The crying stopped. My throbbing head was bathed in blissful, soothing silence. I closed my eyes and slipped into an uneasy dream: green and purple cartoon babies were spinning at me out of a dark sky, their mouths wide and their tonsils vibrating. They formed a cacophonous, whirling spiral, like an ear, a snail, or an artichoke . . .

Then there was a thump and the first strains of Rihanna drifted up from downstairs.

After Obe left for work, once The Toddler was up and there was absolutely no chance of me getting back to sleep again, Eliot drifted off into a deep, blissful-looking slumber. I put him in his cot, covered him with a soft woollen blanket, and watched his smooth, peaceful face for a moment, aching with the desire to swap places. My eyes had retreated back into my head; I was peering out at the world from somewhere far away. The tightness had spread from my temples down my neck, all the way to the tight spot on my upper back. I felt ill, sick. I couldn't imagine how I would get through the day.

There was nothing for it: I put *Bob the Builder* on for Larkin and picked up my phone. The birthday sculpture was eyeing me ferociously from the window ledge; I draped a muslin over it, and then called Bill.

'Morning, Sylvia,' he said as soon as he picked up. I guessed he must recognise my number by now. He sounded livlier than usual; the monotone had been enlivened with a cheery little trill. And that was great; Bill's happiness made me happy. Or it would, as soon as I could think straight.

'Oh Bill, I'm so glad you're there.' I was nearly sobbing with exhaustion.

'Oh dear, dear. At it again, is she?'

'Who?'

'Dawn!'

'Oh, Dawn. Yes, of course she is. But that's not what I was calling about.'

'How can I help, Sylvia?'

I felt a warm wave of love for Bill. I wanted to hug him and for him to cradle my head in his arms and tell me it was all going to be all right. I wanted him to be my dad. Was that weird?

'What do you think, Bill, about leaving a baby to cry? It just doesn't feel right to me, but I've been reading this book . . .'

'Which book?' asked Bill.

I picked up the sleep training book Frankie had lent me. The cover had a picture on it of a fresh-faced, delighted-looking mother cuddling a smiley, baby. In shiny gold capitals across the top it said: AMERICA'S NUMBER ONE BABY GURU.

'*The Great Big Happy Sleepy Baby Book*,' I told Bill. 'By Delilah Rodbaum.'

Frankie had given me the book a long time ago, when Larkin and Caleb were just a few months old. 'You've got to read this,' she had said fervently, pressing the book into my hands. 'It's really a very simple set of instructions. All you have to do is follow them, see? It worked perfectly with Caleb, he's already sleeping through the night.' I had smiled and said thanks, and then I had hidden the book away on the highest shelf and never got it down again – until now. I had never thought of myself as the type of mother who would read a book like this. I thought I was more natural, more earth-mothery, instinctive – until now. Now, I was so desperate I would have jumped off a cliff just for three consecutive hours.

Bill sucked his teeth. 'Personally, I don't trust these baby gurus,' he said. 'The very premise seems designed to make ordinary mothers feel like failures.'

And there it was, the familiar flush of relief that always accompanied these little advice sessions. 'It's so good to hear you say that, Bill,' I said. 'I just need to put the book away, and follow my instincts. Don't I?'

'That's just my view,' said Bill.

'I really don't know what I'd do without you. Thank you so much.'

'No problem,' said Bill. 'Anything else I can help you with? Any more trouble downstairs?'

'Actually, there is a new thing,' I said. 'A strange smell that comes up through the floorboards whenever Dawn has her "friends" round.'

'What kind of smell is it?' asked Bill.

'It's sort of chemical,' I told him. 'But sweet. Like burnt marshmallows.'

The smell had been getting worse ever since the night I saw Dawn and Winston together on the balcony. And I had also been hearing his gravelly voice amid the general hubbub down there. My suspicions were confirmed: the dynamic duo had joined forces. Fortunately, there had been no sex noises. Not yet.

Bill paused. 'Hmmm,' he said, and his voice had an edge I hadn't heard before. 'Would you,' he asked, 'recognise the smell of illegal drugs?'

'Um,' I hesitated. It depended which drugs he meant. Obe and I had dabbled, recreationally, in the brief window before kids came along, but we'd never done crack or smack. We definitely weren't crack or smack kind of people.

'Not necessarily,' I said.

Bill was onto something. The more we talked about it, the more it made sense: the coming and going, the lift clanking up and down all night; the unfamiliar male voices, never the same twice. Dawn's flat was a crack den! This was the best news I'd had for ages. Finally, I felt justified. Noise was so abstract, so subjective an annoyance, that sometimes even I had suspected that the fact that it even bothered me was more to do with me than it was with Dawn. But drugs were a different matter. Drugs, as Bill said using audible capital letters, were Definitely Not On.

'So what do we do?' I asked.

'I'll need to report our suspicions to the police,' said Bill. 'After that, it's out of my hands.'

'Be my guest, Bill,' I said. 'As you know, we're hoping to move out soon, anyway. But we should get it sorted out for the benefit of everybody else.'

'That's what I admire about you, Sylvia,' said Bill. 'Your spirit of public service.'

'Thanks, Bill,' I said. 'I'd say the same about you.'

The weather had taken an unexpected turn. It wasn't raining any more, but just as spring should have been springing the country had been plunged into an unseasonal deep freeze. In the park, the daffodils that had been nosing out of the soil had been clubbed back by the cold; flurries of tiny snowflakes jerked through the air, and the ducks had to pick their way across an icy pond. On the news, Welsh farmers were digging baby lambs out of snowdrifts.

Frankie vetoed the park and insisted that we meet at Tumble in the Jungle, a soft play centre in an industrial estate just off the North Circular. We sat ourselves at a grey Formica table while Caleb and Larkin took turns to leap into a pool full of plastic balls. Eliot was in a high chair, making rapid headway with his first ever portion of chips.

'All you have to do,' she was saying, 'is start calling in your contacts, and increasing your social media presence. Are you on Facebook, Twitter, LinkedIn?'

I reached for my polystyrene cup of horrible, bitter, barely caffeinated instant coffee. I was already almost hallucinating with tiredness, and this place was a bad trip. The heating was blasting out a tropical-style mugginess, and there was a strong smell of mould. Hand-painted not-quite-Disney characters loomed disturbingly from the peeling orange walls; next to our table was an animal that had the eyes of Dumbo but the mouth and body of a crocodile. I guessed it had to look that messed-up for copyright reasons.

With intense effort, I pulled myself back to the conversation. Frankie was taking her usual can-do attitude towards our situation. She was one hundred per cent sure that we'd get the mortgage, despite the fact that I hadn't told the bank about my redundancy, because 'they'll lend money to anyone – all that stuff about learning from the subprime loans crisis was just a load of old blah'. All I had to do, she said confidently, was figure out a way of meeting the repayments.

I swigged, tried to focus. 'I'm on Facebook. And I sometimes look on Twitter. But I haven't got many followers.'

'How many?'

'Er, seven,' I said, and then remembered that the other day @crockettdreamhomes had followed me. 'No, eight! Eight.'

'For fuck's sake,' said Frankie. 'I thought you were supposed to be in public relations. Doesn't that include social media?'

'It probably should have done,' I admitted. Looking back on it, I wasn't sure what I had been doing, career-wise, for the last few years. I'd probably let myself get a little bit sidetracked by having two children. The whole social media thing seemed to really gather pace the year that I was on maternity leave with Larkin, and I'd never quite caught up.

'You're so good at all this stuff, Franks,' I said ruefully, dipping another chip in ketchup and giving it to Eliot. 'It should be you going back to work.'

Before having Caleb, Frankie had been a producer for a film company, making real feature films. She'd worked crazy hours, flown all over the world, won awards. Frankie had great ideas, and she was exceptionally skilled at making people want to do what she said, not exactly because she manipulated them, but because they liked to make her happy.

'Do you ever think about getting another job?'

'Of course, all the time. I've been at home far too long. But Mark is away so much, and in film all contracts are short, and there's no such thing as part-time. You are expected to live and breathe work for months, and then survive until the next contract comes up. I just can't work out how I'd organise the childcare.' Frankie sighed. 'I'm sick of it, to be honest. You know, I have to ask Mark for money every time I need a haircut, or a new coat? It's humiliating.'

'Hmm?' I said, thinking about how much I would love it if my partner – or anyone, really – gave me money for a haircut or a new coat.

'Yeah. I mean, he doesn't like it either, obviously. As you know, Mark's a total feminist. It's not like he wants me to be in this position, it's just that his work is so . . . important.'

As she said this last word, Frankie made a strangled noise, somewhere between a cough and a gasp. This was a shock, as I tended to assume, based on previous life experience, that my best friend was generally okay. Now I looked at her with concern. She had definitely lost weight; Frankie was always slim, but right now she looked stringy and parched, like a neglected houseplant. She swallowed, and said more normally, 'Actually, I got a call last week from Ben, do you remember Ben from Legless Productions?'

'What, that bell-end who didn't invite you to the Golden Globes?'

'That's him.' Ben was the director of a feature that Frankie produced, which won a Golden Globe shortly after she went on maternity leave. She read about the award in the paper: he hadn't bothered to get in touch or to invite her to the ceremony. 'He wants me to work on his new project. It's a big showcase documentary series for the BBC. It would be a whole new area for me.'

'You should totally do it!'

'I can't, Syl,' she said, wiping her eyes. 'Mark's got a crazy few months ahead . . . it's just too complicated.' I wondered where he was in the world, but felt a bit dizzy just thinking about it.

'I thought he was going to cut back on the travel.'

'Yeah,' said Frankie, and if I hadn't known her, I would have said there was a trace of resentment in her voice. 'That's what he told me.'

She got a packet of tissues out of her pocket – even in distress she still remembered tissues – and dabbed at her nose. Frankie was crying! This never happened. I shuffled up my chair and put my arm around her shoulders. She was so thin that I could feel the knobbles of her vertebrae through her Puffa – how had I not noticed this before?

'I'm just going a bit crazy at home by myself all the time,' she said. 'I need to get out, you know? Engage with the world. Talk to some adults. Go to places that aren't . . . this.' She gestured around us, at the detritus of chips and baby wipes, the neon orange-and-green walls, the corrugated-iron ceiling. 'In fact, when Mark gets back, I wanted to invite you and Obe over for dinner. So we can have an adult conversation, for once.'

I narrowed my eyes at her. 'Is this a dinner party?'

Frankie knew I didn't do dinner parties. Once, one of the old Etonian journalists I worked with had invited me to a dinner party at which there was compulsory charades, and I swore to myself I would never go to a dinner party ever again.

She shifted in her seat. 'Okay, I was thinking of inviting

Toby and Phoebe, too, you know, the friends I told you about from Caleb's nursery.'

Just as I suspected: she wanted to integrate me with her leafy street friends. Usually I would have had no hesitation about nipping this plan in the bud, but there was no way I could refuse Frankie in her hour of need. 'Phoebe is the model-turned-environmental-activist?'

'That makes her sound terrifying,' said Frankie. 'But actually she's not like that at all.'

This was the kind of thing Frankie always said. I had tried to explain that they weren't terrifying *to her*, which was a very different thing.

I sneaked one of Eliot's chips. 'And what does her partner do?'

'Toby? He's in, erm, banking.'

'Christ, Frankie!'

'Syl, please. I'd really appreciate it if you made the effort. Just do it for me, okay?'

There was a commotion in the ball pool. Caleb was poised on the edge, shrieking, 'I will crush you!' at my submerged son.

I was trapped holding a lightly greased Eliot on my lap, but Frankie leapt up in a burst of energy.

'How many times have I told you, Caleb? We don't crush our friends.'

'I just wanted to crush him a bit,' protested Caleb.

'Not at all. No crushing. Full stop.'

She sat back down, with a panting and grateful Larkin on her knee. 'So anyway that's great,' she said. 'I'm so glad you can come.'

Back at the flat, another official-looking envelope stared blankly up at me from the doormat. This one was unusually thick and white, and I immediately knew what it was. Sure enough, when I picked it up the name and logo of the mortgage company were emblazoned on the back: Happy Bank it said, above a yellow smiley face, and then below, Decent Mortgages for Decent People.

I held it to the light. The paper was so thick that the envelope gave nothing away. Obe would be back from work soon, should I wait for him? I held it in my hand for a moment, toying with the corner, thinking about ripping it . . .

'Mummy!' Larkin was straining at the straps of the buggy. 'Let me out! I need a poo!'

I shoved the envelope into my bag and leaped into action. I had only just started trying to potty-train Larkin, and based on previous mishaps there was not a single millisecond to waste. I unbuckled him, picked him up and raced to the bathroom. In one swift movement I whipped his tracky bottoms down and dumped him unceremoniously on the potty. He sat there frowning, deeply concentrated.

I left him to it and headed for the privacy of the bedroom, where I sat down on the bed, heart racing. A couple of deep breaths, in and out, in and out. Either way, I told myself, it was absolutely fine. If we did get the mortgage that was obviously brilliant, woop-de-doo we would have our own little family home, no matter that it didn't have a functioning kitchen or bathroom, smelled strongly of rotting meat and fish, and was located closer to the North Circular than was strictly speaking ideal. And if we didn't get it, that was fine too, because we would find another little flat to rent, if Priory Court was knocked down. We'd have to pare down the toy collection and throw out a few books to make room once That Baby got too big for his cot. Perhaps we could even string up some kind of curtain, to make a dining room . . .

A single salutary THUMP from the flat downstairs brought me to my senses. Who was I kidding? If Happy Bank turned us down, I would throw myself into the reservoir and be done with it all.

With a trembling hand, I opened the envelope, pulled out the sheaf of paper inside. 'Thank you for choosing a Happy Bank Ethical Mortgage,' read the covering letter.

'I am pleased to tell you that your application has been approved subject to the Terms and Conditions outlined in the enclosed mortgage offer.'

I jumped up. I screamed. I did a Red-Indian-style war dance around the bedroom.

'Mummy?' Larkin called out plaintively.

'Just a second!' I pulled my phone out of my pocket and called Obe. For once, he answered straight away. 'Obe! Babe! We got the mortgage!'

'Fuck off,' he said, and Obe never swore. 'I can't believe they would be that stupid.'

'They are! They really are! We are moving house!'

'Just tell me –' the background noise died away; he must have taken shelter in the do-it-right room, something he only did in very important moments – 'what *exactly* does it say?'

I skimmed, muttering, through the enclosed Terms and Conditions. 'Repayments take place over a thirty-four year period . . . you may lose your home . . .' I stopped, paused, read one particular section again. 'Oh wow,' I said. 'Listen to this. For every pound we borrow, we pay back £1.91. By the time we've paid this off, this house will have cost us double what we are supposedly paying for it.'

I could almost hear Obe's brain whirring away, hard at work on the calculations. 'Half a lifetime,' he murmured.

'Half a lifetime paying for a smelly, derelict, grey-brick two-up two-down off a major ring road.'

It was hard to fathom why I was feeling so triumphant when he put it like that. But hey, it was best not to overthink things.

'Mummy!'

'Anyway,' I said quickly. 'Gotta go. Yes, Larkin?'

'I missed.'

'Missed what?'

'Missed the potty.'

'How?'

Ending the call, I craned my neck around the bedroom door. Larkin had somehow managed to shuffle the potty from the bathroom into the hall. He was now standing up, legs akimbo, and beneath him, on the pale beige carpet, glistened an enormous turd.

I made sure to breathe, in and out. This was fine. I could deal with it. In fact, it was good to have a distraction – the whole mortgage thing was suddenly feeling a bit overwhelming. 'Larkin,' I said firmly, 'don't move.'

I raced to the bathroom, and pinged on the rubber gloves.

And that was it: the rest of the day was gone, consumed with scrubbing and rinsing and comforting and feeding and wiping. Wiping, in particular, of bums and surfaces and mouths and hands. Once, I had imagined passing tender days with my children, laughing with them, tickling them, making silly faces and playing educational games. At the moment, all that was on hold. As long as I was still wiping, that was good enough.

That night, I got Eliot down by 10 p.m. In theory, I wouldn't be feeding him again until the next morning, but in practice this was the brief window in which I might get a couple of hours' sleep. I felt like Obe and I should use the time to have celebratory sex, but no part of me felt celebratory enough. I tried to summon up a mental image to get me into the sex mood, but nothing really worked: not even Labrynth-era David Bowie, and that was usually a cert.

I breathed a sigh of relief when Obe reached for the laptop and booted up a violent alien film. Thank goodness, he didn't feel like having sex, either. I padded down the hall to the bedroom, tucked myself up and, after a brief internal struggle, opened *The Great Big Happy Sleepy Baby Book*.

On the first page was a large picture of a smiling, overweight woman with a bouffant. She looked a little like Margaret Thatcher, but perhaps that was okay. Perhaps what I actually needed right now was a little more Margaret Thatcher in my life. I cracked on with the introduction, nodding in vigorous agreement after almost every sentence.

Having a new baby can be a daunting task for any parent, wrote Delilah Rodbaum. *Advice can be conflicting. Many parents worry about sleep deprivation and their baby's endless crying.* The Great Big Happy Sleepy Baby Book *will guide you through all of this. Delilah gives you simple, easy-to-follow routines, which will get your baby sleeping through the night, from 7 p.m. to 7 a.m., at between eight and ten weeks. Babies who settle into Delilah's routines are happy, nourished, and well-prepared for life, because all their needs are met.*

So far, this was all sounding very encouraging. It was incredibly good to think that at least this element of our situation might have a simple, common-sense solution. I closed my eyes and just imagined how firm and fair I was going to be next time Eliot woke up. I saw myself patting him gently and reassuringly, just as Delilah Rodbaum described, and then quietly leaving the room. I saw Eliot crying half-heartedly for a moment, and then popping his thumb into his mouth, and drifting off into blissful sleep. Ahhhh. Sleep.

THUMP THUMP THUMP.

My eyes sprang open. The floor of the bedroom was vibrating.

THUMP THUMP THUMP.

'Obe!' I called, querulously. 'Obe, what's that?'

There was a pause.

THUMP THUMP THUMP.

'I guess Dawn is doing that thumping thing again,' came Obe's piercing insight from the sitting room. 'Did we ever find out what it was? Not her head, is it?'

I sighed, and sat up. My whole body ached for sleep. The clock by the bed blinked 11:00 in its harsh red digital letters.

THUMP THUMP THUMP.

The floor vibrated again. From the cot came the first rustle of a stirring baby, the first whimper, the first sign of an impending crescendo. I grabbed *The Great Big Happy Sleepy Baby Book* from the bedside table and turned to the index, scanning desperately for 'neighbours', then 'external noise', then 'crack den downstairs'. But there was nothing. On that subject, Delilah Rodbaum had absolutely zero advice. I threw the book on the floor and, before the crying could start, I picked up Eliot. His head bobbed, his tiny mouth gaped desperately for my nipple. Screw it. I carried him into the sitting room, sat down on the feeding chair, and put him to my breast.

THUMP THUMP THUMP.

THUMP THUMP THUMP.

I looked out over the reservoir. No sign of the man in black, but Mummy Fox was out there, padding through the drizzle, sniffing at an old plastic bag. She had a touch of mange on her tail. I wondered where her cubs were. Come to think of it, I hadn't seen her cubs for days. Was it me, or did she look a bit anxious? She was pacing about, sniffing the bag, sniffing the bushes, sniffing the air.

'Where are they, Mummy Fox?' I asked her, silently. 'What's become of your babies?'

THUMP THUMP THUMP.

8.

I'm a professional

Incident No. 260. 1st March, 5 a.m.

One of the fox cubs is missing. I can see Cub 1 out there, playing about on a rotting mattress. But it's been days now, with no sign of Cub 2. Has he been kidnapped by the man in black?

Perhaps I should raise this at the big meeting with High-Class Homes. Aren't they supposed to be 'creating habitats, fostering bio-diversity'?

Aargh. Enough! What I actually need to do is sleep. That's all. Somehow my body seems to have forgotten that basic function. Might try some meditation. Or alternatively, might just sit here, picking at the scabs on my hands.

Hours' sleep: Not enough. Thanks for nothing, Delilah.

S*YLVIA! So sorry about the delay – but congrats on going freelance! I'm sure you've made the right decision! As it happens, there is something you might be able to help me with . . .*

I re-read Hari's email, to spur myself on. Unexpectedly, he had come up with the goods. He wanted me to edit Deutsche Bank's annual diversity report, at a day rate equivalent to at least a week's work in the public sector. So here I was, sitting at the computer, trying to focus.

The report was 250 pages long, and filled with tables and banking jargon that I could barely understand. I pulled together every fibre of mental strength to deal with the first sentence: . . . *streamlining the governance structures of the organisation for maximum* . . . for maximum what? Cash return? Efficiency? Cabbage? Impact! Impact. Phew.

This was potentially a really big break. If I didn't mess it up there might be more work in the future. It hadn't come a moment too soon. We'd had a menacing letter from the car insurance company this morning. Rob Crockett had called to hassle us for a completion date, and I had managed to put him off – for now. But if I had a new career as a freelance editor for Deutsche Bank, suddenly moving house didn't seem so crazy after all. Maybe we could even get that extension that Frankie had been talking about . . .

The problem was the exhaustion. Last night had been particularly bad. That Baby woke up every two hours all night long. Nothing I did – feeding, cuddling, listless patting – seemed to make any difference. At some point

I found myself sprawled on the sitting-room floor, with him draped across my face.

Strange things had started to happen in my body. There were permanent floaters in my peripheral vision, and a grey, listless fug in my head. I felt jangly, edgy; something in my neck had seized up.

Nevertheless, here I was: a Freelance Writing and Editing Professional. A little weary, perhaps, and smeared in banana, maybe, but still, the Solution to All Your Editorial Needs.

'Syl?' Obe put a dish down on the folding table, which was doubling up as my desk. This was our new, negotiated routine – I had put my foot down about doing all the cooking, and he had agreed to take charge at weekends. Apart from Roberta's rum-and-raisin cake, Obe only cooked one thing and that was macaroni cheese.

'Just a sec.' I looked back to the screen.

Accountability procedures are rigorous at best, but looking forward, stakeholders will demand an end-to-end process . . .

'Can you do that later? Lunch is ready,' said Obe. I ignored him, screwed up my eyes, burrowed my fingers into my temples and ploughed ahead. Surely it wasn't too much to ask for a clear five minutes to focus.

Looking forward, stakeholders will demand . . .

'Urgh! What the – Syl!'

'Just a second!'

. . . stakeholders will demand . . .

'There's something wrong with the macaroni cheese!'

. . . an end-to-end process . . .

'Syl, please. What are you doing?'

'What do you think I'm bloody doing?' I snapped. 'I'm working. Bearing in mind that if we don't keep up with the repayments we will lose our home. And that we still haven't renewed the car insurance. And that my boots have been leaking for months, and I need a haircut and a new coat. So please, just give me . . .'

Obe peered over my shoulder and read the first line. 'I don't understand a word of that,' he said. 'What does it mean?'

'I have absolutely no idea.'

'Listen, Syl, it's lunchtime, and also . . .' Somehow, I rolled my eyes, without moving them from the screen. 'To be honest, I'm not sure that you are ready to take on this work. You've seemed quite –' he hesitated – 'tired recently.'

'Well, of course I'm tired,' I snapped. 'I'm tired, you're tired, we're all tired. What choice do I have? I'll deal with it.'

'But—'

'Oh, for God's sake, Obe.' I had no more patience for his laissez-faire attitude towards the financial crisis. I was beginning to feel that although we, to all appearances, shared one slightly-too-small flat, he and I actually inhabited different planets. 'Do I really need to explain this? You saw the mortgage documents! If we don't keep up the repayments . . .'

He went back to his place, and sat down. 'Syl, please. You don't have to do this. I think if you just tried to – let go a bit, give yourself a break. Things will work themselves out. The world will provide.'

I emitted a small yelp of helpless frustration. 'Try telling that to the car insurance company! Try telling that to Rob "Satan" Crockett! The world doesn't provide, Obe! I provide! Look at me – here I am, providing.'

Larkin was turning his head like a dog at a tennis match as this conversation – I wasn't prepared to acknowledge it as a fully fledged, right-in-front-of-the-kids argument – pinged back and forth. 'Okay,' said Obe, holding his hands up. 'Well, I was just saying. I don't think you are ready to go back to work right now. But obviously, you know best.'

'Thank you,' I said. 'I'm glad we can agree on something.'

'Anyway,' he said. 'Look at this.' At last, I looked up at the macaroni, of which Obe had extracted a spoonful. He was right, it did look curious; the cheese didn't seem to have reacted in the normal way to the cooking process.

Rather than melting, it had separated into grease and gelatinous yellow lumps. I remembered that I had hit a new low while out shopping and bought cheese in the pound shop. 'Signature, a cheese to please', read the label, and then in smaller letters underneath, 'A Cheese Product'. There was no list of ingredients. Was a cheese product the same as cheese?

'It's fine,' I told him confidently. 'Let's just eat it.'

'It's dis-GUS-ting,' said The Toddler.

'It *is* disgusting,' Obe agreed, letting another lumpy spoonful of it fall back into the dish.

I sighed and slammed the laptop shut. 'Okay. Bread and Marmite?'

Larkin shook his head. 'Jam.'

'Not jam.'

'Jam.'

I got him jam. I got all of us jam. Obe scraped the macaroni into the bin, and, remarkably, also washed up the dish.

After 'lunch' Obe took the kids out, so that I would have some space to work on the report. The deadline was on Monday and I was fast running out of time. The plan was that they would be gone for several hours, so I gave him the changing bag crammed with nappies, wipes and expressed milk in bottles. I packed carrot puree for Eliot, in the vague hope that he wouldn't be fed on donuts.

Future-proofing the organisation will require sustained momentum . . .

The saggy old sofa beckoned me enticingly from the corner of my vision. It looked so squishy, so comfy, as if its soft, baggy cushions would swallow me right up. I imagined sinking my head down, taking the weight off my neck, closing my eyes. Surely, I would work more efficiently if I just had a short power nap first? There was little point in battling on, when after a bit of sleep I'd get this job done in no time. I shut the computer, sat down on the sofa, and a delicious wave of relaxation swept over me. I leaned my head back and closed my eyes, just for a moment . . .

I am in a house. It is the Highbury House, I know, even though it looks nothing like it. This place is dark, a shadowy, winding maze of rooms, some accessible only by ladders, others so low I can't stand up. The Toddler is holding my hand. 'Look, Mummy,' he says, pointing. 'Is that your daddy?'

'Where?'

The Toddler is pointing into the shadows. I know Dad is there, but I can't see him.

'Over here. Look.' The Toddler starts to run, and I try

to follow him, but he is so small that he can squeeze down impossibly small corridors, through tunnels. I haven't got a hope of keeping up. I know I'm going to lose him, lose both of them.

The door banged, and something hurtled towards me through a fog of sleep. I opened my eyes; it was The Toddler, his mouth smeared with pink icing. He gave me a sticky kiss.

'She's asleep,' he announced.

Obe's face loomed overhead. 'Did you finish it?'

I wrenched my head from the cushions and stared at him uncomprehendingly, feeling that some important chance had just slipped through my fingers. Then I remembered the report. Finish it? But they had only just gone out. And I'd only got to page three. 'Why are you back? I've hardly even started!'

'We've been out all afternoon,' said Obe.

'We ate three donuts,' said Larkin, proudly.

Obe undid the sling and thrust That Baby into my arms. 'And he needs a feed.'

I tucked Eliot into the crook of my elbow and he dived eagerly in. I closed my eyes and a tear trickled gently down my cheek. 'I'll have to do it tomorrow. Can you take them out again?'

'You lack the season of all natures, sleep.' Obe sat down next to me and stroked my hair. 'I really think you should tell them you can't do it. Look at you. You're exhausted.'

'I can't pull out now!' Hauling Eliot with me, I got up and ran wildly back to the computer, hair akimbo. 'I've committed . . . my reputation . . . have *some* standards . . . I'm a *professional*!'

Obe was looking at me as a doctor might examine an unexplained rash. But I didn't care; something was rising up inside, I couldn't hold it back any more. 'And anyway,' I shouted. 'Why do you think I even took on this work? Do you think I want to? Do you think it's good for me? I only took on this work because of you!'

'What are you talking about? I told you not to!'

'Look around!' I gestured furiously at the poky sitting room, the stained carpet, the hole in the ceiling where the plaster still hadn't been fixed. The birthday sculpture observed us from the window ledge with its haughty tin-can eyes. 'We haven't got any money!'

'Of course we haven't.'

'And do you ever think about *why* we haven't got any money?'

'Do *you* think that, if you had all the money in the world, you would attain some state of everlasting happiness? Think about it, Sylvia. It's an illusion. Life is never easy, not even when you're rich.'

'Easier, Obe it's easier.'

'Oh, right. Well, come on then, tell me what's really going on. Let's have the Sylvia analysis.' Obe held his voice steady, but clouds of rage had gathered over his face.

'You still haven't got your act together.'

'What do you mean? I work, don't I?'

'You are a playworker.'

'And?'

'Well, that's fine if you're twenty-two, single, and fancy-free. It's another thing now, when you've a family. I can't do it all. I'm breastfeeding, I'm doing all the childcare, I'm working my fingers almost literally to the bone at home, I can't support us as well. It's too much. It's time to grow up, Obe. You need to get a better-paid job.'

Bang. The shot had been fired. The reverberations sounded around the entire continent of our relationship. Diplomats scrabbled for their papers, tried desperately to highlight shared interests, while states massed their troops. I glanced nervously at the birthday sculpture, but it was glowering at me even more terrifyingly than Obe. In the hope of pacifying it, I rearranged my face and continued in a calmer, more conciliatory tone.

'You know, a leaflet came through the door the other day, about training courses for environmentally friendly electricians,' I went on. 'Installing solar panels and wind turbines and stuff. Apparently the green electricity sector is growing, even during the recession. Why don't you look into it?'

Obe stood up suddenly. 'Oh please, Sylvia,' he said. 'With your fancy degree and your big ideas. I'm not an electrician, or a teacher, or any of the other things you want me to be. I am what I am. I'm no layabout. But the vibe I'm getting is that nothing I do is good enough for you.'

Perhaps it wasn't, I thought defiantly to myself, after he'd left the room, banging the door behind him. Perhaps I did want more. Would that be so very bad?

From the sofa, The Toddler watched me quietly as I wiped tears from my face. Then, carefully, he picked up the raggedy blanket he had slept with ever since he was tiny, and held it out in his chubby hand.

'You need blankie,' he said.

I lifted The Toddler onto my lap, while he stroked blankie across my cheek. His fingers were still sticky with sugar. He peered at the computer on the table.

'What are you writing?' he asked.

I told him I was writing a story. 'Do you know who it's for?' He shook his head. 'It's for you.'

'Really?'

'Really.'

'Tell it to me.'

I took a deep breath. 'Once upon a time, there was a

small boy, with eyes the colour of beetles, and his name was Larkin . . .'

That evening, after the kids were in bed, the tension in the flat made the rooms feel even smaller, the air thick with resentment. I had to get out. I left the flat heading for somewhere, anywhere. Snow was falling gently, a fine layer of white across the tarmac. It covered up the usual detritus – a bag of nappies, a broken sink, yet another chequered mattress – and made the place look sparkling clean. Every window was bright with warm light; fifty-four families side by side, cheek by jowl, getting on with it. The hoover was whining from the Kosovan family's flat, and I imagined roller-skates girl in there, cooped up in the warmth.

Brenda had stuck one of her fluorescent green posters up in the lift.

'DEFEND YOUR BLOCK!!!', read the felt-tip scrawl. 'FIND OUT THE COUNCIL'S REAL PLANS FOR PRIORY COURT!! Come to the Extraordinary General Meeting of the Tenants and Residents Association! Meeting open to All. The future is in our hands.'

The cold bit into my cheeks and hands as I walked. I didn't think about where I was going, but my feet knew: I was homing. They took me past the park and through

Highbury Barn, towards the Fields. This was a place saturated with my past; it called me whenever I didn't know where to go. Everything around me – the trees, the tennis courts, the little kiosk café – was layered with childhood memories: Lou and I crunching through piles of autumn leaves; the pure freedom of racing down this path on our bikes, the wind on our cheeks. Me, when I was no older than The Toddler, in my buggy with the rain cover on, the warm dampness of my breath fugging the plastic. Every day, Dad used to wheel me this way to Highbury Barn, where he bought his lunch from the sandwich shop. I knew that he was there, behind me, steering me, even when I couldn't see him.

Was he there, now?

I held my hand up to catch a snowflake, and examined its tiny perfection. Perfect as the sleeping faces of my children; too perfect for this world. This weather was all wrong. It was true, we all knew it was true, what the scientists said. How long would it be before the oceans started rising and the food stopped growing? Did anybody know, for sure? I turned my face to the sky, feeling snow fall on it one flake after another. I imagined them burying me up to my knees, my chest, my neck. I closed my eyes and sank into the cool dark inside.

I found myself on the doorstep of the Highbury house. The front window was dark, but through the glass panels of the door I could see a glow from the kitchen. Mum would be in there, dressing gown on, teacup in hand, chamber music playing. I could reach up, now, ring the bell, and she would open it and see me here. She would invite me in and make me hot milk like she used to when I couldn't sleep, and I could tell her about all the things that were on my mind: about the car insurance, and how I hadn't slept for days, and that I hadn't managed to finish this report and the deadline was Monday. How I would go crazy if we didn't move house, but also if we did, and how tired I was, and how Obe hated me, and I hated him sometimes, too, and how I couldn't remember the last time I had felt normal.

I could tell her about the 1980s-man smell, and the strange loud-quiet voice. I could ask her if she ever smelled it, ever heard it, or if it was just me.

I reached my hand up, and put my finger to the bell. All I had to do was push, all I had to do was say, I need you . . . but I couldn't do it. I shoved my hand in my pocket, turned around, and headed back the way I had come.

Back at Priory Court, Dawn and Winston were huddling together on the drunks' bench, sharing a bottle of

Wray and Nephs. Their holey coats and beanies had a light dusting of snow. Between them nestled a sports bag, gaping slightly open. As I got closer, it struck me that the bag was moving. Winston kept patting it, and then peeking down inside it, making little kissing noises.

'You all right, lady?' he said. I narrowed my eyes and squinted through the snow. Now I was sure: the sports bag had something inside it that was alive.

'What have you got there?' I said, peering over. Winston held the bag open and I leaned over to see inside. A pair of frightened yellow eyes met mine. Then a furry head stuck right out and there could be no doubt.

'Winston, you have to put him back!' I cried. 'That's the fox cub that lives on the bank! His mother has been looking for him!'

Winston looked at me as though I was nuts, then threw his head back and laughed. 'Do you hear dat?' he said, nudging Dawn, still giggling. 'She worried about the dog!'

He produced a packet of cheesy Wotsits and offered one to Cub 2, who sniffed it and then greedily gobbled it up. It was Wotsits now, I thought grimly to myself, but how long before that poor cub would be addicted to crack? Then Winston turned to me and spoke very slowly, as if to someone hard of hearing. 'The park keeper gave him to me. He found it, on its own in the bushes. Told me to give it a good home, innit?' He sighed, contentedly. 'I've always wanted a dog.'

Something came over me, and suddenly I was running as fast as I could down the white-dusted road towards the reservoir, with the sports bag clutched to my chest. Was that Winston's limping footsteps, the tap of Dawn's heels, on the pavement behind me? I reached the fence, lifted the broken panel, and looked through: on the other side there was the scrubby grass, a patch of iced nettles, and beyond that the water, glimmering with the promise of something better. I pushed the bag through the fence. The little cub's feet flailed and scratched, ensnared by the straps and zips, but after a second or two he was out.

'Run!' I urged him silently. 'Get out of here, escape while you still can!' He didn't need to be told twice. With a flick of his tail, he disappeared into the bushes.

I finally got the report off to Hari at 11 p.m., pressing send with a sigh of relief. Downstairs, everything was quiet. I had a window, now, when I could get some sleep, but I could feel that mounting edge of anxiety that prevented me from letting go. Seized by an impulse, I piled three cushions on top of one another in the middle of the living room. I knelt down on them and took a deep breath.

I didn't look at the birthday sculpture, but I could feel it behind me, its metal face blank and yet powerful. That was fine. I wasn't scared; perhaps what I needed to do was channel some of its dark, challenging energy.

Obe was sitting on the sofa, watching a film. Recently, he didn't seem to have been reading quite as much poetry. Or reading much at all, in fact. Instead, he had developed an uncharacteristic taste for action films. I wasn't sure what to make of this. From the booming soundtrack, I could tell it was going to involve loud violence and shooting. I wished I had another, more peaceful room to meditate in, but I didn't fancy sitting on the kitchen floor and both bedrooms were currently occupied by sleeping children I couldn't risk waking.

'You know, there's a documentary about the Beat poets on BBC4,' I suggested. 'Why don't you watch that instead?'

'Nah,' he replied. 'I'm not in the mood. What are you doing?'

'I'm practising meditation,' I told him.

'Why?'

'You wouldn't understand.'

'No?'

'No,' I said, firmly. 'You don't need to meditate, because you have a naturally empty mind.'

Obe did not dignify this with a reply. I wondered when, if ever, we would start talking again. 'You need to get a better-paid job' was still hanging in the air like a bad smell – a rotting-meat smell, that no matter how much you scrub, is never going to go away.

I crossed my legs, shut my eyes, and I focused my attention on my breath:

In . . . and out.

In . . . and out.

I wouldn't think about money or car insurance or mortgages or launching my website or Syria or climate change or potty training or whether I should really be giving Eliot chips or green electricity courses. I would just sit here peacefully and breathe. That was all I had to do right now. I settled in. I kept my attention lightly on my warm, solid body as it inhaled and exhaled. And as I did so, something new appeared in my mind. A light horizon, a clear view over flat water. Somehow I knew it had always been there, I'd just never taken the time to notice it.

BOOOOM CRASH PAP-PAP-PAP-PAP.

A round of machine-gun fire echoed across the living room. But I would not be deterred. Buddha wouldn't have been put off by a little background noise.

In . . . and out. In . . . and out.

I was doing this all day without even realising. Breathing. Looking after myself, keeping myself alive. Light was shining over the water, the sea at sunset. I was looking out over it, but at the same time I knew that I was looking in, that this uncluttered scene was actually somewhere inside me. Little bubbles of joy ran up and down my spine.

'Oooh, ouch,' Obe remarked, as the horrible sound of crunching cartilage filled the room. But that was fine. I felt so calm, that it really didn't matter what he was doing. This was about me, not about anyone else.

In . . . and out. In . . . and out.

BOOOOOM CRUNCH.

The seascape cracked and wavered, like the picture on a dodgy telly. Really, I bet Buddha did not have to put up with this kind of provocation. Wasn't he sitting under a nice, peaceful tree somewhere when he reached enlightenment? Would he ever have got there under these conditions? I got it back, momentarily, felt peace descend again . . .

Suddenly there was lots of shouting, and then a man's voice: 'I'M GONNA SPANK YOUR MOTHER'S ASS IN HELL!'

This was more than I could take. I jumped to my feet and shouted wildly: 'For God's sake can't I get a minute's peace in this sodding flat?'

Obe was wearing an expression almost as withering as that of the birthday sculpture. 'Nirvana still some way off then?' he remarked, before calmly unplugging the computer and settling himself down in the hall, resting the laptop on his knees. I closed my eyes again, but it was no good, the beautiful view had gone. I lay down on the sofa, body thrumming with tension, and pretended to sleep.

9.

All aboard the party bus

Incident No. 261. 9th March, 8 p.m. All I can see is a blur. I don't know if we are moving or staying; if I'm ill or well, awake or asleep. I don't know whether to work or rest or try or just give up. I don't know whether to keep fighting, or just . . . let go.

But I know that this book, like Bill, like my job and this flat, has become something other than it was meant to be. So I'm going to send it off into the world now. Who knows, perhaps the world will send something back.

Hours' sleep: I'm just about to go to bed. Wish me luck. Over and out.

I SHUT the logbook, and slid it into a big brown envelope I had bought specifically for this purpose. Over the last week, I'd been sitting down to meditate every day. I did it at odd times, sometimes when That Baby was napping, and The Toddler was engrossed in *Bob the Builder*. Sometimes sitting up in bed, while Obe was in the other room. Sometimes I'd shut myself in the toilet for two minutes, forget about the chaos on the other side of the door, and just close my eyes.

Usually two minutes was all it was, but a couple of times I managed half an hour. Every time, even if only for a matter of seconds, the view opened up in my mind. Now I had seen it, now I knew it was there, I could visit it any time. I had discovered a place in my head that felt warm and safe. Sometimes there were flashes of another feeling, too, a stronger one – love, perhaps.

When I was in that place, ideas would bubble up, from somewhere in the depths of my brain. Yesterday, I realised that I had finished with the logbook. Enough was enough. I went out that afternoon and bought the envelope.

Bill Baker, I wrote on the back. *Anti-Social Behaviour Unit, Hackney Town Hall*. I slipped a note in, too. *Dear Bill, thank you so much for all your help and advice over the years. Here it is, all the evidence. Do what you will with it. Love, Sylvia*. I added one kiss, and then another. I put the package in the hall, to post the next day. Then I ran myself a bath, and stayed in it until it was almost cold.

The phone rang as I was drying myself and wondering whether eight thirty was too early to get into my pyjamas. I usually made myself wait until nine.

'Hey, sis.' Lou's voice was hard to make out; in the background people were talking, laughing, and there was a tinny *csk-csk* of music. 'What you up to?'

'Funny you should ask,' I said. 'I'm actually at an amazing party on a beach in Ibiza. I've been up for three days taking a cocktail of drugs and having a sex marathon with a bartender called Juan.'

'I thought as much,' said Lou. 'Just a standard Friday night in Priory Court, then.'

'He's so hot. He calls me his mamasita.'

I could hear Lou take a drag on her cigarette. I tried to picture my little sister, on a battered sofa in the squat, the phone in one hand, roll-up clamped between the fingers of the other. A free spirit, damn her. 'So are you in your pyjamas yet?'

'No! Don't be crazy, it's only eight thirty.'

'Sylvia . . . ?'

'Well, okay, I was thinking about it,' I admitted, sitting down on the bed and wrapping the duvet around me. Why was she calling? It was usually some drama – a row with Shanti, perhaps, or another run-in with the bailiffs, who regularly showed up at the squat, with vigorous threats but so far no discernable impact. 'So what's happened?'

'Does something have to have happened for me to ring my big sister?'

'I guess you just called to make yourself green with envy about my exciting Friday night.'

'Actually, no . . .' The music was fainter now, perhaps she had stepped outside, to sit by the bonfire. I had a clear mental image of the squat, despite never having been there. It was a cul-de-sac of former council houses, sold off to developers and then never developed. Lou and her gang had taken over the whole road. They'd crow-barred off the metal shutters on the doors and windows, cleared tonnes of flytipped junk. They'd built a wind turbine in one of the gardens and made raised beds for veggies. They even had a solar-powered hot water system, Lou told me proudly ('because we do wash, actually').

'I called because we're having a party here tonight. And I think you should come.'

I burst out laughing. 'Leave my house! In the evening! Get all the way over to the other side of London! Lou, you make me laugh.'

'Why? I'll come and pick you up in the van.'

'Sis, listen. I know this is hard for you to understand. But I've got two kids. I'm exhausted, and it's only two hours until I'll have to feed Eliot . . .'

'Just because you've got kids,' Lou pointed out, 'doesn't mean you can't have a life. All you do these days is sit around and worry. Fuck that. I'm gonna come and get you. Get ready, I'll be there in forty-five minutes.'

She hung up, and the bedroom closed around me like a fist. It dawned on me that perhaps I did want to go out, after all. To go out and get really messed up and tear things up and tear myself up and remember some stuff I'd forgotten about being me. With sudden resolve, I stood up and opened the cupboard, pulled out my old black going-out dress on its hanger, where it had been abandoned months, maybe years ago. I wondered if I'd still fit into it.

At half ten, there was a hoot from the forecourt. I darted out into the front walkway and leaned over the parapet wall. Down below, Lou's battered old van was idling by the wheelie bins, growling unevenly. I marvelled as usual that my sister hadn't been pulled over – the front bumper was hanging off, one headlight was flickering, and there was a large floral armchair strapped to the roof with bungee cords.

She poked her head out of the driver's side and called, 'You ready?'

'Just a sec,' I popped my head back in through the front door. 'Obe, I'm going!' There was a grunt from the living room, which was as close as I got to a reply from Obe these days. 'Formula is in the fridge, okay? Remember to microwave it—'

'—for thirty seconds, I do know. Go on, just go.'

I climbed in next to Shanti and gave him a hug, breathing in hair and the smell of woodsmoke. When I first met Shanti I couldn't get past the hair. There was so much of it, cascading in matted waves over his shoulders, and twined in a small hanging bobble under his chin. And then there were the feet... but when he smiled, all that faded into the background. His smile opened up his whole face, crinkling around a pair of hazel eyes and unveiling a perfect set of white teeth.

'Hey, sister,' he said. 'Good to see you out.'

Hugging him, I remembered that I had something important to do before we set off. 'Wait a sec.' I jumped out of the van and slipped the logbook parcel into the post box in the forecourt, then hopped back in. 'Okay. Ready.' The van was filled with all the usual junk: on the dashboard Lou had arranged a stuffed toy monkey and a collection of quasi-religious artefacts including a garish plastic Ganesh and a nodding Jesus. 'I can't believe you're making me do this.'

'How's that for a thank you!' said Lou, slamming the van into first and skidding off down the High Street towards the North Circular.

The squat was diagonally opposite my patch of north-east London, on the fringes of the south-west. The van growled and clanked its way right around the capital, through endless industrial estates, past petrol stations and scrubby bits of wasteland and car parks and sewage-processing plants and detention centres. It was a grand tour of all the bits of the city that the people who lived in the middle of town didn't want to see.

Eventually we turned off a floodlit, deserted roundabout onto a one-way street lined with small post-war houses. Half of them were boarded up, and even the ones that weren't had rotten window frames, overgrown front hedges. Tattered St George's Cross flags fluttered from front windows. There was a roar of thunder above us as a plane came in to land, its blinking lights close enough to touch. Lou didn't flinch.

'I forget how loud it is,' she said, when she saw me cowering. 'After a while, you don't even notice.'

These suburbs had been on the slide for decades, as the government prevaricated about whether to expand the airport. Threatened with demolition, its housing stock was unsellable, and anybody who could leave had already gone. When residents were evicted from the cul-de-sac, the squatters had spotted their chance, and moved in to occupy it. The place had become a base for a motley collection of protests. 'We're against airport expansion and migrant detention and gentrification and the whole rotten planet-raping neoliberal system,' Lou would explain, when anyone asked.

'Home sweet home!' said Shanti as we pulled up. I climbed out of the van and found myself in a little oasis amid all that barren greyness. Trees lined the road, strung with bunting and twinkling fairy lights. The doors and windows of the houses were open, and people milled about in the front gardens. Some kids were playing in a sand pit on the pavement. Banners hung from the windows read, 'Tar Free Future' and 'People not Profits.'

There were no cars in this street, just sofas and bales of hay arranged in rows, and a few tables set with twinkling tea lights. At the end, between two houses, was a small stage made from pallets, with a big screen set up on it. As we sat down on a hay bale, a man with a long rats' tail appeared on the stage holding a saxophone.

'I forgot to tell you about the Belgian anarchist collective,' said Lou.

'There are anarchists in Belgium?' I whispered.

'Of course! They've come to show an animated film.'

Rats' Tail played one long blast on his horn and everybody fell silent.

'Once upon a time,' he said, sounding incongruously like Hercule Poirot. 'Zere was a village. Ze village was a place where people lived, where zey had families, grew their food, buried their dead, lived, loved and died.'

On the screen a range of green hills appeared, and

small, idyllic-looking village, drawn in the style of a small child. A set of giant black tentacles appeared on the horizon and spread blackness through the landscape. A plane closed in overhead, its belly silver like a giant fish, and the saxophone trilled and squawked amid the roar. I moved closer to Lou and leaned my head her shoulder. She put her arm around me.

The film was long and surreal but I didn't mind. It was just good to be out, to be surrounded by people who thought and talked about things other than sleep training and house prices.

'Gradually, as ze city grew, it outgrew the people who lived on it. It ceased to be a human place, and became a gigantic parasite, sucking in anyone who came wizin its reach.'

The saxophone tootled. Near the front, a lady in a feathered headdress stood up and started to dance, reaching her arms up to the sky.

I gazed at the shifting shapes on the screen and let my mind roam. I wondered what would happen afterwards, whether things would get messy. I remembered partying with Lou in the old days, before either of us had to get up in the morning. The first time I went out with her, she was fifteen, and I was seventeen. I'd had enough of sitting at home imagining crime scenes; if I couldn't beat my sister, I was going to join her. And that weekend she was going to a rave called 'Escape from Samsara' in Kentish Town.

'Why give a party a name like that?' I asked, when she showed me the flyer.

'It's not just a party,' she replied. 'It's a way of life.'

We put our winter coats on over the silver PVC Cyberdog dresses we had bought in Camden market, and caught the number 19 bus to the Rainbow Centre. We headed for the talks area first, where a middle-aged man with glasses and leather elbow patches was trying to give a presentation about outer space. Nobody could hear him above the banging trance.

'You see,' said Lou, proudly. 'It's not just about getting trashed and dancing.' But we gave up on the talk after five minutes and went off to buy a packet of 'speed' from a stubbly Scouser in a leather jacket. He was trying to stand up but as he fished the wrap out of his pocket he kept slowly toppling to one side.

'Do you think that's a bad sign?' I asked, after we'd given him our fiver.

'Only one way to find out,' said Lou, rubbing fingerfuls into her gums.

That night we danced so much we forgot about everything. That crowded sweaty room expanded until it filled the whole world. I discovered that while I was dancing, the heavy cloak lifted from my shoulders.

As the saxophone trilled, the tentacular village turned into a monster city, swallowing up everything around it. When the screen went black there was a smattering of uncertain applause, before the audience scattered. Lou and I walked over to a makeshift bar that had been set up beneath a tree. As she ordered our drinks, my mind buzzed with dangerous and thrilling possibilities.

What would I do now, tonight, if somebody offered me a line?

I was still breastfeeding, clearly I would say a firm no, that's what I would do. It would be completely irresponsible to take drugs. And I could have fun perfectly well on a few rum and gingers.

But then again . . . I'd been so good for *three years*. And I could always 'pump and dump' when I got home. Perhaps a line, just a little one, would do me good. It might help me to forget all the stress over the house, and the job, and fighting with Obe. I could have a dance to some dance music, just like the old days. Perhaps tonight I'd finally have the chance to get into drill, or whatever that new thing was . . .

A man with the facial hair of a werewolf and the eyes of a stoned possum appeared on the stage and sat cross-legged by the mike holding a banjo. A banjo! People clapped and whistled as he started to twang.

I turned to Lou. 'Is this a *folk* night?'

She nodded enthusiastically. 'This guy is great. The Really Wild Creole. He's genuinely from Baton Rouge.'

'So,' I said, slowly. 'Just clear this up for me – I've been at home for a while. This is what people are into these days – banjo music?'

'Well, sometimes,' said Lou, sounding a bit put out. 'Is that wrong?'

'It's not *wrong*,' I sighed. 'It's just – oh, nothing.'

It turned out folk nights were fun once you'd drunk five rum and gingers. At some point I found myself dancing by the speakers, in a country-dancing moshpit, attempting reckless do-si-dos with a guy with a large beard and a plaid shirt. He kept looking at me and smiling and grabbing my hands to whirl me around.

'I don't suppose,' I said breathlessly to him after one particularly vigorous fiddle number, 'you have any drugs?'

'Only this,' he said apologetically, and held up something that looked like a mini shisha pipe. I had to look at it for several moments before realising that it was a vaporiser. I laughed, I laughed, I couldn't stop laughing.

When at last I left the dance floor for a glass of water, I found Shanti sitting by one of the bonfires wearing his usual benevolent expression.

'So is it good to be out?' he asked.

'It's great!' I said. 'Though it would be even more great if I had some drugs.'

'What would you like?' asked Shanti. He put a hand in his pocket, produced a Visit Cornwall tin, and opened the lid. Inside was an impressive assortment of wraps, packets, and strips of pills. 'I've got coke, MDMA, weed,' he said, rummaging around. 'And this thing.' He held up a tiny plastic bag of pink powder.

'What's that?'

'It doesn't have a name,' he explained, 'just a number.' Despite the quantity of alcohol swilling around in my brain, something still told me not to go for the no-name thing. 'I need something familiar,' I said. 'I haven't done this for a while.'

Shanti tugged thoughtfully at his beard-knot. 'I know what you need,' he said, producing a tiny jar. Inside was a tangle of grey thread-like stalks, like a miniature bird's nest.

'Mushrooms!' I took them in my hand. 'Oh God, I don't know,' I said. 'Do you think it's okay, what with breast-feeding, and everything?'

He fixed me with his steady hazel eyes. 'In some native Amazonian tribes, hallucinogenic mushrooms are given to nursing mothers to promote milk production.'

He'd probably made that up, but it was exactly what

I wanted to hear. I pinched the knotty threads between my fingers and put them right at the back of my tongue. I washed them down with a fizzy burn of rum and ginger. That was it, too late. I was on board the party bus, destination unknown.

It didn't take long for things to get weird. 'Lou,' I said, lunging for her arm across a line of people frantically stripping the willow, 'can we go somewhere quiet for a minute?'

'Sure,' she said. 'You're a bit pale.'

'It's the country dancing,' I told her. My head was whirling, and there was a funny little cartoon skeleton dancing in the corner of my eye. 'I'm way too high for do-si-dos. I need to sit still and stare at my hands.'

Lou led me round the back of one of the houses, into one of the back gardens, where sofas were arranged around a fire. After a couple of lungfuls of damp night air, I felt much better. The skeleton was still there, but he was dancing in a more gentle, less frenetic way. It was nice here. People were laughing and talking and lying about. The cul-de-sac was perched up on a hill, and from the back gardens we could see for miles, into the centre of town. On the horizon was a huddle of vast towers, skyscrapers, sheer walls of light. They looked close enough to touch, like a mirage, as though at any moment they might crack, slide into the Thames, and disappear forever. 'One day, no one will believe they existed,' I said, to nobody in particular.

In front of our sofa, two bearded men who were definitely too old to be wearing backwards baseball caps were playing glow-in- the-dark ping-pong. It was mesmerising. Lou and I sat there together, our heads touching, watching the fluorescent pink ball flying back and forth, a tiny planet flying chaotically through space.

Lou snuggled in behind me, so she could play with my hair. This was how Little Lou and I used to pass our Sunday afternoons in the 1980s, when the rain never stopped and all the shops were closed and there was nothing but *Ski Sunday* on telly. We would sit close up like this on the old brown sofa, the air heavy with stale Rothmans smoke, the gas fire giving off lazy clicks, drizzle pattering on the window, and we would plait and unplait each other's hair.

I would have laughed if you'd told me then that I would yearn for the warm, endless boredom of those afternoons. Was it even possible to achieve that feeling now?

'So, sis. Tell me: what's up?'

'I'm fine, it's just this skeleton . . .'

'No,' said Lou. 'I mean, in general.'

'Oh.' I wondered how to explain the gnawing anxiety, the overload, the sense that things had got out of control. 'I've been thinking a lot about Dad,' I said, without realising that's where I was going to start.

Lou's lively, mobile, anarchic face, lit up by the flickering fire, softened as soon as I said the D-word. She seemed tough, my sister, but just under the surface was the child with eyes so huge and blue strangers would comment on them in the street. She looked at me, but didn't reply.

'We don't talk about him much, do we?' I said. 'Do you remember the stories he used to tell us? The killer iguanas and the alcoholic squirrels, and Sylvia with the seaweed eyes?'

'I don't remember,' said Lou, quietly. 'I was younger than you, when – I really don't remember much about him at all.' Her face had hardened again. 'Most of it has just –' she flicked her fingers, a bubble popping – 'gone. You're lucky, Syl, to have all those memories.'

'I didn't always have them. They've started coming back – since I had the kids, really. Being with them reminds me of our childhood. I've been thinking about it – about him – more than I did before. And the really weird thing is I keep feeling like he's still around, watching – even talking to me.'

'Ha!' Lou's laugh was short and dry. 'Well, I hope he's not watching right now. I'm not sure he'd approve.'

'I think he is,' I said. 'I really do. I can feel him, just here . . .' I took her hand and reached it out into the night air in front of us. I wanted her to feel this presence, forever hovering on the edge of my vision, but the air was empty, and Lou's hand dropped back into her lap.

'It's not the same,' she said, and stood up roughly. 'Don't you get that, Syl? It's not the same for me.'

I was tripping now, pretty hard. I found myself squeezing through one of the garden fences, escaping onto a piece of wasteland. There was a tall building on the main road, lit up in green. At the top glared a vivid neon sign, Holiday Inn. I wondered if the people staying in those stuffy green rooms could see me. I waved both arms, but the green windows stared inscrutably back. Behind the building, another plane was taking off. With a roar, it gathered speed and then lifted improbably, impossibly from the ground.

The wasteland was overgrown with brambles and scattered with plastic bags, mattresses, remnants of old building works. I sat down on a pile of girders and looked around at the battered landscape. I thought about Larkin and Eliot, these small beings I had brought into existence, and what kind of world I would like for them. I thought about the squat, and how I had always sniped about it, bitched about it behind Lou's back, told myself that my sister was unrealistic, an idealist, running away from the real world. Something was changing inside me, the plates were shifting. I was glad to be here, it felt like a place where I could breathe.

Because the real world wasn't working, was it? We were all barricaded behind our front doors, clinging for dear life to our sanded floorboards and our period features, trying to keep up appearances as the flood waters rose. Each of us was locked in a lonely, solitary battle that we were doomed to lose. We had been taught that walls would protect us, and that survival depended on defending our territory, clinging on ever more tightly to our foothold on the creaking, cracking social ladder. And it was a great big lie.

'Where are our brains?' I said, to the plastic bags, to the mattresses, to the guests at the Holiday Inn. Just for a moment, the rubbish-strewn landscape cleared, and the view opened up before me. Flat, calm, glowing with a mysterious inner light. 'We have to find a better way.'

I had no idea how to find it, but sitting there that night with mushrooms dancing jigs around my brain, I thought about how much I would like to be able to look my children in the eye when they were big enough to understand and to tell them that I had tried.

* * *

When I got back to the party the music had changed: there was now a band on the stage playing some kind of deep-down-dirty-stompy-swampy-Wild-West music. The drummer had huge sideburns, and he was pounding away at his kit like it had personally offended him. The hay bale seating had been pushed back, and people were standing on the bales, falling off them, knocking tea lights onto them, gurning and going for it.

I discovered that I could still dance. It had been a long time since I used my hips for anything other than carrying a child on, I'd almost forgotten they could move for fun. This music was the sound of sex the morning after a bar brawl, when your breath stinks of fags and you're still drunk on whisky, and you're doing it really slowly and deeply in that delicious limbo between today and tomorrow. It seemed almost indecent to dance to it, but I was past caring. I noticed a man dancing next to me, and from what I could see out of the corner of my eye, he had a pleasing body, full and firm, and it was moving to the same rhythm as mine.

I made sure I absolutely wasn't looking at him. I kept my eyes fixed on the stage. The singer had sideburns too, and he was singing in a snarly kind of way about a black serpent who ate a rat.

The Body was dancing with a girl. She had long flowing sleeves and slender elegant arms. I could tell that girl

183

danced all the time. While they danced they sang along about the snake and the rat. The Body had brown messy hair and a curly moustache. I hated moustaches but this one looked good. It made me think of a Mexican bartender in the kind of bar where you would get drunk on whisky and there would be a bar brawl and you'd end up sneaking upstairs and having the kind of sex you have to this kind of music, to the soundtrack of breaking glass downstairs.

I made sure I was definitely, one hundred per cent not looking at him. I kept my eyes fixed on the stage. The bass player looked a little like Vincent Cassel. I told myself to keep looking at Vincent Cassel and not The Body.

But then the girl with the long flowing sleeves had gone somewhere. Perhaps to the bar. And The Body was still there. I snuck a tiny – the tiniest – little look at his face, which was round and brown and grizzled and smiling in pleasure at the music. And just as I did so, oh hell, he turned his head and looked straight at me.

Rumbled.

I looked away and carried on dancing. I made sure I did not look back. From deep down inside, I summoned up the spirit of THIRTY-SOMETHING MOTHER. I looked at the bass player and the drummer and then at the singer, who was now singing about a temptress called Juanita.

But The Body had turned towards me and we were moving in time.

'Hello,' he said, once the song had blistered into a wall of feedback. He was leaning in and murmuring into my ear.

Oh goodness gracious me.

'Hi,' I said, and I looked him in the face, properly this time. He really did have a good face. Brown eyes as deep and sticky as swamp mud and a mouth soft like clouds. The Body was right next to mine now, I could feel it even if I closed my eyes.

The next song was slower and more grinding and almost impossible to dance to without actually being horizontal. But it was fine. It was only dancing. The Body took my hands and raised them up and pressed in even closer, and I could feel his full firm warmness, and we were moving to the same rhythm, definitely quite a bit closer than we should have been, but it was only dancing, and it was fine.

It was so, so fine.

'Your eyes,' he said. 'I've never seen eyes that colour before. It's like—'

'Seaweed,' I whispered. 'I'm Sylvia with the seaweed eyes.'

He shook his head. 'I was thinking more something – how do you say, like, that stuff on the top of a pond?' he said.

'Algae?' I suggested.

'That's it!'

When the band crashed to a halt, The Body suggested we got some air out by the sofas.

'I might actually just go home,' I said. But even as my mouth was saying the words, my feet were already following him to the back gardens. Something was humming, it might have been inside my head, a noise I had been trying not to hear.

He sat down on one of the sofas and offered me a cigarette. The sensation of his arm against my arm made something vibrate in my stomach. The ping-pong table was glowing, abandoned, in the dark. I hadn't smoked a cigarette since before I got pregnant. The old me had smoked cigarettes, and as the smoke hit the back of my throat I remembered how it had felt to be old me, child-free me, fun me. I exhaled and watched the smoke curl off into space. I wondered where Lou was. She had left me to fend for myself, and now look.

The Body got out a little tin from his shirt pocket and started to expertly roll up a joint.

'Where are you from?' I said.

'Colombia,' he replied.

The Colombian Body had been living in London for three years, studying photography at the Slade. He wanted to be a war reporter. He was about to go back to Latin America to begin a project about Bolivian street gangs. 'And circuses,' he said. 'I want to take pictures of these very colourful street circuses, you know, performing dogs, acrobats in cheap Lycra. It's very – how do you say? Carnivalesque.'

I told him I wasn't sure that was the right word, but I knew what he meant. We shared the cigarette, and then we shared the joint. I liked The Body. He had spirit. He had plans, ambitions, ideas, things he wanted to do in the world. He hadn't been squashed, like me, and like Obe. I hadn't realised quite how squashed we had become, until now; so much that we could hardly breathe.

But as I sat there with him, high as a kite, talking about big stuff like wars and circuses, the towers of the City hanging before us like our own personal light show, I was breathing away like my lungs were on fire. He threw the butt into the bushes where it fell in a cascade of sparks, and then he took my face between his hands and we started to kiss, very slowly at first. He smelled of cigarettes and something deeper and less identifiable that had to do with being a man.

At first I thought, shit, it really really is time I went home.

And then I stopped thinking, and everything fell away.

10.

A diagnosis

'You smell funny,' said Obe sleepily, the next morning. 'Mmmm?' I said, rolling over to face the wall. There was an earthy, cardboard taste in my mouth. I lay there listening to the sounds of the estate waking up: the whine of the hoover from the Kosovans' flat; Zeynab shouting at Hassan in Turkish, a tinny bump of reggae. In my stomach fluttered the remnants of excitement mixed with deep, unfolding horror.

I had kissed The Body. I had kissed him for ages, on the sofas and then on the dance floor and then back on the sofas again. And when he put his hand on my chest it was wet and I realised it wasn't sweat, it was milk, because it was 3 a.m. and I should have been at home feeding my baby.

What kind of a person does that? Nobody does that.

I put a hand to my lips. They felt raw and red from kissing a Colombian with a Mexican barman's moustache. There was no way Obe was not going to notice.

In the cot next to the bed, That Baby was spread-eagled,

still fast asleep. My heart gave a sad bump. He was just starting out in the world, he didn't deserve to have such a stupid mess of a mother. I picked up his soft warm body and lay him next to me in bed; he stretched and yawned and opened his deep black-blue baby eyes. I stared right into them. There was no messing around with those eyes; they knew everything there was to know.

'I'm so sorry, Eliot,' I whispered. 'That was certainly an off-day.'

But he just looked back at me silently, and unblinkingly.

I could hear Obe in the kitchen, the clattering pots and pans as he made coffee. He'd take The Toddler off to the High Street in a little while, that's what he did on a Sunday morning, to get the food for a roast. If I could just stay in bed for long enough, I could buy myself some more time, tidy myself up, sort my head out, before I had to speak to him. Decide whether I had the will to brazen this out, or if I would have to tell him.

I put That Baby to my breast and shut my eyes.

But as he started to suckle, a lightning strike of stabbing pain radiated from my nipple to underneath my armpit. I cried out and snatched his head away. There was a weird yellow spot in the centre of my nipple, which I was sure hadn't been there yesterday. Oh, this was not good. This had to be some kind of instant karmic payback for being a very bad not-quite-wife and mother.

'Obe,' I cried, piteously.

He poked his head round the door and grimaced at the sight of me. 'Oh dear,' he said with mock sympathy. 'Heavy night, was it?' He sat down and sniffed. 'The whiskey on your breath / could make a small boy dizzy.'

The Toddler appeared and curled up in the bed beside me.

'Rum,' I whispered, hugging him. 'It was rum. And I only had three. Or four.' I buried my face in The Toddler's curls to avoid meeting Obe's eye.

'And the rest.'

'And a small pinch of mushrooms.'

'Aha!' said Obe, with the air of a TV detective identifying a murderer. 'Well, there you go, then.'

'But still, I don't think I should be feeling this bad. Look.' I rolled over and pointed at my breast. 'I think my nipple is infected.'

The Toddler took a close look, then reported back to Obe. 'Mummy's boob's all yellow,' he said.

'O-kay.' Obe looked like he was about to gag. 'What does one do about that, then?'

I cast my mind back to the ante-natal classes we had attended before Larkin was born, and dredged up some muddy old memories. 'I've heard something about cabbage leaves. Cold cabbage leaves. Could you check the fridge?'

While Obe was in the kitchen I put Eliot back on my

breast, just to see what would happen. But when he latched on, the lightning struck again, and this time the blood rushed away from my head and a greenish light flickered and sputtered as if it was about to go out. I tried to sit up and, as I did so, a stream of bright-yellow bile spurted from my mouth and nose, frothing onto the too-small duvet. It spread out like a map of somewhere I had never been.

'There aren't any carrots in it,' said Larkin, leaning in to examine it. 'Daddy told me there were always carrots.'

I was possessed by an overwhelming urge to be some-where, anywhere, else. I tried once again to push myself up to a sitting position. The last thing I registered before passing out was that Eliot was crying somewhere in the distance, but it was no good, I couldn't reach him as I was falling, falling backwards into blissful blackness.

'Take a seat.'

The receptionist in the Homerton A&E department had long fake nails decorated with a dramatic feathered pattern and diamante studs. Those nails wanted to be living it up in a glamorous nightclub in Miami, not wasting their time in this drab, sour-smelling room, filled with miserable-looking people sitting uncomfortably on plastic chairs. Obe took the small green token the nails were holding out to him. On my lap I was clutching a bright pink plastic beach bucket, bile swilling around in the bottom. I had no idea where the bucket had come from, but it felt very important to hang on to it.

'Why did we get a green token?' I whimpered as he pushed my wheelchair into the waiting area.

'I think everyone gets a green token, Syl.'

'No. Look.' I pointed furtively at a small Asian man in a salwar kameez suit who had been standing in the queue behind us, retching loudly into a plastic takeaway carton. 'She gave him a red token, and now he's going straight in.'

Obe looked up as the retching man was ushered through the door marked 'Triage'. 'Perhaps you only get one of those if she thinks you're going to be sick on her desk.'

'I've got a baby,' I said, my voice rising and wobbling hysterically. I was gripping the beach bucket so hard that my fingers had turned white. 'I can't feed him. Go and ask her for a red token.'

'I can't do that!'

'Obe!' I fixed him with a furious glare. 'Just ask her!'

Obe trooped off, his shoulders hunched resentfully. From the buggy, Eliot started to cry, just little whimpers for now, not yet the full crescendo. Larkin was doing laps of the waiting room on his scooter.

With an effort I detached my fingers from the bucket, leaned over and lifted Eliot from his buggy and put him to my good breast. As he suckled, the swollen one emitted a slow, aching throb, like the low whistle of a steam train.

Obe returned, still holding the green token. 'She said no.'

'Did you tell her about the baby?'

'She said she can only assess you, not the baby.'

'Even though he's only six months old and I can't feed him?'

'That's what she said.'

My throat tightened, tears rose to my eyes. My neck couldn't hold the weight of my head, my arms couldn't hold the weight of the baby. My body had had enough of carrying things. 'How long?'

'I don't know.'

'Excuse me, madam,' said a porter in a blue hospital smock. 'I'll need to take that wheelchair now.'

I looked down at Eliot in my lap. Slowly, carefully, I stood up, still holding him to my breast. The porter immediately grabbed the chair and wheeled it away. I spread my coat out on the grey lino floor, and sat down on it. Then I lay down, holding Eliot carefully next to me. I tried once more to swap breasts, to ease the pain from the bad, throbbing side. As his mouth met the nipple, my stomach heaved, and a thin stream of pale warm liquid leaked from my lips. I closed my eyes and delivered myself into a white light of pain.

'Madam. Hello? Madam?'

The lino was cold and soothing against my cheek, and a black shoe had appeared in my line of vision. It was highly polished and tightly laced; a shoe of authority.

'I have to ask you to move, madam.'

I moved my gaze upwards, taking in a blue polyester leg and a black belt hung with a crackling radio. Looming above them was the square red face of a police officer. 'It is not safe for you or your baby to be lying there.'

Eliot was sleeping peacefully, nestled on the arm of the coat. I thought about lifting my head, but it seemed to be glued to the floor. I rolled over until I was lying on my back. I was about to say something to the police officer, when a shadow fell between me and the light. It was Obe, his face blazing, his voice calm.

'My wife is sick, officer.' He never called me his wife. I wasn't his wife. 'She has a serious infection and the baby can't feed. If you would like her to move, perhaps you could persuade a doctor to see her – immediately.'

The shoe disappeared, taking the leg and the policeman with it. I sank back into semi-sleep. Soon afterwards, another, softer, female voice called: 'Sylvia? The doctor will see you now.'

'How can I help you, daaaaaarling?'

I'd never been called darling by a doctor before, but I liked it. Dr Ibrahim – that was the name on her badge – was older than me, in her fifties maybe, and dark-skinned, with bright red lipstick. Her consulting room had a heavy, perfumed smell, with a faint undertone of – could it be – cigarette smoke. It was quiet and calm, mainly because Obe had taken the boys for a breath of fresh air in the hospital car park.

After examining me, Dr Ibrahim printed out a prescription for antibiotics and then clicked her fingers, as if she were working a healing magic. 'These can get rid of mastitis just like that, not a problem,' she said. 'But if you're not careful, it can come back. You've got to take it easy when you're breastfeeding. No stress. Mastitis comes when you are stressed out. And make sure the baby's feeds are regular.'

As I scanned the prescription, Dr Ibrahim narrowed her eyes at my cracked, wizened hand. My fingers were stuck in their customary claw-shape, the skin like parched leather.

'And what is this?' Dr Ibrahim took my witchy hand in

her soft plump one and turned it over. 'Are you treating it?'

I shook my head.

'And why not?'

'Well,' I whispered, 'I've been a leeeetle bit busy. With That Baby.'

'How long has your hand been this way?'

I cast my mind back. 'It's been getting worse for about six months.'

'And how old is er, That Baby?'

'He is six months.'

'Hmmm,' she said. 'Okay.' She turned her wise dark eyes to meet mine. 'And everything is going well?'

Tickety-boo, thanks, I thought to myself, but for some reason the words wouldn't come out of my mouth. A small squeak came out instead. The blood rushed to my face, and I quickly looked down into my lap as my eyes misted over. I had patched up the arse-split in these jeans, but I now noticed they had developed a hole in the knee. I was still holding the pink beach bucket, which now felt ridiculous; I bent down and placed it carefully on the floor next to the chair.

Everything was not going well. I had four missed calls on my phone from Rob Crockett, who was doubtless wondering what the hell was going on with our house move, I dreaded to think what the situation with the car insurance was, I could still taste rancid mushrooms in my mouth, and I'd kissed somebody who wasn't my not-quite-husband.

I ruled out saying any of this to the doctor.

'Sorry,' I said instead, wiping my nose on my sleeve. Dr Ibrahim got up from her chair and came back with water in a crumpled plastic cup. I looked up and noticed a packet of red Gauloise peeping from the pocket of her blouse. God, I would kill for a cigarette. Would she give me one? I didn't dare ask.

'Things have been a bit tricky recently,' I admitted, after glugging back the water. 'I haven't been sleeping. We haven't got any money. I've been arguing with my hus— er, boyfriend. And we're supposed to be moving house.'

I told her about some of my symptoms: the anxiety, the doomy thoughts, the creeping insomnia. I didn't mention the voice from beyond the grave.

'That's understandable, darling,' she said. 'You've got two small children. It is a stressful time.'

She sat down and lifted my hand up again. 'You see, the medical term for this is contact dermatitis,' she said, pointing at the crusty knuckles, the cracked fingers. 'But I would call it a little window into your soul.'

I nodded and swallowed. I definitely hadn't been expecting this level of diagnosis.

'I'm going to give you more antibiotics for the infection. And I can prescribe you moisturiser, and steroids, all that,' she said, 'but you know, darling, what you actually need is a rest.'

This was indisputable. I could feel the pressure of sleeplessness on my brain, reducing everything to a dull grey pulp. Through the window, I could see a surprising spring day; the sky was blue, with just the odd fluffy cloud . . . but inside my head, things were still as dark as a December morning. The view was nowhere to be found. It was as though my brain had stopped absorbing any of the nice stuff, while it sucked up doom like a sponge.

'Do you think you can get one?'

I laughed doubtfully. 'A rest? I'm not sure how.'

'Well, think about it. That is what I am prescribing. You can tell that to your husband – or boyfriend, was it?'

'Boyfriend,' I said emphatically. 'If that.'

Dr Ibrahim tapped away at her computer for a moment. 'Also,' she said, 'I am giving you a referral letter for the Mental Health Access Team.'

'The who?' I pulled myself up straight, outraged.

'There is very effective treatment available for postnatal depression, you know.'

I stared at her, blinking. What was she talking about? Did she mean to imply that my problems were just in my head? Did she think that the Mental Health Access Team could somehow make our flat bigger, or make Obe and I like each other again, or get my freelance career off the ground, or save the environment from certain destruction?

'I really don't think that's necessary,' I said, adjusting my holey Puffa jacket to look more imposing.

'Give them a call. Postnatal depression is a common condition, and the right treatment really can help.'

Walking slowly, painfully, like an arthritic old woman, I made my way through the waiting room and out into the car park, where Obe had promised to wait. Spring seemed to have arrived overnight, but the newly minted sunlight wasn't fresh and clear, it was close, like in mid-summer. As I sat down on the blue graffitied bench by the main entrance, a solitary bee buzzed past, looking confused.

Larkin whizzed up and screeched to a halt on his scooter.

'Are you better, Mummy?'

I rattled my box of pills, doing my best to smile. 'Will be soon, love.'

Obe put the brake on the buggy and sat down next to me, pulling out his phone to call a taxi.

'What did she say?'

'She gave me antibiotics.' I stopped there, wondering how to broach the rest of Dr Ibrahim's diagnosis. Larry zipped off for another lap of the car park and I took my chance. 'She thinks I have postnatal depression. She gave me this.' I passed him the referral letter for the Mental Health Access Team. Obe read it quietly, failing to look quite as shocked and outraged as I wanted him to. 'I mean, I think she is over-reaching. I'm fine, really.'

He put a giant bear-hand over his eyes, rubbed them, shoulders sagging. Behind us, the doors to the hospital slid open. A young couple emerged, carrying a tiny baby in a car seat. They fussed about looking shell-shocked, no doubt overawed by the responsibility of carrying this small being across the tarmac and into the car. Embrace that fear, comrades, I thought. It never really goes away.

'I don't know, Syl.' He pulled his hand over his face, making it look as though his eyes were sliding down his cheekbones. 'Perhaps you should give them a call.'

Et tu, Brute? Irritation pierced through the fog in my brain. I stood up and waved my arms around weakly, while my voice rose and wobbled. 'Oh yeah, because I'm the one with the problem, right? It's nothing to do with you not taking any responsibility, and leaving me to sort everything out, from childbirth to washing up to job-hunting for you and sorting out the fucking car insurance. That stuff is all irrelevant, because now I've been given this "depression" badge, meaning that my mental state is yet ANOTHER THING I HAVE TO SORT OUT!'

My voice was now ringing out shrilly around the car park. 'This is not just about me!' I cried. 'I'm not the one who is earning minimum wage! I'm not the one who hasn't even got GCSE fucking maths!'

Obe stood up. He handed me his phone. 'I tell you what, call the taxi yourself,' he said, picking up Eliot, and calling Larkin to follow him to the bus stop.

That night, once the antibiotics had taken the edge off the throbbing pain, I tried to make amends. Obe was on the sofa, watching *Game of Thrones*. We'd been considering embarking on this commitment together for a while, but now he had taken a unilateral decision and started watching it alone. He would put it on as soon as the children were in bed, which meant we didn't have to talk to each other. As there were an apparently limitless number of episodes, we would potentially never have to talk to each other again.

I sat down beside him, hoping that by sharing his TV experience I could find us some much-needed common ground. My main observation was that the sexual politics were questionable at best. A beautiful blonde princess had been raped by her sinister brown-skinned savage of a husband, a problem that she had decided to tackle by taking sex lessons from an attractive brunette handmaiden.

'I don't want to be all politically correct,' I said, 'but there's something a little bit wrong—'

Obe turned to look at me, seemingly with great effort. 'Yes, but Sylvia,' he said. 'Look at her tits.'

This felt like quite an aggressive comment, but I decided to let it pass.

'She has got nice tits,' I conceded.

The scene cut and the princess was back in her marital bed, giving the rapist husband a great time and seemingly enjoying herself, too. I watched for five minutes, finding the storyline ridiculous and the acting wooden. But Obe seemed to be enthralled by it. He didn't lift his eyes from the screen. Even when I moved closer to him on the sofa and tried for a cuddle, he lifted his arm stiffly, a gesture of no discernible affection.

I sat up, huffily, and stared at him for a minute or two.

'I kissed someone,' I said. It came out like a mild apology, in the kind of tone I might have used to tell him I'd forgotten to buy peas, or shrunk his jumper in the wash.

'O-Kay.' Obe was sitting very still, staring at the screen, with the corners of his mouth turning down, like one of those men who paint themselves silver and stand motionless in Covent Garden. The princess was riding through a bamboo forest. She was happier and more confident than before, thanks to her new-found prowess in the bedroom. Perhaps I needed sex lessons. Perhaps if I wasn't exhausted and mostly indifferent at the prospect of ending our sex drought, then Obe would actually care that I'd kissed somebody else.

'At the party last night. A Colombian. With a moustache.' He still didn't react. I leaned forward and pressed pause. 'Did you hear me?'

'Yup.'

A long echoey howl drifted across the reservoir; it was definitely the foxes this time. Outside, the water observed us like a giant black eye; it was nearly mating season, and the foxes didn't make it sound like much fun. The way I was feeling right now, I could understand why.

'I'm sorry,' I said. 'I was drunk.'

Obe didn't reply, he just leaned forward and pressed play. The princess was back in bed again, with her tits out.

'For God's sake!' I exclaimed, despite myself. 'I thought *Game of Thrones* was supposed to be quality drama! This is just . . . soft porn.'

Obe pursed his lips. 'Enter not into judgement with thy servant: for in thy sight shall no man living be judged,' he said, forbiddingly. I didn't understand what this meant, but I knew things were really bad when Obe started quoting the Bible. He had been raised to be God-fearing; he didn't do it lightly. After another couple of minutes I snapped the laptop shut. Obe snatched the computer angrily and jabbed at the power button. 'I was watching that!'

'I know, Obe,' I said, 'but we need to talk about this.'

The spinning beach ball appeared on the screen, followed by the loading bar, and Obe watched it creep along notch by notch, as though he had never seen anything so fascinating before. 'So you kissed somebody. What do you want me to say?'

I picked at the fraying edge of the too-saggy sofa. 'That I've let you down. That I've been disloyal, and you're disappointed and hurt.' I pulled at a thread and the cushion cover split a little, revealing its grey, polyester insides. 'That you care.'

There was a long silence. 'Obe?' The loading bar had almost reached halfway. I took one of his bear-hands between my hands, but if I'd hoped for any warmth or responsiveness, I didn't get it. 'I'm so sorry.'

'No, you're not,' he said, as the loading bar stalled, inexplicably, at three-quarters. 'You did what you wanted to do.'

'But I didn't—'

'You did. You wanted to. Otherwise you wouldn't have done it.'

Now it was my turn to go quiet.

'Anyway, I *don't* really care about you kissing someone – it's everything else that bothers me. The way you treat me. You think I'm not good enough, you make that very clear.'

Obe bit his lip. I'd only ever seen him cry once, at Roberta's funeral, and he wasn't about to give me the satisfaction of crying now. He had a quote for every occasion, but his own feelings were a firmly closed book. Why were we hurting each other so much? Neither of us wanted to do it; but somehow, we couldn't work out how not to. After four years together, our decent, kind, presentable facades had been chip-chipped away by relentless broken nights, by the ever-present financial crisis. We had reached some kind of nadir of each other's personalities, a stripped-back place where his insecurity rubbed against my insecurity, my need against his.

'You always want more: a new job, more money, a better house,' he said, his voice tense, but calm. We both knew he had the upper hand now; I'd relinquished my traditional claim to martyrdom. 'But if we get any of those things, you'll only start wanting something else. Whatever I do will never be enough. Trying to make you happy is like trying to fill in a bottomless pit.'

We sat there staring hopelessly at the screen. I knew how that beach ball felt, stuck, going round and round. Finally, the loading bar inched up to the top, the beach ball disappeared, and the computer made a glorious sunrise noise. A luscious green field appeared on the screensaver. Obe turned and looked me in the face. 'Life is difficult, Sylvia. Did you think it was going to be easy?'

'I don't know,' I whispered. 'I don't know what I thought.'

And it was true. I had no idea what my expectations were, until they were not being met. But however sick Obe was of me, I was sicker of myself. I stood up and the sofa gave out an ominous creak. I walked down the hall and got into bed, curling up around the central emptiness. Obe called it a bottomless pit; Frankie called it The Hole. No matter what I did, it was always there.

With something like relief, I let myself sink down into it, into the place I'd never left. I was twelve years old, on my knees, on the floor, by the bookcase. I could see the corner of the old brown sofa, the familiar spines of my childhood books – *Where the Wild Things Are*, *Not Now Bernard*, *Winnie the Pooh* – but their colours blurred into jagged lines. This was where I fell, the moment that Mum told me he was gone, the moment The Hole opened up. It was a physical sensation, my insides scooped out. Even now, decades later, I could still feel it.

Perhaps I had thought I could leave The Hole behind when I met Obe, and had a family of my own. But I'd been kidding myself; it was there the whole time, waiting to swallow me up. All I had to do was let go, and fall.

* * *

I was pulled out of sleep by the sound of a phone ringing. Early morning sunlight was glowing behind the curtains, but there was no sign that Obe had slept next to me – perhaps he was on the saggy old sofa. I reached for the phone through treacle, glanced at the screen, and swiped before I'd really thought about it.

'Hello there, Sylvia,' said Bill, in his scrupulous monotone.

'Oh, Bill,' I croaked. 'I'm so glad you called. I am not well, not at all. Do you know anything about mastitis?'

Bill said he knew a little about mastitis, but his voice didn't sound as sympathetic as I had come to expect. I wondered if something had happened. Come to think of it, it was very unusual for him to call me – I always called Bill, that was how our relationship worked. He cut to the chase.

'This is a little awkward,' he said. 'But we have received a complaint about you.'

'What?' Someone had complained about me, a young mother and pillar of the community? I never played my music too loud, or threw nappies around the bottom of the bins, or pissed in the lift. I never did anything anti-social – I only wished I did. 'What kind of complaint?'

'It's from a Mr Winston Shillington,' said Bill. 'He says you stole his dog.'

'It wasn't a dog,' I whispered weakly, clutching my breast and leaning up on one elbow. 'It was a fox. He had taken it from its natural habitat.'

'That's not what he says,' said Bill.

'I didn't steal it, Bill,' I said, but my voice was flat and unconvincing. 'I set it free.'

'Well,' said Bill. 'I don't know the ins and outs of it, dog, fox, fox, dog. I'm just telling you what I've been told.'

Bill said he wouldn't pursue it, as it was my first warning. He just told me to keep things calm until the police dealt with Dawn.

'Also, Sylvia, I received your logbook this morning,' he said, and I detected a slight hesitation in his voice, as though even Bill, my rock, my guide in this hostile world, was having a wobble.

'Oh yes,' I said. 'The logbook. Is that going to help our case, do you think?'

Bill sighed heavily. 'I just have to ask, Sylvia,' he said. 'Have you considered seeking professional help?'

11.

Emergency services

THE next morning, after Obe left for work without saying goodbye, I took myself over to Mum's house, and this time I knocked on the door. When she answered, in her lilac silk dressing gown, smelling of peppermint tea, I tumbled inside followed by a small avalanche of children, nappies, buggies, potties, snivels, and snotty tissues.

'Good morning, darling. What a surprise!'

She managed to make it sound like a nice surprise. As usual, the place was immaculate, every surface white and gleaming. In the kitchen the hyacinths had been replaced by a pot of narcissi, which filled the room with the delicate scent of spring. As I sat down with That Baby on my knee he lunged for them, ripping off two perfect white flowers, stuffing them in his mouth and then grimacing and spitting them out again. Meanwhile, The Toddler was banging with his hammer on the glass pane of the back door. For a brief moment Mum's smile acquired a frazzled edge.

'I tell you what, Larkin dear, how about I get the drawing things out?'

She produced a large roll of paper and some felt tips from the cupboard in the hall, and Larkin immediately set to work with intense concentration. I gave Eliot a breadstick, which usually bought at least seven minutes of quiet.

Mum sat back down and looked at me, at my blotchy face, my red eyes, the hair I hadn't managed to even think about brushing since my Night of Shame.

'Is everything alright?'

I tried to reply, but something had seized up in my throat. I made the squeaking noise again. Then I coughed, blew my nose, and tried to talk normally. 'I've been a little bit under the weather.'

Mum took one of my hands and examined it, front and back. 'Have you been to the doctor yet?'

'I went yesterday,' I managed to say, before telling her a strategically edited version of the whole sorry situation: the mastitis episode, how Obe and I were barely speaking, how I didn't think we could really afford the house but I was too scared to tell Rob Crockett for fear of what would happen to me, mentally, if I had to accept that we were staying in Priory Court for ever. I didn't mention the Night of Shame, and I didn't mention The Hole. There were certain areas – drugs, sex and Dad – that were off-limits with my mother. 'The doctor thinks I've got post-natal depression,' I told her. 'She's referred me to the mental health team.'

Mum regarded me with her cool blue eyes, and she didn't judge. 'I didn't realise it was that bad,' she said, in the end. 'Tell me: are you keeping up your meditation?'

I knew she was going to ask that. And I had been trying. Only this morning I had closed my eyes in bed and tried to summon up the view, even for a single second, but where the calm clear sea had once been, all I could find was a murky old pond, littered with shopping trolleys. Even sitting right in front of the birthday sculpture hadn't helped my focus. 'It doesn't always happen.'

'Don't give up,' she said. 'It's not easy, I know. But I can only tell you what has helped me: in the end, all we can do is move through life's difficulties one breath at a time.' She stopped for a moment and looked out of the window into the garden, and I wondered whether she was remembering times when life's difficulties had felt almost insurmountable. She had kept going, my mum; she had never given up. One thing I had learned from her was that it was possible to get through hard times. Maybe that is the most important thing any of us can teach our children. 'When is your appointment?'

'I haven't got one, yet,' I said, head in hands. 'I have to call them, and I haven't got around to it.'

When I looked up, she was holding out the phone.

'So how long have you been having these irrational thoughts?'

I stared up at the picture in Mum's sitting room while I thought about how to reply. Lou had painted it at school; it was two small girls holding hands in front of a sunset. She had based it on a photograph of us when we were on holiday in Devon. That was the last holiday we had together, all four of us. I wiped my nose, again.

'I'm not sure,' I told the lady from the Mental Health Access Team, playing for time. It was important to give the correct answer; I had to strike just the right balance. If she thought I was not mentally unstable enough, she would not refer me for free counselling, which was what I wanted. But if she thought I was too mentally unstable, she might call in the social and tell them to take my kids away.

Would she actually do that? On balance, probably not. But nevertheless, I needed to tread carefully.

The honest answer was that I didn't think my anxiety and depression *was* irrational. It was based on hard, objective facts. To name a few: we were moving into a derelict house that we couldn't afford; Obe was sick of me; our collective incomings did not match our outgoings and we had no savings or pensions; the destruction of the environment continued unchecked, with consequences that were likely to prove utterly disastrous for humanity within my children's lifetime. These were surely reasons enough to legitimately feel less than one hundred per cent.

'It started a couple of months ago. The baby stopped sleeping. We've been trying to buy a house . . .' I went through the litany.

She sounded pleasingly concerned. This was going well. 'Any suicidal feelings?'

I hesitated. Should I tell her about the crack in the ceiling thing? It was not really suicidal, not in the active planning sense, more like a train of thought that I found relaxing, like scratching an itch. 'No,' I said firmly, before adding, 'not as such.'

'Good,' she said briskly. 'So what I'm going to do is recommend that you come in for a full assessment session with one of our mental health nurses. You should receive a letter in the post.'

'Great. Thank you.' Result. I couldn't wait for them to make me better again. 'And how long will it take to get the appointment?'

'It shouldn't be more than six weeks.' SIX WEEKS!!! I

couldn't wait six weeks. Obe was already on the brink of disowning me. I was on the brink of disowning myself. I took a deep breath.

'Right. Well, thank you very much for your help.' As I hung up, the tears had already formed a puddle on the keypad.

Back in the kitchen, a pair of familiar leopard-skin-clad legs were sprawled out on the floor next to Larkin. My sister was doodling anarchy signs and elaborate tropical flowers on the giant paper.

'Lou! What are you doing here?'

'Didn't Mum tell you?' Mum surveyed us all from her seat at the table, as That Baby drooled over her silk dressing gown. She hadn't had a chance to tell me anything much, I'd been too busy talking about me.

'Auntie Lou got evicted,' announced The Toddler.

'Not quite,' corrected Lou. 'Served with an eviction notice. Not actually evicted. Yet. We just woke up the morning after the party to find a bunch of bailiffs on the doorstep.'

'Bummer. Well, I woke up with mastitis.'

'I'd take that over bailiffs.'

'Easy to say when you've never *had* mastitis.'

'Come on, girls, this is not a competition.' Mum didn't

say 'a mother's work is never done' verbally, but her face said it all right.

'It's about time we both had a crisis, though,' said Lou, putting her pen down and surveying her doodles with satisfaction. 'Mum's life was going far too well, there was a genuine danger of her forgetting all about us.' Mum rolled her eyes: fat chance.

'So, Mother . . . when are we going to meet William?'

'Oh,' she smiled shyly. 'I'm sure you will, soon. He's been very busy at work, with some particularly challenging clients. It takes its toll. We've been getting together for evening meditations, to help him manage the stress.'

A distant chime sounded in my head . . . why did something about William seem familiar to me? I groped through the brain fog, but came up with nothing. Mum handed me That Baby, and bustled about packing us a bag full of frozen soup. She told me she would come round twice a week, from now on, to help out with the boys, so I could have a rest and get some more freelance work.

'And I tell you what, girls,' she said to Lou and me. 'Why don't we go away for a break? I think we all need to get out of London.'

'No money,' we both chorused.

'This is on me,' she said firmly. 'I'll ask Angela if we

can use the Devon house. A bit of fresh air might help to put everything in perspective.'

The Devon house was where we had gone on holiday as a family when Lou and I were kids. It had belonged to our grandparents, and then later partly to Dad, until he sold his share in it to his sister Angela. Although we didn't own it any more, Angela still encouraged us to go and stay. Going there with the boys gave me a warm feeling of continuity, as I'd gone there at their ages, too.

The Toddler scrambled to his feet and held up his drawing for us all to admire. Lou examined the riot of multicoloured scribbles with great seriousness. 'That's great, Lar. What is it?'

'It's Darth Vader. And his best friend, Mr Hairy.'

'Do you know, I'd never heard of Mr Hairy,' said Mum, tactfully. 'Is he in the film?'

'Oh, yes,' said Larkin, with great authority. He prided himself on his knowledge of *Star Wars*, despite never having seen it.

Once Mum had taken Larkin outside to water the plants, I got the full lowdown about Lou's situation. She rummaged around in the back of the kitchen cupboards and found an illicit, half-empty bag of coffee, which she immediately set about brewing. Waves of its delicious aroma wafted temptingly across the kitchen. One upside of my diagnosis was that I could now definitely not rule out giving up coffee. I grabbed another cup and lined it up next to hers.

The squatters had been served with a notice to leave within three months, or face a forced eviction. 'They probably won't do it, but it just creates this atmosphere of stress and chaos.'

'I thought you loved chaos.'

'Maybe I did, once upon a time.' She filled both cups and sat down next to me at the table. 'You know, I'm getting to that age, I've started to think about the fact that I want to have kids soon. I can't really do that with this level of instability. Sometimes I really think – you're going to laugh, now: should I just give up and marry a banker?'

I almost choked on my coffee. These were not words I ever expected to cross my sister's lips. She and Shanti had spent five happy years hitch-hiking around India, skinny-dipping in lochs and attending festivals wearing full anatomically correct monkey suits. The day Lou married a banker would be the day the final nail was banged into the coffin of the hippy dream.

'I'm getting the fear,' she said. 'Of course, Shanti and I could carry on as we are, but I've just started to realise . . . that I don't think I want to.'

Here was a question I never thought I'd find myself considering: should Lou bail on the hippy life and try to find herself a stockbroker with a detached house in Surrey? Or follow the path of true love, regardless of material considerations? High on caffeine, I found myself full of practical advice.

'If I had my time again,' I said airily, 'I'd put money much further up the wish list. Of course, it's nice to be in love, blah blah. But you might as well admit that a relationship is not just about soppy stuff, it's an economic arrangement. Read Jane Austen: at least in those days they were upfront about it.'

No sooner had the words left my mouth than a disturbing thought occurred to me. What if Lou followed my advice and found some stinking rich sugar daddy who sorted her out with a terraced house in Islington, complete with a wisteria over the door? What if her kids got to go to private school and learn debating and Latin? What if she were able to avoid paid employment entirely and dedicate her time to art and charitable works?

It would be more than I could bear. The comforting knowledge that Lou was broker than me was fundamental to my sanity.

I drained the last drops from my cup, and cleared my throat. 'On the other hand . . .'

* * *

Later, I called Frankie to let her know that I would not be able to make her dinner party, for mental health reasons. To take the edge off this announcement, I said it in a jokey, I'm-your-wacky-friend kind of tone.

'Whatever, Syl,' she said. 'See you later.'

'But—'

'Look, I know how you feel. You're not sleeping. You're drowning in nappies and breastmilk. You've forgotten who you are. Join the club. Which is exactly why a nice evening with some interesting new friends will be good for both of us.'

'I don't think—'

'Why don't you stay here afterwards, give yourself a bit of a break and catch up on some sleep? Obe can go home and deal with the kids.' That gave me pause; it sounded like a really good idea. 'Anyway, Sylvia, you bloody well promised. I know you're not going to let me down. See you at seven thirty.'

So that evening, I found myself in front of the mirror, patting layer after layer of concealer onto the dark circles beneath my eyes.

'Please remind me why we are doing this?' asked Obe, who was even less of a dinner party native than me. The wrinkles under his eyes made sad star shapes; I hadn't noticed them appear. I shook my head vigorously, as though I could shake the tiredness out of my ear hole.

'Because I said I would. And I'd really appreciate it if you came with me.'

In recent days Obe and I had settled on a kind of strained politeness. Neither of us wanted to argue; neither of us wanted to be upset. We both knew we had to stop hurting each other, and that meant falling back on basic good manners: saying please and thank you, not leaving stuff around for the other person to clear up, and not indulging in any character assassinations. It was amazing how much this seemed to be helping. *Sit upright, walk tall; manners maketh the man*, Earl had written to Obe in one of his postcards.

'It might be nice for us to spend some adult time together. Don't you think?'

'Well, that depends,' said Obe, without specifying what it depended on. 'You do realise this means I'm going to have to talk to Mark?'

'Is that bad?'

'It's not so much bad, as impossible. I just look at him and every word I know disappears from my head.'

'Perhaps you could express yourself using dance,' I suggested, but for some reason this didn't seem to cheer him up.

* * *

Toby and Phoebe were in the living room when we arrived, stretched out on the sculptural sofa like a couple of magnificent lions. They were leafy streeters, all right. Toby was wearing a beautifully fitting suit, with trainers, a funky touch. Phoebe had long wavy blonde hair, feline eyes and a slow, radiant smile. Her dress was cream lace with pearly buttons, the kind of thing I might have worn to a wedding – my own wedding.

The only sign of Frankie was a clatter of pans from the kitchen. So Obe and I did the handshakes and settled down awkwardly to attempt some pre-dinner chitchat. It had been a while since either of us had made small talk with other adults. What did adults talk about these days? The appalling state of the country? The even more appalling state of the world? I racked my brains for a subject of conversation that wasn't horribly depressing. But there was a grey, listless feeling in my head, and permanent floaters in my peripheral vision.

'Yes, I'm afraid Afghanistan was very disappointing,' Mark was saying. I admired him sitting there across the room, in the grey velvet armchair by the open fire: Mark was very good-looking, tall and athletic with blond, sweeping, confident hair. Private-school hair. I could understand why the Afghans had trusted him with their constitution, with hair like that. 'The political structures just aren't there; it's still the military who are running the show.'

Phoebe shook her head sorrowfully. 'It's such a shame. Makes you think, we'll never learn.'

'And what about you, Obe, how's your work?' Mark said kindly, as though national constitutions and local authority playschemes were all the same to him. 'Not too badly affected by the cuts, I hope?'

'Hanging in there,' said Obe, and then explained to Phoebe and Toby: 'It's an after-school and holiday club for autistic children. I'm a playworker.' They assumed the charmed expressions of American tourists in a Cotswold village.

'That must be *so* rewarding,' said Phoebe.

'It is,' said Obe, his face lighting up. He started telling Phoebe and Toby about Jase. Obe had a really good collection of Jase anecdotes: the time he tried to eat a crash mat, the time he stole the playscheme's credit card and used it to order fifty ham and pineapple pizzas, the time he ran away and the police found him trying to break into the hyena enclosure at London Zoo. Everyone was in stitches; Obe was acing this dinner party.

'And how about you, Sylvia,' said Toby, wiping his eyes. 'Do you work?'

I hesitated. There was nothing unkind about Toby's face. He had boyish chubby cheeks and teddy-bear eyes.

In the abstract I obviously hated bankers, but now I had one sitting in front of me, my righteous moral superiority dribbled uselessly away. I opened my mouth, and then shut it again. Everyone in the room was looking at me. 'In a way,' I said.

There was a brief silence. Obe coughed. 'Sylvia is being made redundant,' he said. 'It's been a bit of a shock.'

'Oh God,' said Phoebe. 'I'm so sorry.'

'No it's fine, it's really—' To my horror, I felt blood rush to my face, and tears prickle in my eyes. I could not start crying. Not now, before I'd even bloody said anything. Crying was not sophisticated dinner party behaviour. 'It's really fine.'

Phoebe reached out and put her cool, slender hand on my cracked, witchy one. 'No, it's not fine, it's really crap,' she said. 'I know, I was made redundant last year – also when I was on maternity leave. I'm still not over it, to be honest. It's just so unfair.'

I was touched by her genuine sympathy. 'But Frankie told me you were doing all this amazing environmental stuff,' I said, sniffing. 'Setting up a green law firm, or something?'

'I've just got going with that,' said Phoebe. 'I guess it took me a while to figure out that getting kicked out of my old firm was actually an opportunity – to think about what kind of work would be meaningful to me.

I'd had enough of other people bossing me around, anyway, and enough of solving property disputes between millionaires. And the environmental crisis has been completely terrifying me and obsessing me for years – after Aurora was born, it was pretty much all I could think about.'

Phoebe was one of my kind! I was gripping her hand now; I didn't want to let go. 'I know *exactly* what you mean,' I told her. 'I mean, I lie there at night, unable to sleep, or think about anything else, because it's all so terrifying. The only thing worse than the terror is the complete helplessness, really.'

Phoebe gave my hand another kind but firm squeeze and removed hers from its grip. 'But we're not helpless, are we?' she said, the slow smile returning to her lips. 'Don't get me wrong – I felt that way, too. But once you start facing up to it, and working with other people who feel the same way, the helplessness kind of evaporates. The terror doesn't – if anything, the more I know about it, the more terrified I feel. But the terror has a purpose: it's propelling us to act.'

I remembered the night at the squat, the landscape with its strange inner glow. *We have to find a better way.* 'I know you're right,' I whispered. 'I'm nearly there, I really am.' Some slight hesitation, some flicker in her eyes told me that Phoebe thought I should get on with it, but she was far too nice and well brought-up to say so.

Halfway through dinner, things took a funny turn. Frankie had made a beautiful spread: roasted pumpkin with feta cheese, a beetroot dip, three different bowls of brightly coloured salads, a whole salmon, and cheeses from the cheese-on-a-pedestal shop were laid out on the kitchen table. She'd been at the Ottolenghi cookbook, I could tell.

'So it's Cuba again next month,' Mark was telling Toby as we sat down and dug in. 'We've just got permission to visit that client I was telling you about, the Guantanamo detainee . . .'

Frankie glanced up sharply. 'Is Cuba definite now, darling?' she said. 'I thought perhaps you were going to turn that one down, because of Caleb's birthday.'

'No, it's definite,' said Mark, without looking at her. Frankie carefully picked up her glass, and took a long swig of wine.

'Refill, Sylvia?' she asked, and before I could respond, she drained her own glass, and poured herself another one, almost to the top. I wondered if she drank this much every night, when Mark was away and she was on her own. We'd never really talked about it. When she looked back at me her eyes seemed to be focusing on the middle distance, somewhere over my shoulder. Then she stood up, wobbled momentarily, and then tapped her knife against the side of her glass, like the best man announcing his speech at a wedding. The table fell silent, and all eyes turned to her.

'I have a very exciting announcement to make,' said Frankie, swaying slightly and beaming out her megawatt smile. 'I'm going back to work!'

Phoebe raised her glass in an enthusiastic toast, but put it down again when she realised that nobody else was joining her. Mark had frozen with his bottle of seaweed-infused craft beer halfway to his mouth.

'I spoke to Ben from Legless Productions this morning, and as of next week I will be working full-time on his documentary. As assistant director!'

Mark coughed, put the bottle down. 'Franks, perhaps we could discuss this . . .'

Frankie beamed at him even more widely. 'I would be so very happy to discuss it with you, my darling. And we'll have plenty of time to do that, as you'll be taking several weeks off work to help me make the transition. You'll need to cancel Cuba, so you can look after Caleb, organise his birthday party, and help set up our future childcare arrangements.'

Mark finally managed to take a gulp of his beer.

Frankie turned to Phoebe and me, waving her hands expansively. 'I'm sure you ladies will agree,' she announced, 'that it's wonderful we all share our lives with such ardent feminists.'

Phoebe raised her glass again. 'I'll drink to that,' she said, and this time I joined her. Obe was looking thoughtful, as though he were trying to decode what message there was in this for him, but after a couple of moments, he raised his glass and clinked, and Toby followed his lead. It took a few more before Mark grinned nervously, and held up his bottle.

All in all, I actually enjoyed the dinner party. After Obe went home to mastermind That Baby's sleep training, and Mark took his jet-lag to bed, Frankie and I sat up drinking hot chocolate.

'You *told* him?' said Frankie, incredulously. 'Why?'

'I don't know.' I covered my face with my hands, and peeped at her through a crack in my fingers. 'It just seemed like the right thing to do.'

'*Never* tell,' said Frankie. 'That's the golden rule of infidelity.'

I closed the crack and sank into the blankness of my eyelids. It was too late, what was done, was done. Too late for rules, and too late for good advice.

'More to the point,' said Frankie, 'next time Lou has one of her crazy parties with sexy Mexicans, invite me, you cow.'

'Colombian,' I said. 'He was Colombian.'

'Just tell me one more time,' said Frankie. 'What did he *smell* like?'

In the spare room, I got into the bed and sank my aching limbs into the clean, crisp white sheets. Around me, everything was quiet. Not the kind of dread quiet that you got in our flat, which was laden with the knowledge that within two hours it would be shattered by baffling, implacable screams of red-faced outrage, or R'n'B, or thumps, or howling. This was real quiet. It's-going-to-stay-quiet quiet. I shut my eyes and took a breath; the view appeared, shimmering. The shopping trolleys and murky depths had gone; peace and serenity reigned. In fact, I wasn't just looking at the water now, I was immersed in it, floating naked in it, like a baby. Everything here was clean, everything was pure. I had no responsibilities, nothing I had to do.

Snatches of the evening's conversation floated across my mind like clouds: *it is rewarding, yes; wonderful to share our lives with such ardent feminists!; the terror has a purpose, it's propelling us to act.* Above all of them I could hear Dad's voice, loud but quiet, travelling through time and space: *you've got brains. You know there's a better way*. I lay like that for quite some time, and when I opened my eyes I knew something perfectly clear, perfectly obvious: we couldn't do it. We couldn't move to Jewel Road. It didn't matter if it was a once-in-a-life-time opportunity, because we could only stretch ourselves so thin without snapping. If that meant we had to stay in Priory Court for ever, then that was the way it had to be.

For a moment I imagined Obe's long and bitter laugh when I told him about this epiphany, but before I could think about that too much a huge, white wave of sleep swept over me. I dived gratefully into its very heart, and let it bear me away to a distant, longed-for shore.

12.

Come together

'So. Would either of you like to tell me why you are here?'

Silence. Obe and I sat opposite each other in the sad grey plywood cubbyhole, the clock ticking away on the little table. I couldn't think of any decent answer to this question, even though I must have had a reason for booking us an appointment with a couples' counsellor. I had insisted that we do this together, instead of having therapy on my own. And Mum had lent us the money for a private appointment. Obviously, Obe didn't want to come. 'Why should I?' he asked. 'I'm not depressed!' And he pulled a crazy-fun face to show how very un-depressed he was.

'Because if you don't,' I said, in a very calm, reasonable tone, 'I'm going to borrow more of Mum's money and book one-way tickets to Rio for me and the kids.'

Ironically, ever since I booked the appointment, we had continued to get along much better. We'd kept up the politeness thing, and I'd kept up my meditation. We'd agreed that soon – after giving ourselves a little cool-down time – we would tell Rob Crockett that we were not, after all, going to buy his rotten house. Obe had stopped watching *Game of Thrones* in favour of a drama about a funny-but-anxious thirty-something woman (my choice). The sleep training had worked, so we'd been getting at least four consecutive hours a night. Together, in a great show of domestic co-operation, we had renewed the car insurance.

And now here we were, raking up the whole hornets' nest all over again.

'What would you like to get out of these sessions?'

The following silence seemed to drag on for light-years. Obe was sitting very, very still in his cheap foam chair, as though if he didn't move a muscle, we would both forget he was there. I was staring at a picture on the wall with intense concentration. As the only decorative touch in the otherwise plain consulting room, it did draw the eye. It was a very surreal painting: a blue horse floating against a deep blue background, and next to it something that might have been a toy cow. Around the edge of the canvas was an irregular geometric pattern. I wondered if Dr Gordon chose it, and if so what he wanted to imply. Were the horse and the cow having relationship problems? Did the geometric pattern hemming them in represent their subconscious?

The clock on the small table next to Dr Gordon was

ticking softly. We were already five minutes into our appointment. I considered trying to work out how much of Mum's money each one of those ticks was costing. Then decided it was probably best not to.

Dr Gordon's eyes flicked around the room and then fastened on the clipboard he was resting on his lap, upon which he appeared to have a checklist. He was not at all what I had had in mind. When I pictured a therapist, I had imagined somebody like Mum: a wise old woman with spectacles, short grey hair, flowing floral skirt and an air of hard-won empathy. But Dr Gordon was wearing tightly belted beige trousers and his face was strangely immobile. I definitely didn't look at him and think 'emotional intelligence'. I looked at him and thought 'fish on a slab'.

There was probably a deep-seated psychological explanation for the overwhelming hostility I was feeling towards him. But at that moment I felt like it had more to do with those trousers, which were hitched up way above his belly button. I didn't know if I could accept advice from a man who seemingly took his fashion cues from Simon Cowell. But having got this far, I felt obliged to give him a chance.

Ten minutes in; this was ridiculous, somebody had to say something. I cleared my throat and said, 'I'd like to resolve some of our differences about money.'

Dr Gordon nodded gravely. I paused, trying to identify what my feelings actually were, and express them in the least unreasonable terms. 'I've always been the main breadwinner,' I said. 'And that has been fine. But now we've got two children, and most of the domestic respon-sibilities have fallen to me as well. 'Obe and I have . . . different approaches to life. I love it that he is so passionate about poetry, for example. But perhaps it would be possible for him to combine that passion with earning more than the minimum wage.'

Dr Gordon shifted in his seat. He looked supremely unbothered. Was it me, or were his eyes a little glazed? Was he sleepy? Or on some kind of medication? Perhaps he was on that new cannabis oil that everyone was talking about. Perhaps I should find out what he was on, and get some for myself.

Obe still hadn't moved. I wondered whether he had actually slipped into some kind of waking coma. Perhaps he had a severe allergy to talking about emotions, and his body had shut down.

'Thank you, Sylvia,' said Dr Gordon, after a short pause. 'How does that sound to you, Obe?'

Obe took a long, slow breath. 'It sounds,' he said sonorously, 'like soundless wailing, / The silent withering of autumn flowers / Dropping their petals and remaining motionless.'

I raised my eyebrows at Dr Gordon expecting some solidarity, but he was scribbling furiously on his clipboard. He hadn't scribbled at all while I was talking. I felt like pointing out to him that I was using my own words, whereas Obe was just nicking someone else's. But when Dr Gordon stopped writing he looked up admiringly.

'*The Four Quartets*,' he said. 'In my view, the greatest poetic work of the 20th century.'

Obe inclined his head, giving this statement due consideration. 'I'd put *The Wasteland* just ahead, personally.'

'A close second,' conceded Dr Gordon.

This interaction transformed the atmosphere in the room. Obe was now lounging back on his chair, his legs confidently crossed. Dr Gordon was smiling matily at him. I cleared my throat again, just to remind them I was there. 'Anyway. As I was saying about the money—'

'We were getting to that, Sylvia,' said Dr Gordon, sounding tetchy. 'Perhaps you'd like to explain – when you talk about money – what does money actually *mean* to you?'

'Well,' I said. 'It means being able to pay the bills. And live in a house. And feed the children.'

'Yes, yes, on a *completely mundane* level, that's obviously what it means. But I'm asking you to think *symbolically*. What does money mean to you as a *system of value*?'

'Exactly!' cried Obe. 'This is my question!'

There was a pause as Dr Gordon scribbled on his clipboard again. He seemed to be ticking boxes, but I didn't know what the boxes were, or what they were telling him. Perhaps he was rating us both out of ten, and he'd hold up our scores at the end. It was pretty clear to me who was ahead. As every second ticked by, I felt more annoyed and frustrated.

'For example,' Dr Gordon went on. 'You are paying me seventy-five pounds an hour—'

'Sixty,' I said.

'What?' Dr Gordon's face at last displayed some genuine concern.

'When I booked, the website gave me the option of paying sixty, as we are low-waged.'

'Oh, I see. You're on the discount rate.' Dr Gordon seemed unimpressed at this, but I was too busy imagining a world in which Obe retrained as a therapist and charged his clients seventy-five pounds an hour. Or even sixty. Sixty would be just fine.

'The point is,' said Dr Gordon, 'that the true value of this session has nothing to do with the amount you are paying.'

Too right, I thought, but did not say. There was no point in antagonising him, it would only make him side with Obe even more. 'I was hoping,' I explained, 'that we could use this session to discuss how to share our responsibilities more equally, so the burden doesn't fall on me. Because this situation has nearly broken me. It's nearly broken all of us. Physically, emotionally . . . well, in every way, really.'

Dr Gordon blinked. His face had resumed its impassive expression. 'Perhaps you'd like to explain why this issue of responsibility is so significant to you,' he said.

'We're not just talking about me!' I cried, exasperated. 'We're also talking about Obe!'

'We are talking about both of you. Because I could turn it around. The question might be not why Obe doesn't assume enough responsibility, but instead why you feel compelled to assume so much.'

That was the last straw for me and Dr Gordon. I had not paid to come here and be told the whole thing was my fault. I shut my mouth firmly and slumped down in my chair. Suffice to say, I hated therapy. Obe was delighted. I would never make him go, ever again.

'I liked him more than I thought I would,' Obe said afterwards, as we sat recovering in an artisan-style coffee shop on Charlotte Street. My coffee had a fancy oak-leaf pattern in the foam, which failed to make me feel it had been worth paying £3.50 for it. 'He seemed to understand the situation.'

'I think he fancied you, Obe! He hardly looked at me

for the entire hour! And who did he remind me of? His eyes were so weird. Blank.'

'That one from the Addams Family,' said Obe immediately. 'Lurch.'

'That's it!'

We cracked up. 'Oh Syl, your face,' said Obe, wiping away a tear of pure hilarity. 'There was a reason he couldn't look at you: he would have turned to stone.' I could at least say one thing for Dr Gordon: we hadn't laughed like that in quite a while.

By the time I slipped quietly into the Priory Court community room that evening, the Extraordinary General TRA meeting was already in full swing. Full swing, in this case, meant that there were two men sitting with Brenda behind a fold-out table: a pale-faced man in a suit, with a Hackney Council badge that read 'Darren', and a perma-tanned guy with the shoulders of a scaffolder wearing a red T-shirt with 'High-Class Homes' in crisp white lettering. A splay-legged flip chart was propped up against the wall.

Facing them, twenty chairs were arranged in two semicircles. Three of the chairs were occupied. Despite Brenda's extensive publicity campaign, the only attendees from the block were Abraham, dressed in his black robes and a large furry hat, Zeynab, and me. Zeynab gave me a little wave, as I slid into a chair as close as possible to the door.

'Aha!' said Brenda triumphantly, springing up to pour another cup of tea from the chipped enamel pot. 'I knew there would be more! We were just getting started.'

I'd never been inside the community room before. It had been easy to overlook the small, square brick building just next to the car park, as there was nothing pretty about it from the outside. Inside, it was a magnolia-painted box, with a little kitchen in the corner, complete with a sink, a kettle and a packet of biscuits, and one barred window, too high up the wall to look out on anything other than a patch of sky. It had that musty, dusty smell of a room that isn't used often enough.

But there were signs that once, long ago, somebody had given the place some love. In faded paint on the wall behind Darren and Brenda there was a giant rainbow, made from kids' handprints – perhaps somebody had once run a playgroup here, back in the days of Cora, when all the mothers knew one another.

'So,' said Brenda, smiling encouragingly at us past the empty rows of chairs. 'I think we might as well start, and hopefully more people will join us. As you'll know, I called this meeting because the council have informed the TRA about regeneration plans for Priory Court. This is big news with far-reaching implications for the future of the estate, so Darren, housing officer from the council, and Mike, from High-Class Homes, have kindly come here to talk us through the plans. Darren, over to you.'

'Thank you, Brenda,' said Darren as he stepped to the front rubbing his eyes. He looked like he hadn't slept for weeks. He took a deep breath, but before he could say anything the door creaked open. We all looked around to see Dawn standing in the doorway, wearing her tracky bottoms and beanie and clutching a can of Tennent's. She hesitated, blinking, and then sat down with a bump in the chair next to the door.

'As you will be aware, Priory Court is long overdue for core improvements,' Darren was saying. 'Hackney council is committed to continually raising the standards of our social housing, and we are fortunate to now have the opportunity to go into partnership with High-Class Homes, a respected property developer.' He gestured to the man in the red T-shirt, who grinned toadily through his tan. Darren gave him a wan smile back. 'Mike will now talk you through the plans, and I hope you'll share my excitement about this transformative initiative.'

Mike stood up. He was roughly the same width as he was tall. He reached up and turned over the first page of the flip chart, to reveal a larger reproduction of the image from the leaflet: there were the shining glass towers, the photoshopped children, the bright blue reservoir. 'Thanks,

Darren,' he said. 'So here you can see our vision for this area. It's nothing less than a total transformation. High-spec blocks, constructed from the latest modern materials. A mixture of affordable and luxury properties, all with a waterside view. This is housing for the 21st century.' He grinned, exposing too-white teeth. 'And it's an eco-development: as part of our commitment to corporate social responsibility, we will be transforming the reservoir into a wildlife sanctuary.'

There was a brief silence after he sat down, before Zeynab put up her hand. 'Can I ask about the other animals who live here, the human ones? Where are we in this picture?'

Mike glanced at Darren. Darren glanced at Mike. Mike's tan had deepened, while Darren seemed to have turned even paler, as though the colour was being drained out of him. Darren coughed.

'High-Class Homes' proposal is to demolish the current block,' he said. 'In order to replace it with two high-spec towers, constructed from the latest . . .'

I caught my breath. Abraham leaned forward, blinking through his glasses.

'And when that happens,' he interrupted, nervously, 'where do we go?'

'Council tenants will be rehoused,' Darren said, quickly.

'But where?' asked Zeynab. 'Not here, I guess, as you'll

need to knock down our homes in order to start building this new development. So where will you put us, as you get on with your lovely project?'

'That's a great question,' said Darren. Darren seemed to be becoming ever whiter and more spectral; Mike was now staring at a wall and obviously visualising how much cash was trickling into his bank account for every minute spent in that room. 'Obviously we can't give any guarantees, but we will try our best to find housing for you within the Greater London area . . .'

Zeynab laughed. 'The Greater London area? And there's no guarantee even for that? What, so we could end up in . . . in Birmingham? Or the middle of the countryside?' Darren got another degree paler. 'Because I'm telling you, Darren, you might as well rip me to shreds right now. We come from Turkey ten years ago, and it has taken us all this time to make a life – to learn English, to find work, to settle in. Everything we worked for is right here – my husband's work, my son's nursery, the only people I know in this whole country. Right here. Not in Greater London. Not in Birmingham.'

'And obviously for members of my community, moving is out of the question,' said Abraham. 'None of us can live without our schools, our synagogues and community centres. If one of us has to move, we all move.'

Mike unleashed those white teeth again, as if he might

blind us all with their brilliance. 'I think what my colleague here is saying is that every effort will be made—'

But he stopped because, at the back of the room, Dawn had sprung to her feet. For once, she was standing perfectly steady; she uncurled a finger, with its long, yellowing nail, and pointed it straight at Mike. Her usually blurry eyes were full of fire. 'You put that smarmy smile away, young man,' she said, as he visibly shrank in his chair. 'You think you can come in here and smile and get us to agree to this? To you knocking down our homes? Do you think we are stupid? There is nothing wrong with this block. It is made of brick, not no fancy glass rubbish. It is solid. All it needs is repairs, some paint, some care and attention.' She turned to Darren. 'I didn't understand this word, regeneration. Now I know: it means get rid of people.'

With wobbly dignity, she retrieved her can from the floor, turned on her heel and left, banging the door behind her. Darren shifted uneasily in his chair. After a second, Abraham stood up, and started to clap. One by one, all four of us joined in.

After Darren and Mike left, hurriedly packing their flip-chart into a High-Class Homes van and skidding out of the car park, the rest of us stayed for another cup of tea, to discuss tactics. Darren had told us that he didn't know how long it was going to take for the plans to go through, or whether it was even certain that they would, or what the timetable for the building work would be. He didn't know how much the new flats would sell for, or whether any of them would be affordable, or what affordable really meant. All he could say, and he repeated this several times, was that the council was dealing with the impact of the central government's austerity measures, and 'having to explore all the options at increasing its sources of revenue'.

'So, Brenda,' said Zeynab. 'Tell us. What's the plan? How do we take on the council?'

Brenda ran her hand through her tin-hat hair. 'I thought we could start by writing them a letter about the demolition plans. A letter of complaint. Strongly worded, you know.'

Zeynab snorted. 'You think that's gonna do anything?'

Brenda's stocky body sagged back into the chair; it was the first time I had seen her look less than one hundred per cent determined. 'I don't know what else we *can* do. We don't have many options.'

'A letter's going to make zero difference,' said Zeynab. 'They don't care what we think.'

Abraham had been sitting there fiddling with his hat.

The strip light on the ceiling flickered and a football rattled the bars over the tiny, cell-like window. There was a long low whine from outside; one of the kids was driving a moped around the forecourt again. 'If we actually want the council to change their plans, we need to make their lives difficult,' he said. 'We're going to need publicity, to get the story into the papers.'

'Oh, that's a good idea,' said Brenda. 'But I wouldn't know how to begin with all that. What we need is somebody with some experience in dealing with the press.'

I sat very, very still. Perhaps if I didn't move a muscle, the conversation would move on, and I wouldn't have to let them know that I had nearly ten years of communications experience. As soon as I did that, there'd be no end to it – I'd get sucked into this whole problem. I had enough sleepless nights, without trying to take on the powers-that-be.

'Let's think,' said Brenda. 'There must be *somebody* in the block who knows about the media. Somebody who works in that area . . .'

'Perhaps somebody who works in a communications department,' said Abraham, brightly. 'Or has some kind of experience with political lobbying.'

The terror has a purpose, it's propelling us to act. We need to find a better way. 'Me,' I blurted out. 'I work in political communications. I used to be a journalist. I deal with the press all the time.'

'Oh!' said Brenda. 'I had no idea! That's brilliant, Sylvia. So you can draft a letter to the editor of the *Hackney Gazette*.'

I nodded. Then I thought: no, if I'm going to do this, I'm going to do it properly. 'The council won't care about a letter to the editor in the local press,' I said. 'If we want to make them sit up and take notice, we need to get this onto the national news. Abraham's right, we need a story.'

'We need to protest!' said Zeynab. 'All this writing-things-down rubbish, you guys are kidding yourselves. We need to find out where these High-Class Homes guys live, the big bosses. Go and shout outside their houses and make their lives hell!'

Brenda shuffled a pile of papers in front of her. The council had given her an information pack with an approximate timeline for the decision-making, as well as lots of shiny leaflets showing the regenerated estate in all its glory. She picked one paper out of the sheaf and read it over. 'Look here,' she said, pointing to one entry on the timeline. 'In August, the chief executives of High-Class Homes are going to visit the estate for a special event. It says here that they will meet residents to answer questions, and present the new plans in detail.'

My mind was working now. Some long-submerged instinct kicked in, and I switched into professional mode. 'Right,' I said. 'So that's our story. We need to get a protest together for that day. Confront the big High-Class Homes bosses when they come into the estate. The media love that kind of thing: the little people take on the fat cats.'

'What, just the four of us?' Abraham laughed. 'Big story!'

'We'll get everybody on the estate out!' said Zeynab. 'We need to wake them up, make them realise that they can't just sit in their flats watching telly – or soon they won't have any flats to sit in.'

'That'll be the day,' said Brenda. 'I've been trying to get people out of their flats and into this meeting room for years. They don't want to know. I've all but given up.'

I thought about the squat where Lou and the squatters had created a different kind of life for themselves. I might not know how to organise a protest – but I knew some people who did. I fished my phone out of my pocket and called Lou. It went straight to voicemail. 'Call me back, I need to ask you something,' I said. 'Something – political.'

Abraham and I walked together through the damp forecourt towards the lift. His robes flapped in the wind, and catching sight of this dark silhouette a question rose to my lips. 'Abraham, do you ever sit out there, by the reservoir, late at night?'

He put his head down, hiding his face behind his wide-brimmed hat. 'Occasionally,' he said. 'You might have seen me out there once or twice.'

'Why? What are you doing? Are you fishing, or something?'

'No, no, I don't fish.' Abraham smiled shyly. 'It's amphibians that are of great interest to me – particularly newts.' This somehow made sense; there was something slightly newt-like about Abraham's big blinking eyes, long, thin face. 'Perhaps you don't know that in this reservoir here we have a very rare species of newt, the Greater Crested. These newts are famed for their courtship dances, and these tend to happen late at night. So occasionally, when I have a break in my studies, I go and wait out there. I like to watch it.'

He seemed embarrassed by this confession, and scurried off. But it was good to know I wasn't the only one who loved watching the water; I wasn't the only one who found a much-needed piece of calm on the reservoir. Just as we were leaving, I thought to myself, the mysteries of Priory Court were beginning to reveal themselves.

* * *

I was sitting in front of the birthday sculpture, enveloped in the power of its forcefield. Its tin-can eyes seemed to look directly into mine, giving me the strength I needed to conduct this conversation. Because I had my phone in my hand, and Rob Crockett was angry. His usually chirpy cockney patter had given way to something a little harsher and more menacing.

'Can you just explain *why*, please madam, because I will obviously have to tell your vendor, who is going to want to string me up . . .'

I had just told him that, at the very last possible moment, we were pulling out of buying the house. Why? Because we couldn't bloody well afford to move, that's why. And the place was a rip-off. It smelled, it had no functioning kitchen or bathroom, the roof was about to fall down, and we would be paying for it for the rest of our lives. I'd heard of a worse deal, but it was struck at a crossroads, at midnight, with a cloven-hooved stranger.

'We just thought better of it,' I replied, and the birthday sculpture almost seemed to smile. I closed my eyes, drew myself up tall, sucked in its power. Finally, I could stick it to him, after months of having to laugh at his jokes, tolerate his nauseating shiny clothes and generally suck up to him. 'It's too expensive.'

'I see. Well, obviously I think you're making the wrong decision.' He sounded really pissed off. 'You do realise that this is absolutely the only house you are going to get in this area for this price? If you drop out now, you are staying right where you are.'

'I know. I'm okay with that.' And the funny thing is, I was. Though the kids would miss out on having a garden, they would hopefully appreciate having parents who weren't out of their minds with stress. Also, seeing as we were saving *tens of thousands of pounds* by not moving, I might be able to get myself a new coat, once the pay cheque from Deutsche Bank came in.

'Right. Well, I'd better make the call, then.' Rob Crockett sighed. Dammit, despite myself I was starting to feel a teensy bit sorry for him.

'Look, just tell him circumstances changed. There are redundancies at work, and we don't feel able to take the risk.'

'Ah! I see. Now I understand.' Clearly, redundancy was an obstacle Rob Crockett had encountered before, and his voice took on a hint of its previous cockiness. 'But you mustn't let that worry you, my dear. If you lose your job you can always come and work here with me. We're run off our feet!'

13.

Crime and punishment

'I HAVE desired to go / Where springs not fail,' murmured Obe, as we sat in the car watching the wipers flick pea-sized balls of ice across the windscreen. 'To fields where flies no sharp and sided hail.'

'Tell me about it. Marbella?' I sighed, and cranked up the car heater. We were on our way to Westfield, because Obe had grand plans for improving our quality of life. Apparently what we needed was not a new home, but a new duvet. And not just any old duvet; he had been researching it online. It had to be super king-sized Hungarian goosedown, the bedding of fat cats and oligarchs. If those bastards could get a good night's sleep, he pointed out, then so should we. The duvet was to be paid for on a new nought-per-cent finance credit card that Obe had sent off for especially.

'We can pay off twenty-five quid a month from the child benefit money,' he explained. 'After all, it's in the children's best interests that we get a good night's sleep.'

So now here we were, idling in neutral outside Topps Tiles, with Big Yellow Storage a garish smudge on the horizon. The kids were asleep in the back seat, lulled by the heat and the poptastic melodies of Smooth FM. We should spend more Saturday mornings in traffic jams, I thought. It was relaxing.

'So, are the council supposed to be getting the police on the case downstairs?' Obe asked. I'd actually managed to sleep last night, but according to Obe, who was up with Eliot, it had been particularly riotous. 'I don't buy it, though – I've never smelled crack down there.'

'Haven't you? That sweet, marshmallowy smell?'

Obe tutted. 'That's not crack.'

He sounded so confident that I had to ask: 'Have you ever *done* crack?'

A nostalgic expression came over Obe's face. 'A couple of times,' he said. 'Years ago, in Birmingham. Great drug.'

'*Great drug?*'

'Best one I ever tried. I had to promise myself never to do it again. I could see where that was leading.'

'Wow, Obe.' Obe's tales of his youth in Birmingham often surprised me. I had to remind myself that my poetry-quoting gentle giant could easily have ended up a junkie, or in jail, like a lot of the people he knew back then. It was easy to forget how different our backgrounds were, now our lives were so closely entwined.

'I don't remember it smelling anything like marshmallows,' Obe went on. 'Perhaps she's just having lovely marshmallow parties with her friends. You never can tell, with Dawn.'

We inched forwards. I wasn't entirely sure we were going the right way around the North Circular, as after we'd loaded everyone into the car we had realised that the sat nav wasn't working. The screen was displaying an endless twisting white spiral alongside the words 'Waiting for GPS . . .' as though Samuel Beckett had got into the machine.

This was bad news, because Obe and I had fundamentally different approaches to navigation. I liked to be told what to do, at least three steps ahead, and in a calm and decisive tone of voice. He preferred to 'freestyle'. There was nothing more calculated to send me into paroxysms of expletive-laden rage than a car journey with Obe doing the map reading.

'Hey, I heard from Titania. She wants to come and visit.'

'Oh God, really?' I loved my sister-in-law, but after her last visit, she'd left our sofa stained with gold body-paint, the bath clogged with feathers and the fridge filled with some kind of pungent fermented yoghurt. 'When?'

'August. She's got some plan: a community art project on the estate, or something.'

'Sounds ominous.'

The traffic moved forward another couple of inches, and we pulled up level with a turning labelled 'Isle of Dogs'. My foot itched on the accelerator. I was longing to get somewhere, anywhere.

'Can I take this one, Obe?'

'Why not?' he said.

Gratefully, I hung a left, and we barrelled off down the deserted A-road.

'Where is the Isle of Dogs, anyway,' I wondered a couple of minutes later, once the towers of the City came into view. 'East or west?'

'Darned if I know,' said Obe.

'But, love,' I said, trying very hard to keep my voice level, 'you're supposed to be map reading.'

Obe looked vaguely down at the map on his lap. Glancing over I could see that he had it open on page 37, Devon and Cornwall.

'Where the fuck are we?' I hissed.

He flicked over a few pages, and studied the map intently. 'I guess you could take a left here,' he said. 'Or if not, then you could go for the next right.'

'*OBE, DO WE HAVE TO GO THROUGH THIS AGAIN? TAKE SOME FUCKING RESPONSIBILITY. JUST TELL ME*

WHERE TO TURN!' I yelled. In the back seat, both children woke and started to whimper. With a screech I pulled over onto the hard shoulder. The car behind us hooted, loud and long.

'Look. Just shut up and let me try to fix this,' muttered Obe, waving the sat nav pointlessly above his head. In the back seat the whimpers turned into wails, with all the soothing effect of a couple of cheesegraters on the cerebral cortex. I turned to him and I didn't even shout: *'If you don't give me the map right now I'm leaving you. I mean it. And you can keep the bloody kids.'*

'Wait!' Obe peered at the sat nav screen, upon which a little spinning egg-timer had appeared. Then – oh miracle! – a tiny map, and a second later a well-spoken woman's reassuring voice: 'After three hundred metres take the next left, and then, stay left.'

Immediately, the atmosphere in the car lightened. I pulled into the left-hand lane, and the children were lulled back into silence by the forward motion. Obe switched the radio on and hummed along cheerily to 'Girls Just Wanna Have Fun'.

'I think I fancy that woman,' he said, as I turned with brisk confidence onto the A13.

'Which woman?'

'The voice of the sat nav.'

'Oh her. Yeah, so do I.'

'She's so calm and consistent, she never changes her mind.' I couldn't help but feel this was a pointed remark.

'She is so helpful and supportive, I know I can completely rely on her,' I retorted.

The sat nav beeped. 'Stay left, and then turn left. In three hundred metres you will reach your destination.' Right on cue, the sleek form of Westfield appeared on the horizon. It looked like a gleaming spaceship that had crashed amid the pigeon-shitty tower blocks of east London.

If only there were an equivalent of sat nav to guide us through the other tricky areas of our family life: a sat nav child behavioural expert, say, or a sat nav financial adviser. Now that was a bloody good idea. I made a mental note to take it on *Dragon's Den,* it could make millions.

Westfield was heaving. There was a queue to get into the car park, a queue to get out of the car park, a queue to get up the escalators. Everything was bright, from the glass shopfronts to the gleaming spotlights. It was ages since I'd been anywhere so clean. Security men in fluorescent tabards were strutting about like peacocks on steroids.

Outside Carphone Warehouse the crowd was so huge I thought there must have been a stabbing, but it turned out people were queuing up for a new model. I took a moment to remind myself that we were supposed to be living through a period of austerity.

'It just doesn't make any sense,' I said.

'Tell me about it,' replied Obe, staring at the map at the top of the escalators. 'We should be outside John Lewis right now. This map is useless.'

'Of course it is,' I snapped. The Toddler was waving longingly at a giant bear standing outside the Build-a-Bear store. The bear waved enthusiastically back, but before this relationship could develop any further I grabbed Larkin's hand and hissed at Obe, 'Don't you understand, the powers behind Westfield want us to get lost? We'll buy more stuff that way.'

I relaxed a little once the distinguished insignia of John Lewis appeared before us, like an oasis in the desert. Inside, the air felt cooler, the atmosphere less frantic. We made our way to the bedding department, breathless with excitement. And lo, there it was, on the top shelf – the king of duvets, its outrageous price tag winking beneath the strip lights. It had been so long since we bought anything expensive that I felt sure we would be apprehended at the till and told to put it back.

We chose a duvet cover and some sheets, paid, and left carrying our bounty. Halfway back to the car park I noticed Obe was looking peaky; in fact, he was practically hyperventilating.

'The lady at the till,' he panted. 'She charged us for the sheets but not for the duvet.'

'Are you joking?'

'No.' He held up the receipt. Sure enough, we had only paid for the sheets. The helpful John Lewis lady must have removed the security tag and then forgotten to put the duvet through the till. My mind was suddenly in a frenzy of frantic calculations. Clearly, we should take it back. John Lewis! The shop you can trust! Stealing from John Lewis would be like shagging in a church, or swearing at a granny. It just wasn't right. Now, if we'd been in Tesco . . .

We prevaricated, stricken, in front of a brightly lit EXIT sign. Its green arrow seemed to be pointing us towards a new, more reckless, less dutiful kind of life: Obe and I, screeching off with the duvet in the boot, outlaws on the run from the cops. We could be like Bonnie and Clyde, only warmer, and better rested.

But Obe had my hand and was dragging me towards the car park, cackling. He loaded the boxes and bags into the boot, strapped in the kids, and drove away at full speed, pausing only to direct a jaunty wave at a grim phalanx of security bots at the car park gates. Surely somebody would stop us? Surely we couldn't just get away with stealing two hundred and fifty quid's worth of bedding?

But within minutes we were back on the North Circular, Topps Tiles on the horizon, stationary in a traffic jam. Smooth FM was playing Sam Cooke.

Obe and I listened to that song a lot before I got pregnant. We went to stay on a friend's houseboat in the Norfolk Broads for the weekend, and every morning Obe would wake up and open the curtains so we could watch the boats glide by, while we made coffee and listened to Sam Cooke. One day, I promised myself, we would manage another romantic weekend minibreak, somewhere foreign. After the kids left home, perhaps.

In the driving seat, Obe was grinning like a lunatic. He leaned over and planted a sloppy kiss on my neck. I turned to look at him, and our eyes met.

'I really can't wait to go to bed,' he said.

I narrowed my eyes. 'Is that just because of the duvet?'

'Ooooh,' he said, putting an arm around me. 'Could there be another reason?' He pulled me closer and our bodies pressed together. I squeezed myself as close as I could into his bear-like warmth, hoping that the traffic would remain stationary for the next few minutes. 'Mmmm,' he said, burying his head in my neck. He was warm, and he smelled like home. We hadn't hugged for a long time.

'I do love you, you know. Most of the time,' I mumbled. He said nothing, until I pulled back and looked at him reproachfully. 'That's your cue.'

'Oh. Yeah. Well, I guess I love you, too. Most of the time.'

'That's probably good enough, isn't it?'

'Probably.'

We kissed, long and deep. Then he drew back and looked me up and down.

'Are you undressing me with your eyes?' He nodded. 'Let me remind you that we're on a public highway, and you are responsible for this vehicle.'

'But that's me, isn't it? *Irresponsible.*' He put his hand inside my ancient, holey Puffa. Outside, the cars around us had started to move. A tiny beam of sunshine shone through a gap in the clouds.

'Well, go on, then,' I said. 'Put your foot down.'

The duvet was good – really good. Light and yet warm, just as Obe had promised. We spent that night snuggling under it, making up for lost time. We even slept a bit, too.

'Don't you feel guilty?' I whispered into Obe's warm neck, as we lay cocooned in the heavenly, cloud-like folds.

'Terribly,' he whispered back.

'You don't think they caught us on CCTV, or something?'

'Even if they hunt us down tomorrow, it will have been worth it.'

The next day the police arrived. The kids and I were in Zeynab's flat at the time; she had kindly invited us to Hassan's birthday party, and in my new-found spirit of acceptance, I had accepted.

That was the day I got to know Ali, too. I'd never spoken much to Zeynab's husband before, but he answered the door and waved us inside as if we were old friends, took my coat, showed Larkin into the living room while I got Eliot out of the buggy, and then folded it with a practised motion, opened the bathroom door and stashed it neatly in the bath.

'We keep Larkin's bike in the bath,' I told him, and he laughed.

'So do we! Usually. I just moved it today, for the party. Our whole flat is like, how do you say, a giant game of Tetris.'

Ali opened the bedroom door to show me where they had stashed Hassan's bike. I could just make out a room stuffed full to the rafters. As well as the double bed, there was a toddler bed crammed up against the window, and towers of stuff – clothes, scooters, toys – were piled up from floor to ceiling. There was barely a spare centimetre.

Zeynab and Ali's flat was different to ours. I had always assumed that all the flats in Priory Court had the same layout, but theirs only had one bedroom. Their living room faced out over the car park, and seemed darker and more enclosed than ours. One thing of many I had not appreciated enough: how lucky we were to have that view out over the water. That view had meant a lot to me over the last few months.

The living room had been decked out with balloons and a blue shiny Birthday Boy banner. There was a white plasticky sofa and a little glass-topped table covered in snacks: Wotsits, mini-rolls and Haribo. Two other mums who I recognised from around the estate were sitting on the sofa, and they scooted up to make room for me. There was a huge flat-screen telly mounted on the wall, and Larkin joined Hassan and two other kids watching *SpongeBob SquarePants* on Cartoon Network.

'Welcome! Welcome!' said Zeynab, coming in from the kitchen with a tray of syrupy Turkish pastries. 'Eat!' She pressed a napkin and a pastry into my hand. 'These are very good for you.'

I definitely didn't believe her, but I took a pastry and ate it as I fed Eliot. Hassan's birthday party was different from the ones we had been to in the leafy streets. There was not a carrot stick or a cherry tomato in sight, and nobody seemed inclined to organise any kind of improving activity. Instead, the children did what they wanted to do: ate sweets and watched cartoons, while the adults drank strong Turkish coffee and ate pastries and chatted. It was very relaxing.

One of the other mothers, whose name was Valentina, lived in the flat next door to the Kosovans.

'Does she ever stop hoovering?' I asked.

'Only on Sundays,' said Valentina. 'One day of rest. It's not easy being a mum, hey? She's mine, there.' She pointed out her daughter, a studious-looking girl with glasses and long brown hair, who was sitting next to Larkin. 'Her father's not around, and all I do is work. She's in childcare all week long. And my job is just crappy admin. No good for me, no good for her, no good for anyone. I hate it. I'd rather be at home with the hoover.'

I was more used to anguished conversations with career women about maternity breaks and missed promotions. 'Don't you think,' I said, cautiously, 'that it's good for us, to have our own money, and our independence?'

'The government should pay us,' Zeynab said straight away. 'What is this system all about in this country? They hand out money to all the people who can't be bothered to work. But when you say you're a parent and you want to stay at home with your kid – nothing. You're on your own.'

'Listen to her,' said Valentina, laughing and doing a very Italian upturned chin thing. 'She's crazy. She want to start a revolution.'

'Maybe we will,' I said. I turned to Zeynab, who was resting her fluffy-slippered feet on the little table. 'Do you remember we talked about organising a protest in that meeting? I'm going to talk to my sister. She has friends who are kind of revolutionaries. I'm hoping they'll come and help us out.'

'Now you are talking!' said Zeynab. 'That's just what we need around here.'

The other mum, Sofi, shuddered. She was skinny with a tired face, and her T-shirt said 'Come On, Boys' in diamante letters. 'Believe me, we don't,' she said. 'Where I come from we had too many revolutions. You think everything's going to get better, but it just gets worse.'

'But our revolution is going to be different, Sof,' said Zeynab. 'All those were bullshit man revolutions, and you know men, they can't get anything done. This one is going to be a mothers' revolution, innit? We're gonna do it for these lot.' She waved her hands at the kids, who were engrossed in *SpongeBob SquarePants*. 'Are you with me?'

Sofi, Zeynab, Valentina and I clinked coffee cups. I was having much more fun at Hassan's party than I had expected to. As we drank, Ali stuck his head into the living room. 'What are you ladies up to?' he said. 'You only alone five minutes, and I hear all this crazy chat.'

Zeynab waved her hand dismissively. 'Don't worry, Ali,' she said. 'I will look after you. After the revolution, you can be my driver.'

Larkin loved the party. Zeynab and Ali did eventually organise a game of pass the parcel, and at the end they gave out party bags with real flashing lightsabers. We were just about to leave when there came a huge crash from upstairs. Then another, and another. Then the sound of splintering wood, and a man's voice shouting: 'Open up! Police!'

My mind filled with panicked thoughts about the duvet. Obviously, the idea that we might get away with our crime was too good to be true. Of course they had traced us through CCTV, and probably had Wanted notices up all over the Internet, and we'd be publicly shamed. How did one get rid of a duvet in moments? Was it too late to hide it? Or burn it?

'Oh my lord. What is this?' Zeynab ran outside into the forecourt, and the rest of us followed. There were three police vans parked there, lights flashing. It wasn't our flat: on the second floor, Dawn's door was swinging open. All around the horseshoe-shaped estate, doors were opening, people were coming out and leaning over the parapet wall to see what was going on.

'It's Dawn!' said Zeynab. 'The police, they raided Dawn!'

Sure enough, a burly black-clad policeman emerged onto the walkway, holding a handcuffed Winston, still wearing his dressing gown. Behind him was another, gripping Dawn firmly by the arm. She was wearing tracksuit bottoms and flip-flops and clutching her hands over her face. She looked so wobbly and wizened, so battered down by life, so hopeless. I wanted to rush over and tell them to let her go. But I didn't. I didn't know what I wanted any more. I didn't want to be a bad person.

Zeynab and I held the boys' hands as we watched Winston and Dawn get into separate vans. Larkin and Hassan watched the police vans with awed reverence as they drove away, sirens blaring, blue lights flashing.

'Mum?' Larkin said, taking my hand. His mouth was stained orange with Wotsits, and the lightsaber was flashing away, tucked into his belt.

'Yes?' I braced myself for the inevitable awkward questions, trying to think how best to explain the crack den thing to a three-year-old.

Larkin looked up at me solemnly. 'This is the best day of my life,' he said.

Before going back up to our flat we stopped off at the second floor. Outside Dawn's flat there was a rotund policeman leaning on the parapet wall, with an ice cream in his hand. The Toddler kept his eyes fixed on it as it travelled to the policeman's mouth and back again.

'Good afternoon, officer,' I said. 'I live in the flat upstairs. Can you give me any information about what's going on here?'

The policeman took a lick of his ice cream, and then wiped his mouth on his sleeve. 'Cannabis factory,' he said. 'It was stuffed to the rafters in there. We've filled up a van full of these.' He gestured to a stack of large blue plastic flip-top storage boxes piled up next to the front door. A heady fragrance hung about them, a sweet smell that I recognised.

My first thought was: Cannabis! I LOVE cannabis! If only I'd known.

I did not say this to the policeman.

'What are you going to do with it?' I asked.

'They incinerate it,' he said. 'It's probably worth thirty grand.'

Ouch. I started to think of all the things I could have done with thirty grand, and then stopped. Cannabis farming was definitely not the way forward for Obe and me. The Toddler was still looking at the ice cream. The policeman looked down at his yearning face. 'Look, love,' said the policeman, 'why don't you just go and get him one of his own? The way he's looking at me . . .'

'I will, officer,' I said, feeling like he might arrest me if I didn't. 'But can I just ask – do you know what's going to happen to Dawn? The lady who lived here?'

'She got herself in with a bad lot, didn't she?' said the policeman, taking a thoughtful lick. 'It often happens. The dealers seek out people who can't say no, people who just want a friend. They wheedle their way in, then take over their flats for, shall we say, their own purposes.'

He popped the end of his cone into his mouth, and crunched it. 'She probably won't go down for it. At least, not for long. It might even mean that they move her on, sort her out some kind of supported accommodation.'

'Really? That sounds good,' I said, though I suspected the policeman was just trying to be reassuring. A flat, tinkling rendition of 'Three Blind Mice' drifted up from the forecourt; the pastel-pink ice-cream van was parked right opposite the remaining police van, like a reflection in a happy mirror.

'Oh no!' cried The Toddler, gripping the railings in distress. 'He's playing the music! That means all the ice cream has run out!'

The policeman and I both turned to look at him, and then caught each other's eye. 'Larkin,' I asked, 'what do you mean?'

'Daddy told me: when the tune plays, it means all the ice cream has gone.'

The policeman and I looked at each other, and then both creased up with laughter. 'That's evil,' he said, 'who would think up a thing like that.'

My heart swelled with pride. 'His dad has a way with words, officer,' I said.

14.

Getting away from it all

A CROSS the wide stretch of shingle, The Toddler crouched with his fishing net. The late spring afternoon was slightly too warm, but I wasn't going to let it bother me. We were on Sidmouth beach, breathing in fresh clean air and looking for fossils.

As we drove away from Priory Court that morning, I had looked back at the estate in the rear-view mirror, watching its grey bulk recede until we turned the corner. We hadn't left London in so long. Every time we did, I swore to myself that we would do it more often. During our last holiday as a family, in a friend's caravan in Essex, Obe and I had as much as decided to leave London for good. Obe had it all worked out: we could move to the north, where you could buy houses for a pound. He would get a job in the local care home, and take up whittling in his spare time. I would do freelance proof-reading. We'd split the childcare fifty-fifty. For a few weeks, we were convinced we had the answer.

But once we got back, moving felt like too much effort,

and expense, and I couldn't imagine leaving Mum, Lou and Frankie, and before long we had both forgotten the brief glimpse we had allowed ourselves of a different life, away from the concrete and fumes and rubbish and hordes upon hordes of grey shuffling people. I only remembered again today, once we had turned off the M25, leaving the skyscrapers behind on the horizon like a row of cracked teeth, and the sky revealed its true hugeness and I felt a physical sensation of relief, as if I could stretch out to my full height and stop holding my breath.

Now there I was, perched on a rocky outcrop, warming my hands on a polystyrene cup of tea, and watching The Toddler, who was wearing just his wellies and a jumper, his trousers having met with a rock pool earlier. He looked like Christopher Robin, all ruddy-cheeked and wholesome. It was a novelty to observe my son at a distance. In Priory Court, he was constantly under my feet. He tripped me up in the kitchen; watched me intently as I sat on the loo; woke me up by shouting 'porridge time!' only millimetres from my ear. When I thought of him, it was always in close-up, like my own hand or foot.

But over there across the sand, he was content, absorbed. He looked like his own person. I took in a deep breath of salty air and sighed it out again. I felt like my own person, too.

It was almost obscene how much space there was in the countryside. On the journey I watched mile after mile of empty green fields reel by through the car window. There weren't even any animals in them. It just didn't make sense that so many families were stuck in the city, crammed into tiny flats with no outdoor space at all. People made such a fuss about battery chickens. What about battery children?

'I've got one!' The Toddler was waving. He had caught a tiny fish. I went over to look at it for a moment and then we put it back in its rock pool. When the tide came in, it would be able to swim wherever it wanted, the whole sea would be its playground. That was a nice thought. As we walked back along the beach Larkin slipped his hand into mine.

'I like the countryside,' he said. 'I want to stay here all the time.' He always said this when we went on holiday. His face even looked different when we were not in the city; more open, happier. He liked the cottage, too, especially the kitchen with a nice big table in it. 'It's so huge you can run around indoors!'

'I know, darling. Well . . . maybe one day.'

When we got back to the house, Obe was sitting underneath the apple tree in the garden reading Kate Tempest – 'Are you trying to get me up to date?' he asked suspiciously when I gave it to him, but he'd hardly put it down since. Mum was inside, laying the table for lunch.

'GRANNY!!!' cried Larkin in delight, as he did every time he saw her. She crouched down and threw her arms around him, and he disappeared gratefully into the folds of her soft mauve cardigan.

'Hello, little darling,' she said, kissing him on the top of the head. Then she stood up and kissed me on the cheek. 'And hello, big darling. How are you feeling?'

'I'm fine,' I replied, and I really meant it. I felt like a functional human being, a person who had more to offer than wiping.

It had helped that Mum had been around much more, recently. She came to the flat every couple of days and did sensible things like clearing up the mouse droppings in the kitchen cupboards and chucking out the mouldy vegetables in the fridge, and then went home, leaving a little trace of radiant calmness behind her. Obe, too, had been stepping up. He had taken over night duties, so I'd had several weeks of unbroken sleep, and he'd bought an Indian cookbook, and spent his evenings constructing complicated curries. The other day, I'd even noticed him cleaning up the coffee grounds.

Meanwhile, with my new time and energy, I'd been helping Brenda, Abraham and Zeynab plan the protest against High-Class Homes. I'd taken Lou out for a drink in the last remaining old-fashioned boozer on the High Street, to ask whether she could link us up with her activist friends. At first, she had crowed when I explained the situation. 'You're not into protest!' she said, spluttering into her five-pound pint. 'What was it you said to me, once, about the Birkenstocks and banners brigade?'

But she came up with the goods, as I knew she would. Her old friend Rose was part of an organisation called the Revolutionary Housing Network. I'd never heard of them, but Lou explained that they had helped out a lot of the big housing protests, the ones that had been on the news.

'I thought those campaigns were run by residents.'

'They are,' said Lou, taking out her baccy and laying a Rizla carefully on the table. 'But with a little bit of support in just the right places. If you know what I mean.'

'No, explain.'

'Okay,' Lou slowed down, as though she were talking to a child. 'Do you think any of those campaigns would have got as far as they did if they were just run by residents, with no back-up? These things take planning. They take experience, years upon years of organisation. They take strategy, networks.' She tucked her fag behind her ear. 'What happens is exactly what has just happened with you. The council will develop some outrageous plan. The residents will start trying to make a noise, but they won't really know what they're doing, they'll all have kids and complicated lives and no idea how to organise. And that's when the Revolutionary Housing Network comes in. They have media experts, direct action experts, they've been doing this stuff for years. They go along and give the residents whatever support they need.'

'I've never even heard of them.'

'That's the point – you're not supposed to have heard of them. They work behind the scenes. They are enablers, if you like. Help other people to get their voices heard.'

Lou had promised to call Rose, to see whether she would be interested in getting involved at Priory Court. She hadn't joined us in Devon yet as she had 'a few things to sort out' in London – but she was arriving tonight, and I was looking forward to finding out what they had said.

After lunch, Mum took the boys out to the stream at the end of the lane, so I could have a rest. I lay down on the sofa but my mind was buzzing; I couldn't get the idea of leaving London out of my head. Eventually I went out to find Obe under the apple tree. I sat next to him on the grass, watching light dance through the jigsaw of branches.

'Do you think we should move out of London?' I asked.

'Yes,' he said, immediately, without even looking up from his page. 'I've had enough of it. Such an angry city.'

When Obe had said this kind of thing in the past it had annoyed me as a native Londoner. I had never thought London was angry. The city I loved had been about friends, lazy summer days on Hampstead Heath with spliffs and reggae on a stereo, swimming in the Ponds, Sundays in the pub with roasts and papers. It had been about living alongside every kind of person from every country in the world. Of course, it wasn't perfect, but London had always been part of me.

I didn't feel that way any more. The last few years had changed the city, and changed me too. I knew that all we would ever be able to do in London would be hang on by our fingertips. It was no way to live. Rather than continue to live in a place that really didn't want us any more, perhaps it would be better to find somewhere that did.

'To the countryside?'

'I can't live in the countryside, Syl. I can't be the only brown person in the village – and I don't want that for the kids.'

'I'm not going right up north,' I said quickly. 'It needs to be somewhere . . . familiar. Birmingham?'

'No way. I'm never going back there.' Birmingham, for Obe, meant his mum – now she wasn't there any more, there was no point even visiting. There was a pause. 'Brighton?'

Brighton. Hmmm. I knew Brighton well. I had lots of

friends who had been to uni down there. I'd spent many a sunny afternoon drinking cider on the beach, eating fish and chips. It was a fun place. I wondered what it would be like to live and work there.

But Obe already had his phone out. He held it out to me with GoodMove.com open in the browser, and a list of Brighton properties to rent filling the screen. I scrolled down them wonderingly: for just a little bit more than the price of our monthly rent in Priory Court, we could get a three-bedroom house with a small patio garden, just a few minutes' walk from the beach. Obe directed me towards one with a mint-green front door, stripped floorboards and an open fireplace.

As I flicked through the pictures, I felt a flutter of excitement. This was an actual family home, a real one, with space for all of us. It could have been the home I had been seeing in my dreams for all these years.

'It's got period features,' Obe said, pointing out some nice cornicing in the living room. 'The garden looks pretty small, but it's south-facing. And look –' he clicked on an exterior shot. There it was, small and bare and wintry but unmistakable: a wisteria growing in a pot by the door.

'But it's too expensive. We can't afford to pay any more than we're paying now.'

'Hmmm,' said Obe, ponderingly. 'Well. Maybe one day.'

'Maybe one day . . . after you do that green plumbing course.' Obe glared at me. 'Okay! I'm joking, all right?'

Lou arrived later that night. When I came down after putting the kids to bed, leaving Obe dozing, she was curled up on the sofa, nursing a small mountain of crumpled tissues.

'Lou has a bit of a cold,' said Mum.

Lou waved weakly and blew her nose. 'I'b fide,' she said, but it was clear from her voice that this was not just any cold. It sounded as if her whole head had been stuffed, like her words were being stifled somewhere deep in her sinuses. Her eyes were leaking yellow goo.

'Jesus,' I said, recoiling and making my fingers into the sign of the cross. 'I'm not coming anywhere near you.'

Wracked with coughs, she had enough energy to flick me the V-sign.

Mum, Lou and I sat quietly together in front of the open fire. We had drawn the curtains, as the darkness outside was proper darkness; the quiet was proper quiet. This house really was in the middle of nowhere.

The clock ticked in the corner, just like it always had, and the fire made faces loom from the wallpaper, with its cabbagey green flowers. This room had barely changed in my lifetime. It had exactly the same feeling as when I was a child; a feeling of peace, but also of presence – Lou and I always used to think the Devon house was haunted.

Lou said nothing until Mum put her hand on mine, and said: 'Lou has broken up with Shanti.'

'Oh God.' I'd never expected her to take the plunge. I thought sadly about the gorilla suits and the skinny dipping, the Visit Cornwall tin and Shanti's crinkly smile. 'He's such a lovely human being,' I said. 'Maybe too lovely for the real world.'

'Whed I think aboud the future with him I dond feel excited, I feel like I'm lookig dowd a dark hole,' Lou managed to say through a wall of mucus. 'Thad's nod good, is it?'

I shook my head and Mum nodded sympathetically. We'd both liked Shanti, but we could also see her point. Lou blew her nose again and closed her eyes.

'Id doesn't help that life just seems impossible ad the moment. We have this expectation that we'll have stability, somewhere to live, to have a family. But it's not looking good. It's difficult to stay with someone whed the practicalities feel –' she wiped her eyes – 'imbossible.'

We sat there for a moment watching the flames lick the coal. Through the thin cotton curtains, the darkness outside pressed in all around. The fire crackled and sparks flew up the chimney.

'I've been thinking about that,' said Mum. 'And perhaps they are not so impossible.' She wriggled her toes in the warmth, and smiled. Flames glimmered in her pale-blue eyes. 'Perhaps it just has to be . . . a team effort.'

'Whad do you mean?' said Lou, but Mum just smiled enigmatically, and then yawned.

'I'm going to bed. But I have a plan.'

'Oooh! Do tell!' I raised my eyebrows, but Mum wouldn't say any more.

'Let's talk about it tomorrow.'

At breakfast the next morning Mum outlined her plan. It was an amazing plan. It was a plan that would change our lives.

I gave Larkin and Eliot two gingerbread biscuits each so I could fully focus on what she was saying. Mum was proposing to rent out two rooms in the Highbury house to students, and give the proceeds to Lou and me.

'They'll be mature students, so they won't be out drinking all night and what-not. It'll probably do me good to have some more people around,' she said. 'So I'm not just rattling around in there by myself.'

The money would be enough to cover almost all of our rent in Priory Court, so all Obe and I would have to worry about would be paying the other bills, and eventually finding an alternative rental. Lou could move out of the squat permanently, and rent her own place. Mum told us that she was not planning to sell her house yet, but she and William had already had one conversation about moving in together, so in a year, we would review the situation.

'What do you think?' she asked. 'Would that help to take the pressure off for a while?'

Lou and I were too busy grinning ecstatically. Suddenly there were so many possibilities. Obe and I could find somewhere we actually wanted to call home. I could stay off work for a bit longer with the children. Maybe Obe could even do a course in poetry or whittling. I sat smiling stupidly for several minutes before noticing that Eliot had smeared his gingerbread man all over the carpet and was eating ash from the fireplace. I picked him up, buried my mouth in his chubby neck and blew a big raspberry. Then Lou and Larkin piled in, and Mum spread her arms around all of us.

After breakfast everyone else went down to the stream, and I snuggled up in the big double bed with Eliot for his morning sleep. If there was anything better in life than having a little morning nap with a lovely warm squidgy baby in your arms, I couldn't think what it was. Outside, it was grey and cold but that was fine. It made being here in bed all the nicer.

I opened my eyes so I could drink in Eliot's sleeping face. It was the vision of a soul at peace: his eyelids were perfectly still, his forehead smooth. His arms and legs were thrown out wide, skydiver-style. I wished I could sleep like that. There were so many things I wanted to learn from Eliot, but to do so I'd have to be patient, and I couldn't be distracted. If I didn't start paying attention soon, he wouldn't be a baby any more, and then it would be too late.

Poor Eliot. He'd been the calm in the eye of the storm over the last few months. It was only now I felt that I could see it. Obe and I had been whirling around with our worries about money, life, and each other. Larkin had been whirling around with his scooter and his Bob the Builder fix-up schtick. And all the while Eliot had been quietly, unobtrusively learning how to live in the world. All the milestones I made a huge song-and-dance over with Larkin – first solid food, first tooth, first crawl – had slightly passed me by this time around.

The thing about having experienced The Hole is that once you begin to emerge, everything looks better and brighter. I knew all along that Eliot was beautiful, of course I did. I'd just been distracted by a million less beautiful things, I hadn't drunk him in enough. Now he was here, right in front of me. I reached out and stroked his perfect plump cheek. His eyelid flickered. I drew my hand back; I didn't want to wake him up. I leaned in so close that I could feel his wispy baby hair against my lips.

'Darling baby,' I whispered, so gently it was almost just a breath. 'We're going to be all right.'

That afternoon I went off on my own to visit Dad's grave. Whenever we came to Devon on holiday when I was a child, despite there being no reason to think he might die soon, he had always said with an odd insistence that he wanted to be buried here. The house had been special to him since childhood; his parents had brought him and Angela here for all their holidays. So his ashes were buried with a small stone in a beautiful, isolated churchyard a mile's walk from the cottage. On the walk there I picked wild flowers from the hedgerows. It was something I always did when I came here, partly so there was something to leave behind as a marker of my visit, and partly as a task, a mental preparation for the moment when I would see the stone, and allow myself to think about him, and talk to him, which until recently had only happened on my rare visits to this place.

It was a clear day. Tiny white clouds were drifting across the sky, and the wild flowers were nodding in the soft breeze. Sheep grazed sleepily on the steep banks of grass at the side of the path. Walking along without the buggy, without a little hand in mine, I was light and free. I reached the wrought-iron gate of the graveyard and pushed it open. Dad's stone was by the gate, on the left. I sat down beside it and pulled away some of the grass growing over the top. The stone looked old, now, covered in lichen. It was hard to believe that it had been there for more than twenty years. I sat down on the grass and looked out over the valley in front of me, blue and green and timeless.

At first my mind was blank; surely there had been questions I wanted to ask him? But I couldn't remember what they were. Only one came to mind, the biggest of all, the one that hung in the background of all the other questions. 'What *is* the better way?' I asked him silently. The loud-quiet voice didn't reply; perhaps there was no answer to that one.

Now I was a parent, I had a different perspective on Dad's death. I could see how it had changed my world; I'd learned to be hyper-vigilant, ready for anything, always poised to avert the next disaster. That was the real difference between Obe and me. He hadn't had it easy, he had his own things to work out. But in some fundamental way he trusted life. No matter how low the bank account, no matter how poor the employment prospects, or how messed up the state of the world, he assumed that things would be okay.

Could I start to trust life?

I closed my eyes and visualised myself on the edge of The Hole, peering down into the nothingness below. Summoning all my mental strength, I imagined myself taking a deep breath, and then one step backwards, away from the edge. Now I could do it, I just didn't know why it had taken me so long. I took another step, and another, and another, until the precipice was too far away for any gust of wind to blow me off. When I reached that safe place, I crumpled to the ground, my energy depleted, everything spent.

I opened my eyes. The sun was a little higher in the sky, and I was curled up on the slab of stone. It no longer felt chilly, having absorbed some of the warmth of my body. After getting up to go, I rested my fingers on the stone, feeling the warmth linger for a moment, before it faded away.

15.

Fight the power

THE day of the protest dawned, a squally August morning, fretful clouds scudding across a fresh blue sky. Titania was sitting in the kitchen when I got up. She was, as always, quite a vision, in a gold shell suit, with her hair wrapped in kente cloth. She had drawn a feathery pattern around her eyes with eyeliner giving her the look of a voodoo priestess.

'The fates are testing us with this weather,' she observed, taking a sip of her morning drink, a watered-down version of the fermented yoghurt stuff; Titania stuck to a strictly pro-biotic breakfast. 'We need to work fast this morning. Get everything in place before it rains.'

'Do you have the ropes?'

'Strong ropes, firm hearts, spirit guides . . . everything is ready.'

For the last two weeks, Titania had been staying with us at Priory Court and working on her latest project, a fifteen-foot-high mask made from materials she found around the estate: old mattress springs, bits of broken furniture, rusted bikes. It was now downstairs in the community garden, wrapped in tarpaulins, ready to be suspended from the parapet wall on the second floor. She'd given me a preview of the finished piece the day before: it was an elongated oval with a sharp chin, six pairs of tubular eyes (sawn-up car exhausts), curved horns (twisted willow withies from the tree by the reservoir) and a beard (the shredded fibre from inside an abandoned sofa). 'It's modelled on a Grebo war mask,' she explained. 'Designed to intimidate the tribe's enemies.'

'It's just what we need.' With deep satisfaction, I pictured the suits from High-Class Homes arriving in their four-wheel drives, to be confronted by this proud and terrifying visage. 'We can't fail with this on our side,' I told Titania, and she grinned her gap-toothed grin.

Over the last few months, our preparations for the protest had been all-consuming. Shortly after the trip to Devon, I'd arranged a meeting with Lou's friend Rose to get her advice on how to fight the demolition. Brenda, Abraham and Zeynab joined us in the community room with Hassan, who sat quietly on his mum's lap. Rose was blonde and northern and wore combats with nerdy wire-rimmed glasses. There was something purposeful about her, she was unlike many of Lou's other squatty friends. She had an inner confidence, a seriousness.

'So. Have you got a name yet?' she asked, reaching for one of Brenda's Rich Tea.

'The Priory Court Tenants and Residents Association,' Brenda told her.

'Hmm,' said Rose, munching thoughtfully. 'You might want to think about something a little . . . punchier.'

'How about Priory Court Power?' suggested Abraham, after politely putting up his hand.

'Or the Hackney Hornets?' suggested Brenda.

'I've got it – the Priory Panthers!' shouted Zeynab, and Hassan leaped off her lap, growling and holding out his claws. 'Each one of us might seem weak like a kitten, but when we get together, watch out, we bite your head off!'

This got a laugh, and Rose noted down the name at the top of her paper.

'And how many of you are involved?'

'Just us, at the moment,' said Brenda. 'That's one of our problems. It's really hard to get people out.'

'Okay, so that's your first step,' said Rose. 'Get people on board. Let's have the first meeting of the Priory Panthers next week, and beforehand make sure that everybody knows about it. There's nothing like face-to-face contact, so don't just put up notices – go and knock on doors. Tell people what's happening. They need to properly understand that their homes and their futures are at stake, and that they are important contributors to your protest group.'

'I will speak to my community leaders,' said Abraham. 'I'm pretty sure we can add to your numbers.'

'You see? No problem,' said Zeynab. 'Just you wait. Next week, we're gonna have three hundred people at our meeting.' Brenda guffawed. 'No, really,' Zeynab told her. 'You're not on your own now, Brenda. We're going to make this happen.'

The following weekend, Valentina, Zeynab, Abraham and I helped Brenda to leaflet the whole estate about the first meeting of the Priory Court Panthers. We knocked on doors, we told everybody personally about the demolition plans, and we didn't take no for an answer. On the evening of the meeting, Valentina and I went up to the second floor and knocked at the Kosovans' door. After a moment, the hoovering sound stopped, and hoovering woman popped her head around the door. When she saw us, she shook her head and said, 'No English.'

'Doesn't matter,' said Valentina, smiling and grabbing her by the arm. *'Non importa. N'a pas d'importance. Comprende?'*

She followed us meekly downstairs, still holding the duster nozzle.

I had never seen the community room as full as it was that day. We may not quite have reached Zeynab's three hundred target, but at least fifty people were perched on the rickety plastic chairs. Abraham had brought along a large cohort of men in robes and hats. They occupied the whole of the back row, and spilled out of the door. In the front were Lou and Shanti, who had decided they could still be comrades, and Rose, who had come to advise us on direct action tactics. Next to them sat Mark, who had agreed to be our legal adviser, and Frankie, who was filming us for a freelance documentary. I'd contacted Phoebe to suggest that her environmental law firm might be interested in the development, and she had come along too, while Toby had agreed to help us raise some cash for banners, Frankie's film, and any bail payments that might become necessary. Rose had advised us when we first met her that we should ideally identify a few people who were willing to get arrested. 'Only do what you feel comfortable with,' she said, when she saw our eyebrows go up. 'Everyone has their own contribution to make.'

First on the agenda that day was a presentation from the squatters about direct action. Rose made her way to the front.

'What does direct action mean to you?' she asked.

'Is that when they take the money straight out of your bank account?' asked a man in tracky bottoms in the front row.

'It means Revolution!' shouted Valentina, who had clearly caught the radical bug from Zeynab.

'Taking things into your own hands,' said Zeynab.

'Taking control,' said the shy West Indian man from the fourth floor, blinking through his glasses.

Rose quietly agreed with all of it – except possibly the bank thing. 'It can be anything from refusing a plastic bag in the supermarket to getting naked in the Houses of Parliament, or gluing yourself to a building,' she said. 'There are many different levels of action, and not all of them will be right for all of us. So that's the first thing we're going to think about.'

She divided us up into small groups to discuss our campaign objectives. My group included Abraham, Valentina and Phoebe, and we went outside to talk in the communal garden. It was a bright day, and the reservoir was looking almost blue. There was no sign of the foxes; in fact, I hadn't seen them for ages – perhaps they had moved to Beckstow. We sat down around the picnic table.

'So – what is it that you guys want to achieve?' asked Phoebe, pulling out a tablet to make notes. She was wearing a chic trouser-suit today, and the slightly shy manner I remembered from the dinner party had a tougher edge. Phoebe also had her professional mode.

'We want to stop them knocking down our homes,' said Valentina. 'Simple.'

'But in order to do that we need to get as much publicity as possible,' I said. 'We have to shame the council into standing up to the developers.'

Phoebe nodded, but narrowed her cat-like eyes. 'Publicity is great, but that is just one approach,' she said. 'If you actually want to stop the demolition going ahead, you might need to also consider some legal routes.'

'Like what?'

'Well, there are certain rules and regulations governing a development like this.

'We might also want to explore other reasons why we could argue that construction on this site might be illegal – for example, that residents haven't been consulted adequately on the project. Or conservation, for example. Could it be a site of archaeological or natural importance? According to the Habitats Directive, construction cannot take place if it is likely to have a detrimental effect on an endangered species.'

Abraham leaned forwards, intently. 'Yes,' he said. 'Now you say that – yes. I can tell you all about this. Besides the residents, there is another endangered species here at Priory Court.'

After the group discussions, Shanti took over, and asked us to get into pairs. He asked us to think about the most effective way to physically prevent the representatives from High-Class Homes from entering the estate. We tried different formations – sitting in rows with arms linked, lying down.

'And then, of course,' he said smiling his glorious smile, 'there is always the lock-on. Has anyone here done a lock-on?'

The three other squatters raised their hands, and there was a brief discussion about the pros and cons of bike locks, chains, padlocks, plastic tubing, and super-glue.

We practised in pairs: I was the protester, Zeynab was the police. She had to come up and ask me to move, and I had to refuse. I found by far the most effective way to resist was to curl up in a ball and refuse to meet her eye. As soon as I looked at her, I just wanted to be nice and to do what she said.

'Most people find it is best,' said Shanti, 'to refuse to engage completely. Just don't interact with them, human to human, at all. We can all resist pushing and pulling, but eye contact is far harder.'

At the end of the session Shanti handed out a form; if we were prepared to face arrest, we had to tick a box marked 'up for it'. My pencil hovered over the box. I thought about The Toddler and That Baby, and how much they needed me. I thought about all the different ways in which I wanted to be a good mother. It was about being around for them, giving them time and love. It was about earning money. It was often, unavoidably, about wiping. But it was also about raising my head every once in a while to look at the world they were going to grow up into.

I looked back at the form in my hand. Was I 'up for it'? Before I could change my mind, I ticked the box.

We did everything we could to tell the world what was happening at Priory Court. Zeynab, Brenda and Abraham manned a stall on the High Street, handing out leaflets about the prospective eviction of the estate to any passer-by who would take one. Rose and Jez had helped me link up with other protest groups and news organisations on Twitter, and I'd been spending every nap time and evening on the computer, getting the message out to local and national journalists and politicians. To get some publicity before the big protest, the Priory Court Panthers staged a warm-up sit-in at Hackney Town Hall. A group of residents led by Zeynab invaded the central chamber with banners hand-sewn by Valentina: Social Housing Not Social Cleansing! Decent Homes For All!

After that I started getting calls from journalists wanting

to interview Priory Court residents about the potential evictions. Legless Productions also agreed to finance Frankie's documentary.

'What inspired the campaign?' Frankie had asked, when she interviewed me a few days before. It was not easy to sum this up in a few words. 'It's not because I think it will make any difference,' I said. 'I mean, I'm sure that, in the end, the estate will be sold off, and the residents will get kicked out, and those gleaming towers will be built, and everyone who sees them will think this is a great achievement, and the area has been cleaned up. Just like I'm sure that before long there will be a third runway, and all the squatters will move into little two-up two-downs in the suburbs, and the earth will heat up, and the human race will be wiped out in an apocalyptic flood, no matter what any of us do.'

'So . . . ?' said Frankie.

'I'm not expecting results. It's about . . . expressing something.'

'Expressing what?'

'I don't know! Hope, I suppose. We all know we can't go on like this, but we're all too afraid to try anything different.'

Frankie nodded. 'So you're expressing your hope for a different future?'

'That's it,' I said. 'And maybe this protest, and other

protests like it, will inspire more people to stand up and do the same, in whatever way they need to.'

The mask wouldn't fit in the lift, and it took four people to carry it up to the second floor. Obe and Abraham hoisted it over the parapet wall outside Dawn's old flat, which was now sitting empty. *This is for you, too, Dawn,* I said silently to myself. *I hope, wherever you are, you're still shining like a diamond in the sky.*

Obe fastened it with ropes, and Titania and I went down to the forecourt to have a look. Just as the birthday sculpture had in our living room, the mask changed the whole energy of the forecourt. Under its six-eyed gaze, that grey, mundane space looked ready for battle.

'Is it doing the job?' asked Titania.

'Fierce,' I said, approvingly.

Half an hour before the arrival of the High-Class Homes delegation, I left Obe in the flat with the kids and made my way down to the forecourt. This was my first ever civil disobedience; I had even managed to miss the anti-Iraq War march. But I needed to do this now. *You've got brains. You know there's a better way.*

The publicity drive had worked. The estate was teeming with people, some residents of the estate, some squatty types with dreadlocks, a large contingent dressed in full Hasidic gowns, some middle-aged diehards who had been protesting since the 1960s. The parapet wall was strung with Valentina's banners, and a bike with a sound system mounted on the back was playing old-school funk. It looked like a party, but at the entrance to the estate there was a grim row of riot policemen dressed in black, holding plastic shields.

One thing I noticed was that police came in several different varieties. Some of them wore blue jackets with 'Police Liaison' on the back. They looked quite smiley and cuddly, podgy with round friendly faces. They mingled with the crowd and chatted in an amicable kind of way. They didn't carry any noticeable weapons. Then there was another variety that looked like Robocop. Those were the guys by the gate. They had mean chiselled faces and black rubber body armour. Their belts bulged with Tasers and other fearsome implements.

'You ready?' said Zeynab. She had worn a special, glittery headscarf today ('For the cameras, honey!'). Together we found a spot by the gate, just in front of the row of policemen. This was where we were meeting Lou. We sat down on the road, facing the estate. The idea was that we 'arrestables' would lock ourselves to the gate, to prevent the High-Class CEO's car from coming in. We were sitting next to one of the squatty types, who was wearing a monkey suit, with the giant monkey head gripped under his arm. He nodded a friendly hello.

'Ready for it?' he said.

'We've been ready for months!' said Zeynab.

'Er,' I mumbled, and she hit me on the arm.

'Sylvia,' said a familiar voice, and I looked up. There was a middle-aged man standing in front of me, dressed in a Panthers T-shirt. He had grey hair, kindly eyes, and sandals protruding from the bottom of his beige slacks. I had never seen him before in my life, but something about him seemed familiar . . .

'Hi, darling.' Mum appeared at his side. She had the same T-shirt on, above flowing culottes. The pair of them looked like they had taken a wrong turn on the way to the National Theatre. 'Goodness, look at all these people!' I scrambled to my feet, and gave Mum a hug. 'I realise that perhaps this isn't quite the moment, but . . . I'd like you to meet William,' she said.

The man held out his hand. He winked. 'Otherwise known as Bill.'

I stared at him for a moment. It was his voice that was so very familiar – calm, understanding, ever-so-slightly monosyllabic. Just hearing it made me feel warm, relaxed, protected . . . but where did I know it from? Suddenly, with an almost audible clunk, the penny dropped. 'Oh my goodness. You are William – and Bill? My Bill? From the Anti-Social Behaviour Unit?'

Bill / William beamed at me with bright-blue zen-like eyes. 'It's a real pleasure to finally meet you. I'm so glad we got that very difficult situation sorted out in the end – even if it did take us a while.'

A smile spread slowly across my face. Bill was exactly as I had always imagined. And even better, he was also William, which meant he was practically family. From now on, he would potentially be available to give me advice on a helpline-free, in-person basis. 'I'm just so glad it's you!' I managed to stutter. 'And about the fox / dog thing—'

'It's forgotten,' said Bill, patting me on the shoulder. 'I always knew that must have been a misunderstanding.'

In front of us, Phoebe, Rose and Shanti were sitting on the pavement outside the estate with their arms linked. They started chanting 'Our fight! Your fight! Decent housing is a right!' Mum and Bill joined in enthusiastically. But in front of them there was movement in the line of Robocops. We needed to get a move on.

'Hey, Syl!' Somebody was waving at me from behind the line of police. I could see a TV camera, a flash of Frankie's bright yellow mac. I waved and she gave me a thumbs-up, but she disappeared from view as the Robocops raised their shields. The monkey suit man beside me donned his giant monkey head.

Deep breath. *Peace is on the inside. May everyone be well. May they be happy*. I reminded myself that even the Robocops were people with families. They loved their children just as much as me.

Finally, Lou appeared at my side. She pinched my arm and mouthed *you all right?* I smiled *yes*. This was all fun and games to her. Not to me. But alongside the fear was a low buzz of adrenaline. It was the *right* thing to be doing.

'Right, come on, you two, let's get out of the way,' Lou ushered Mum and Bill aside. Then she turned to me. 'You ready?' she said.

I closed my eyes again, leaned my head back against the bar of the gate, and took a couple more deep, deep breaths. I found myself immersed once more in that well-worn daydream.

There it is, the open-plan living room. It's a Saturday morning, and I am holding a steaming cup of coffee. I could stay here, luxuriating in the peace and quiet, but my feet take me on the usual route through the kitchen and out into the garden. It is sunny, of course, but I find a patch of cool shade under the pergola. The wisteria is in bloom. I settle myself down and look out over the velvety lawn, fringed with lavender and rosemary. There is salt in the air, the distant lapping of waves from the nearby beach. It's so real now. I could almost reach out and touch it. The dream is taking on the flavour of reality: I'm so close to finding my place.

Only I wasn't. I was here, on the tarmac, and Lou was in front of me, with a black bike lock in her hand. I nodded, and she got my head into position, with the bar of the gate behind it. Then, with loving kindness in her eyes, she slipped the lock around my neck.

I called Obe from the police station later that night.

'Hi, babe!' He sounded distracted. I could hear Eliot squealing in the background. Of course – it was bath time. Not a good moment to talk. 'Did they nick you, then?'

'They did. For blocking a public highway. They cut the lock in the end, and Zeynab's, too. That was the worst part, those great big cutters right next to my neck.'

'Well, it's what you wanted, Syl. I guess this is a nice adventure for you.'

'Using my privilege, you know?' Obe had laughed when I told him about my plans; getting arrested didn't hold the same appeal for a man who had been stopped and searched at least once every six months ever since he hit puberty. There was a muffled sound on the line, and then Obe's voice shouting: 'Larkin, stop that! It is not okay to put your willy in Eliot's face!'

There was the sound of intense splashing, then a wail. I closed my eyes and pictured my boys, boisterous as ever. They had no idea where Mummy was right now. I imagined the heaviness of them in my arms, their slippery, wriggling bodies. I'd never been away from them for this long before.

Obe's voice came back on the line. 'So where are you?'

'Stoke Newington police station.'

'In a cell?'

'Yeah, but it's – we're fine. It's small, but, you know, we're used to that.' Obe laughed. 'We'll be getting bail tomorrow, I think. Mark's on the case, he's been amazing. The police seem pretty terrified of him. Anyway, I just wanted to see how you all were.'

'Fine. We're fine. Listen, I've just got to get them out of the bath, could we talk . . . ?'

'Sure. Of course.' There was a brief silence. 'Love you,' I said.

Across the airwaves, I heard Obe sigh, long and weary. 'Most of the time,' he said.

In the cell, I found Zeynab lying stretched out on the concrete bench. There was only one of them; it looked like we were going to be top-and-tailing tonight. She shuffled up to give me some room, and we put the scratchy blanket over both of us. There was a high, narrow window on the far wall, and through it the view was oddly spectacular: the full August pink sunset, streaked with orange and purple.

There was a scuffle and a clank from the neighbouring cell; an inebriated voice was shouting something incomprehensible.

'This reminds me of living next to Dawn,' I said.

'But imagine how that must look over the reservoir,' Zeynab replied, pointing at the window. 'I never thought I'd be watching it from here – did you?'

'Well, we did tick the box.'

Zeynab giggled. Was it me, or had her face softened a bit? Her eyes were less harsh and glittery these days, or perhaps it was just that I knew her better. 'Up for it,' she said. 'Do you think our boys will forgive us?'

'I think they'll be proud of us, one day.'

'I hope so.' Zeynab yawned, and wriggled her feet against the small of my back. 'So, have you decided whether to stay?' she asked.

'Not yet,' I told her. 'We're thinking about moving to Brighton. But it probably won't happen. I don't know.'

'You should go,' she said, her eyes fixed on the window with its gaudy changing colours. 'You're moving on. Good for you. If I was in your position, I'd do the same. Go off and have a lovely life by the beach. We don't need you.'

I laughed. 'I know you don't. But perhaps I need you.

It's funny, I've spent so long hating that block. I mean, really hating it, with all my might, and wanting to get out. But when I think about leaving, I realise how much Priory Court has inspired me. It's got under my skin, you know? Wherever we live next, I know it won't be the same.'

Zeynab looked at me, and raised one eyebrow. 'You'll get inspired by the sea, and the beach. You'll get inspired by nice things, pretty things. And if you ever get bored and want a bit more nitty-gritty, you can come and visit, we'll still be here.'

'I hope so,' I said.

'Oh, we will,' said Zeynab, sleepily. 'Just wait and see.'

She closed her eyes, and her breathing slowed. I watched for what felt like hours as little by little the sky darkened to purple, then blue, then black. There were clanks and murmurs from the cells around us; the soundtrack to dramas we'd never know. At some point, almost despite myself, I drifted off to sleep.

16.

Sea view

O BE was actually twitching with excitement. He'd come back from work with big news: he had secretly applied for a managerial job in a playscheme in Brighton – and he'd just been offered the job. I was speechless. Almost.

'But I thought you didn't want to be a manager?' I stuttered eventually.

'I don't,' said Obe, cheerfully.

'And had we definitely decided on Brighton?'

'Well. No. Not as such.'

'But you just went ahead and . . .'

'Listen, Sylvia. I remember what you said in that stupid therapy session. You wanted me to take more responsibility, didn't you?'

'Yes. But—'

'Well, that's what I'm doing. I think we should leave London and go and live by the sea. And now I've got this job, so we can probably get that house if you want it.'

I opened my mouth. I shut it again.

'The one with the wisteria?'

'And the period features.'

'Get lost.'

'What?'

'Just – are you joking?'

Obe took my hand. 'The intellect of man is forced to choose / perfection of the life, or of the work, / And if it take the second must refuse / A heavenly mansion, raging in the dark.'

I attempted to decode this, but it was no good. 'I'm still not sure if you are joking, or not.'

'I'm not joking, okay? I've got a new job, and I'm going to work really hard at it, and we are going to do this.'

I couldn't think what to say. I stared into the middle distance, grinning like an idiot. For some reason the very thought of it made me want to laugh: Obe and I, living in a real, grown-up house. I tried to imagine us strolling nonchalantly from room to capacious room; sitting down to lunch at a real kitchen table; pottering about in the garden on a Sunday afternoon. But I couldn't do it, any more than I could picture a miniature poodle performing *Swan Lake*.

'Well, that's it, then,' I said at last. 'We're going.'

'Here, pass us the computer,' said Obe. 'Just going to ping a quick email to GoodMove.'

And so, in that way, the concept of Brighton became a possibility, and the possibility became a reality.

That Saturday morning, Brighton put on its best for us. We pushed the double buggy along the sea front, the boys pointing things out as we went. Look! The sun glinting off the sea! A cutesy tea room! A row of dinky pastel-painted houses! It was all so lovely, and bracing, and fresh. I could almost feel the cobwebs in my brain being blown away by the sea breeze, the skin on my face tautening, my step getting lighter.

'Is it me,' asked Obe as we passed a playground heaving with ruddy-faced kids, 'or do the children actually look healthier here?'

'It's all that sea air,' I said. Larkin had got out of the buggy and was running ahead of us, excitedly chattering about all the new things: seagulls, pebbles, an old-fashioned carousel.

'Are we on holiday?' he kept on asking.

'Well, Larkin,' I explained. 'We've actually come to see if we want to live here.'

'What, for ever?' he said, puzzled.

'Maybe. What do you think?'

He considered this for a while. 'But what if we get to Brighton and make new friends and get to be happy and then we have to move again?' he asked, with a worried frown. Like most children, Larkin was deeply conservative. Even the most minor deviation from his daily routine – a cheese sandwich cut in the wrong way, or served on the wrong plate – threw him into a spin. He was going to take a bit of convincing to move to a whole new city.

'The idea is that we won't have to move again,' Obe told him. 'Not for a long time.'

Larkin was still frowning. 'But how do you *know*?'

We didn't know, of course. It could all be a disaster. We had no friends in Brighton, no family, and no childcare. We would be taking a punt on it . . . but I didn't say that to Larkin.

'Let's just go and see the house,' I said. 'And see if we can imagine living there.'

The house was only a short walk from the sea front, on a pleasant street, not far from the centre of town. Surely, I thought as we approached, there would be something wrong with it. There were so many potential disasters to consider: nightmare neighbours, a disintegrating kitchen, or an infestation of wood-boring insects. We stopped at the bottom of the little flight of steps leading up to the mint-green front door. There it was, the wisteria, beginning to lose its leaves and still small, but perfectly formed. It looked just like it did in the photographs.

'So far, so good,' said Obe nervously, as he rang the bell.

Inside, the nice surprises kept on coming. It had a fully functional kitchen and bathroom. It had an almost leak-free roof and double glazing. It was, in other words, a fully fledged family home. The owner, smiley in baggy orange trousers, showed us around. Her children had just left home, and she was moving to Portugal. 'We've been here for fifteen years,' she told us. 'I couldn't think of a better place to bring up kids. Great schools, lovely neighbours. But I'm done now. Time to rediscover my freedom.'

Afterwards we went to the beach. The blue sea cut a straight line across the blue sky, just like it did when I shut my eyes and let the view form in my mind. We threw stones into the sea, and ate deliciously soggy chips, and the whole time I turned the Brighton plan over in my mind. There was only one discernible flaw: Brighton did not have Mum, Lou or Frankie in it. Could I survive without them? The question had always terrified me, but now I felt some inner confidence that I could handle it.

Couldn't I?

Food for thought. I popped another chip into my mouth.

* * *

'I think we're going to do it,' I told Frankie when I next saw her. We had met up in IKEA Edmonton, because after several weeks of actual summer it was raining again, and I was too broke for Tumble in the Jungle. At IKEA, Larkin and Caleb could spend the morning jumping on the giant beanbags in the children's bedrooms section and, as long as I managed not to buy anything, it was completely free.

'But how could you bear to leave all this?' Frankie gestured around us at the IKEA café. It had a woodland theme; the tables were spotted red and white, and the chairs were shaped like toadstools. We had chosen a table with a view out over the North Circular and the car park, where somebody had arranged a display of summer deckchairs on a rotting square of astroturf.

'It's gonna be tough,' I said. 'Shall we get the meat-balls?'

'You're so dirty. They're made of horse, you know.'

'But they're so good. And only £2.99!'

'It's a no-brainer,' agreed Frankie.

'The meatballs?'

'Brighton!'

'Oh, that. Yeah, I know.'

I hadn't seen Frankie much lately. She'd been so busy; after getting her short documentary about the protest onto Channel 4, they had given her several more commissions. She'd finished shooting the dance documentary for Century, but she didn't want to continue working for Ben, her boss, who wouldn't even consider letting her work part-time. She was thinking about setting up her own production company. 'I've reached the awkward age,' she told me. 'Can't work for other people any more.'

We headed over to the self-service counter, where clingfilm-covered plates of drab smoked salmon and browning salads glistened in refrigerated rows. I ordered the meatballs and progressed to the dessert counter. What should our treat be this time, a cranberry cheesecake, or a Chelsea bun?

Larkin was jumping up and down excitedly. He loved IKEA, and this was the high point of his day. 'I want a chocolate cake and I don't want to share it. I want it all to myself.'

Eliot, meanwhile, was looking less like a baby, sitting up in the new single buggy, eating a mushy banana and wearing Larkin's old dungarees.

I had always resented the fact that my children spent so much of their infancies in corrugated iron hangars just off the North Circular. But now those days were nearly over, I felt almost nostalgic about them. Larkin and Caleb had spent many happy hours in IKEA, Westfield and Tumble in the Jungle. Would there be retail parks for rainy days in Brighton? I made a mental note to check. Then I took one of the immense slabs of chocolate cake out of the refrigerator and put it on our tray for Larkin and me to share. I added extra ice cream. And sprinkles. I banished thoughts of childhood obesity from my mind: today, I just wanted to have a nice time.

'Mark seems pretty pleased with the result of the case,' said Frankie once we'd settled back onto our toadstools. 'Has he been in touch?'

'Yes, he popped round to see Zeynab and me last week.' Mark had pursued our case as if it were genuinely more important than the Afghan constitution. Not only had Zeynab and I been bailed the morning after the protest, but, according to Mark's latest report, the police had decided not to press charges. The Priory Court Panthers had been all over the news, and even though Hackney Council were sticking to their guns about the demolition, the last thing they wanted was a high-profile court case.

Meanwhile, Abraham and Phoebe had been putting together a case that any development on Priory Court would endanger the Greater Crested Newts in the reservoir – the existence of which Abraham had painstakingly documented over several years. Phoebe and her firm of environmental lawyers seemed to think that this could be enough to delay – if not permanently postpone – the regeneration project.

'I'm going to miss you, Syl,' said Frankie, and for a moment she almost looked sad.

'You too, dude,' I told her. 'Almost enough to keep me here.'

'Almost.'

'But not quite. Will you come and visit?'

'Only if you treat me to fish and chips.'

'Done.'

The next morning before he left for work, I asked Obe: 'Do you ever think we should have another baby?'

The words were out of my mouth before they had even passed through my brain. Where did they come from? Had my womb established some kind of direct line to my vocal cords?

Obe's eyes widened and he went as pale as it was possible for him to go. After a few seconds he gathered himself sufficiently to stutter out one single syllable: 'No.'

'Oh,' I said. 'Okay.'

And he was totally, one hundred per cent, right. There was nothing I wanted less than to go through the whole messy business all over again. I had sworn I never would after the last pregnancy, which incapacitated me for five months with relentless, broiling nausea. I swore it the morning I was sick on a businessman's shoes on the 8.42 to Liverpool Street (he was amazingly nice about it), and again after the mastitis episode. I swore it every single time Eliot woke up more than four times in the night. Which was every night. For months.

Now things had calmed down and life was moving along more smoothly again it would be so easy to forget what a tremendous palaver the whole process was; to look at my two beloved boys and imagine, ever-so-idly, how lovely it would be to have another.

I had to resist. I had to stop myself thinking about cute chubby baby legs, and the pure animal exhilaration of giving birth, and how fun it would be to have a great big noisy gaggle of a family. No, no, no. I had to think of the practicalities: I had to get back to work, we still had no money, and there was the move and the campaign to think about. We had a lot of stuff to figure out. The more I thought about it, the worse the idea most definitely was.

I hummed a satisfied little tune to myself as I got the boys ready for nursery. If only all decisions in life were this straightforward. I grappled Eliot onto his changing mat, stripped off his clothes, and tickled his pudgy tummy. His legs were so big now, they were hardly baby legs any more. He could walk, and say *hiya* and *car* and *teddy*. Soon he wouldn't be a baby at all; he'd be a little boy. And then I would never, ever have a baby again. We'd move to Brighton, and Larkin and Eliot would grow up and go to school and my life would move on to its next phase. Was that what I wanted? Was it? Yes, I told myself firmly. It was.

Epilogue

From the top of Kite Hill, London was spread out before us like a grubby blanket. A layer of fine smog hung over the skyline, punctured here and there by the City skyscrapers, a defiant cluster of one-fingered salutes. I narrowed my eyes against the spring sunlight and said goodbye to it all, bit by bit.

Goodbye to Holloway Road, ungentrified and ungentrifiable; to the popcorn-smelling, sticky-carpeted Odeon where I went on my first ever date. Goodbye to the Highbury Fields playground and the football pitches where Lou and I used to roller-skate on a Saturday morning, the bench where Dad used to sit and smoke on summer evenings. Goodbye to the Whittington Hospital where I had seen his face for the last time; goodbye to the Homerton Hospital, where I first looked into my babies' eyes. Goodbye to Buckingham Palace, which I had not visited once in thirty-four years. Maybe I would, when I wasn't a Londoner any more.

'So,' said Obe, staring out across London towards the

twin protuberances of St Paul's and the Gherkin, with cranes bristling all around them. 'We're really leaving.'

We stood next to one another in silence. Over the last few years, the city and I had been going through a protracted divorce, characterised by all the usual stages of relationship breakdown: denial, rage, grief and finally acceptance. We were no longer right for each other. It was time to move on.

'It'll still be here, you know,' said Obe. He took my hand and I took Larkin's. Eliot stirred in his buggy, swept awake by the chilly breeze. It was nearly tea-time. We walked slowly down the hill to the station, where our train was waiting.

Acknowledgements

Tʜᴀɴᴋ you to:

Kerry Glencorse, for seeing a glimmer of something in a scrappy manuscript and never losing sight of it.

Jo Moulds and Charlie Rolfe, for telling me to make it funnier. (So right).

Jason Cowley and Sophie Elmhirst, for commissioning the Squeezed Middle column that made this book possible.

Miriam Toews, Xiaolu Guo and Pedro Juan Gutierrez, for inspiration.

Will Skidelsky, for publishing clairvoyance.

Hannah Black, Helen Crawford-White and the team at Coronet for 'getting it'.

For feedback and advice along the way: Scott Bradfield, Marina Lewycka, Tobias Jones, Polly Samson, Paul Laity.

Karolina Sutton, for giving me permission.

Mandy, Richard and Jessica O'Keeffe, for a lifetime of love.

Jonny, Stanley and Bowen, for everything.

This book was created by
Hodder & Stoughton

Founded in 1868 by two young men who saw that the rise in literacy would break cultural barriers, the Hodder story is one of visionary publishing and globe-trotting talent-spotting, campaigning journalism and popular understanding, men of influence and pioneering women.

For over 150 years, we have been publishing household names and undiscovered gems, and today we continue to give our readers books that sweep you away or leave you looking at the world with new eyes.

Follow us on our adventures in books . . .

 @HodderBooks /HodderBooks @HodderBooks